DYING IN THE DARK

Sally Spencer

This first world edition published in Great Britain 2005 by
SEVERN HOUSE PUBLISHERS LTD of
9–15 High Street, Sutton, Surrey SM1 1DF.
This first world edition published in the USA 2005 by
SEVERN HOUSE PUBLISHERS INC of
595 Madison Avenue, New York, N.Y. 10022.

British Library Cataloguing in Publication Data

Spencer, Sally
   Dying in the dark
   1.   Woodend, Charlie (Fictitious character) - Fiction
   2.   Police - England - Fiction
   3.   Detective and mystery stories
   I.   Title
   823.9'14 [F]

   ISBN 0-7278-6186-7

Typeset by Palimpsest Book Production Ltd.,
Polmont, Stirlingshire, Scotland.
Printed and bound in Great Britain by
MPG Books Ltd., Bodmin, Cornwall.

Prologue

Maria Rutter was sitting on a bench in Whitebridge Corporation Park, thinking about what she knew – and what she didn't!

She knew it was a *bench* she was sitting on, because she could feel the wooden slats pressing against her bottom. ('Your perfect little bottom,' her husband had called it – but not recently.)

She knew it was a *park* because she could hear ducks calling to each other across the pond. (And where else would there be wildfowl so close to the hum of the passing traffic?)

She knew it was *autumn*. (She had only to move her feet a little to have them brush against the brown, brittle leaves; only to rotate the toe of her shoe to hear them crackle as they disintegrated.)

She knew it had been *raining*. (The earth, the grass and the flowers all had a distinctive smell which came only after rain.)

And she knew it was the *Corporation* Park, rather than any of the other parks in Whitebridge, partly because of the time it had taken to drive here, and partly because her husband had told her it was – and why should he lie? (Why *should* he lie? Why should he *lie*?)

She was sure he hadn't lied to her when they'd first started walking out together. Sure that he hadn't used their marriage certificate as licence to stop telling her the truth. But that had been then – and this was now.

She heard a clattering sound, coming from beside her.

Damn! she thought.

Her white stick, which she'd balanced against the edge of

her seat, must have somehow managed to fall over. She groped around with her foot – rustle, rustle, rustle went the dried leaves – and managed to locate it.

She couldn't be bothered to pick it up if it was only going to fall down again. She'd retrieve it when it was time to leave.

Her keen ears – even keener since the accident – detected the sound of thrashing about in the bushes behind her, and she understood immediately what it was.

The lovers' passion must be burning strongly for them to chance making love in the middle of the park, she thought. And with a cold wind blowing in from the moors, *public* exposure was not the only kind they risked.

She smiled briefly at her own play on words, but the dark preoccupations of her mind soon melted the smile away.

She and Bob had once been like this couple, she thought. Not just in love, but in lust. *So much* in lust that they, too, would have risked almost anything to satisfy each other.

The rustling behind her stopped, to be followed by the sound of zips being zipped, studs being popped back into place, and other articles of clothing being adjusted.

'That was lovely, wasn't it?' a man's voice said.

His partner made no reply.

'Just like it used to be,' the man said, a hint of concern creeping into his voice.

'You said I was the only one who mattered to you,' the woman said.

'You *are* the only one who matters to me!'

'You said we'd be together for ever.'

'We will be.'

'Then what about *her*?'

'She's a complication. No more.'

'She seems like more than that to me.'

Was she suddenly going mad? Maria asked herself.

Was this dialogue – which she'd *thought* was taking place in the bushes – actually only being played out in her own fevered mind?

Because while she had never actually *had* this same

2

conversation with Bob, she had certainly *imagined* it often enough in the previous few days.

The lovers – whether behind her, or only in her brain – had fallen silent. Now she heard a new sound – the noise of rubber wheels bumping over the uneven flag-stoned path.

'Are you all right?' Bob's voice asked, worriedly.

'I'm fine,' Maria said.

'Well, you don't look it. In fact, you've gone quite pale.'

'Is the baby asleep?'

'Yes, I thought we were going to have real trouble with her dropping off at first, but by the time we'd got past the duck pond—'

'Sit down,' Maria commanded.

'Don't you think we should be getting back home now? I know the baby's well wrapped up, but it's still turning quite chilly. And anyway, I'm worried about you.'

'Sit!' Maria said, and felt the bench give slightly, as Bob lowered himself down beside her.

'What's *really* the matter?' Bob asked, sounding like the concerned husband she'd thought he always would be.

'Are you looking at me?'

Using your seeing eyes to look into my lifeless ones?

Bob laughed. 'Of course I am. I thought you could always tell whether I was or not.'

'I *used* to be able to tell.'

There was a pause, then Rutter said, 'What have you heard?'

'What *is there* to hear?'

Another pause. 'I had an affair,' Rutter admitted. 'But it's over. It's been over for nearly a year. If . . . if you can forgive me, I'll make it right again. Things can be just like they used to.'

Maria felt a shiver of horror run through her whole body, a horror which only deepened when she heard the words which came, without her willing them, from her own mouth – 'You said I was the only one who mattered to you.'

'You are!'

'You said we'd be together for ever.'

3

'We will be.'

Am I mad? Maria wondered. Did I only imagine I heard these same words earlier? Am I saying them now? Did I say them earlier and am *now* only imagining them? Or have the words *never* been spoken? Is all this just my thoughts? Do Bob – and the baby – only really exist inside my head?

Once – long ago – she would have focused her eyes on some solid object, in the hope that would bring her back to reality. But now she couldn't see – and any focusing she did would have to be accomplished in her *mind's* eye.

How could she make this seem real? she asked herself. How could she make it seem concrete?

'Who did you have this affair with?' she demanded.

'Does that really matter?'

'Yes, it bloody well does! Was it with Monika Paniatowski?'

'You seem to know already, so why ask?'

'She came to my house!' Maria said outraged. 'She sat down to dinner at our table! We laughed and joked together!'

'She likes you. She really does.'

'Is that why she stole my husband?'

'She didn't steal me.'

'What *did* she do then? *Borrow* you?'

'I love you,' Rutter said helplessly. 'I always have. I loved you even when I was betraying you.'

'So why did you go with her? Because she's a *whole* woman? Because she can *see*?'

'*You're* a whole woman. And it wasn't like that at all.'

'So you loved *her*, did you?'

'Yes, I suppose I did.'

'And you *still* love her?'

'I haven't so much as touched her on the arm since we broke up,' Rutter said. 'We don't even go out drinking together, unless we know that someone else is going to be there.'

He knew the words were a mistake the moment they had spilled out of his mouth.

'You *still* love her,' Maria repeated.

'Not in the way I love you.'

'Could you pick up my stick for me?'

'Yes, of course. But—'

'I want to go home now.'

'I want to put it all behind me,' Rutter repeated desperately. 'I want to make it up to you and the baby.'

'It might be too late for that,' Maria said.

'Might be?' Rutter asked, the anguish evident in his voice. 'Do you mean you still haven't made up your mind?'

'That's right,' Maria agreed. 'I still haven't made up my mind.'

One

'I tell you, I wish I'd been lucky enough to work with Paco Ruiz when he was in his prime,' Chief Inspector Charlie Woodend said enthusiastically, as the barman placed another round of drinks on the table. 'What a bobby that man must have been! An' as to the conditions he had to work under, well it makes you think twice before you complain yourself! The boss he had in Madrid, before the Civil War, makes our Chief Constable seem like gentle Jesus.'

He paused, and examined the faces of the two people sharing the table with him. Monika Paniatowski – blonde hair and a figure to die for, even if her nose was a little too large for Lancashire tastes – had a glazed look in her normally vivacious eyes. Bob Rutter – sharp suit, looking more like a rising young executive than a rising young police inspector – seemed equally far away.

'He could have cracked Kennedy's assassination, could Paco,' Woodend continued.

Still no response.

'In fact, that's just what I was tellin' President Johnson the other day,' Woodend said. 'I went over to see him, you know. Me an' the Beatles together. I suppose we could have flown on a plane, like everybody else, but John Lennon thought it'd be much more fun if we went by hot-air balloon.'

'What?' Bob Rutter asked.

'I said that me an' the Beatles went over to the United States by hot-air balloon.'

'That's what I thought,' Rutter replied, puzzled.

'I'm sorry if I've been borin' you with my tale of how I

7

cracked open a complicated murder case on my holidays, an' still found time to get a nasty case of sun-burn,' Woodend said tartly.

'The Beatles went to America by *hot-air balloon*?' Monika Paniatowski asked, as if his previous remark had only now penetrated her brain.

What was the matter with the two of them? Woodend wondered.

They couldn't have restarted their affair, because, even if they'd tried to hide it from him, he would have known.

Perhaps it was simply the lack of serious activity which had dulled their edges. Both of them worked at their best under pressure, and since he'd returned from Spain there'd been no major crime to speak of in the whole of the Whitebridge area. So maybe that *was* it. Maybe they'd let their brains go into hibernation, in order to build up strength for their next serious challenge.

Or maybe the answer was even simpler, he told himself with a sudden shudder.

Maybe the reason they hadn't been listening was because it hadn't been worth listening *to* – because, even without realizing it, he was turning into a boring old fart.

'Sorry, sir, I was miles away,' Monika Paniatowski said. 'You were telling us about Inspector Ruiz.'

'Forget it, lass,' Woodend said, feeling both more self-conscious *and* more self-critical by the minute. 'Let's talk about somethin' *you* want to talk about, shall we?'

But from the look on her face, it was plain that there was nothing she *did* want to talk about – at least, not to him.

'Mr Woodend!' called the landlord, from behind the bar.

'What is it now, Jack?'

'The station is on the phone for you.'

Woodend gave a sigh which he meant to sound like exasperation – but came closer to relief – stood up, and headed for the bar.

The moment he'd gone, Rutter said, 'If she does divorce me, she'll want custody of the baby. And there's no guarantee she'll stay here in Whitebridge if she gets it. Why should she? All her family live in London.'

'She won't get custody,' Paniatowski said in a whisper. 'She's blind, for God's sake!'

'And I'm a proven adulterer, with a job which hardly ever allows me to get home,' Rutter said mournfully. 'If you were the judge, which one of us would you consider the better bet?'

'It won't come to that,' Monika said earnestly.

'It'd better not,' Rutter told her. 'Because if it does – if she takes the baby away – I don't think I could go on. I think I'd probably kill myself.'

'Don't talk like that,' Monika hissed. Then, in a louder voice, she said, 'But you don't always get that kind of lucky break on a murder investigation, you know, Bob.'

'What are you talking about?' Rutter asked.

'The boss, you bloody fool,' Monika said, her voice lower again. 'He's coming back.'

He was indeed. And there was a look as grim as a granite tombstone on his face.

'Finish your drinks, an' then grab your coats,' the Chief Inspector said. 'We've copped a particularly nasty one this time.'

Woodend and Paniatowski stood on the bridge, looking down at the dark water in the canal below.

The canal cut straight through the centre of old Whitebridge, passing all the dark satanic mills which had once thrived there. In its heyday, Woodend thought, countless stolid, plodding bargees had walked along the towpath, leading their equally stolid and plodding horses. Sometimes they'd even allowed the local kids – little Charlie Woodend among them – to hop on to the cotton-cloth-laden barge which the horse was towing behind it.

'We used to love ridin' on them barges,' Woodend said.

He thought he'd spoken softly enough for no one else to hear him, but he must not have done, because Monika Paniatowski said, 'Loved riding on the barges? Why?'

9

'God alone knows!' Woodend replied.

Certainly it would have been quicker to walk than ride. But perhaps the speed at which they were going had not mattered so much, because it was where they were *going* that was really important.

Those stolid men and stolid horses were leaving the grimy town of Whitebridge behind them, and heading for the port of Liverpool, which the kids were certain – though they had never seen it – was a golden and glorious place to be. Yes, maybe that was it. The barges were escaping Whitebridge. The kids knew – or at least believed – that they never could. But for just half an hour or so – until it was time to get off the barge and go for their tea – they could live under the illusion that such an escape *was* possible, even for them.

The dead woman was lying on the towpath, in the shadow of the old Empire Mill. Two uniformed officers, torches in their hands, stood on guard over her. Other officers had been posted further up and down the canal, in order to keep civilians away.

If that was where she had actually been killed, then the murderer had chosen his spot well, Woodend thought. Because since the mills had closed and the barges had stopped coming, hardly anybody – apart from the occasional angler – used the old towpath any more.

'I suppose I'd better go an' take a look at her,' the Chief Inspector said, with a heavy sigh. 'After all, that *is* what I get paid for.'

'What do you want me to do?' Paniatowski asked.

'Go back to the car, get on the radio, an' see if Bob's come up with anythin' interestin' at headquarters yet. Then, I suppose, it'd be a good idea if you had a look at the body yourself.'

Woodend made his way down the steps to the canal side. The towpath was made up of cobblestones set in clay, but he avoided that, walking instead along the thin concrete strip which topped the edge of the bank.

It was a hundred yards to where the body lay. Two uniformed constables were standing guard over the woman. But they were not looking at her. Instead, they had their eyes fixed on the darkness at the other side of the canal.

The constables heard him coming, shone their torches on him, and saluted when they saw who it was.

'It's Beresford, isn't it?' Woodend asked the senior of the two.

'That's right, sir.'

'Well, Beresford, let's get on with it.'

The constables shone their torches over the body. The woman's skirt was hiked up around her waist, and her knickers had been dragged down around her ankles. From her general physical condition, it was possible to estimate that she was somewhere between twenty-five and thirty-five. But there was no clue to her age to be gained from her face. That was just a mess!

'Who found her?' Woodend asked.

'A tramp,' Beresford said. 'He's well known to most of the bobbies on the beat. Wally the Wanderer, we call him, though nobody's got any idea what his real name is.'

'What was he doin' here?'

'Accordin' to him, he was seein' if there was any way he could get into the mill, so he could doss down for the night. I don't blame him. It's goin' to be a cold bugger.'

It was, Woodend agreed silently. The wind was blowing in hard from over the moors, and there would be ground frost in the morning.

'Do we know who she is?' he asked.

'No, sir. She hasn't got a handbag – or at least we haven't found one yet – an' there's nothin' in her pockets.'

Woodend forced himself to look at the dead woman's face again. Whoever had killed her had gone to work on it with something sharp and heavy – an axe, he would guess, by the depth and width of the cuts.

'Do we have any idea how long she's been dead?' he said.

'Couldn't have been too long, sir. She was still warm when we arrived.'

'How many of you were there?'

11

'Three of us, sir.'

'So where's the third now?'

'I told him to go an' get a cup of tea, sir.'

'Did you, now?' Woodend said. 'How did you approach the scene of the crime?'

'Same way you did, sir. Along the concrete strip. I didn't think there was much chance of there bein' any footprints – the ground's rock-hard tonight – but I didn't want to take any chances.'

'Good lad,' Woodend said. 'An' make sure that goes down in your report – that I said you were a good lad.' He sniffed. 'I can smell somethin' unpleasant. Puke, at a guess. Was it her, while she was bein' attacked, do you think? Or was this bloody mess too much for even the feller who did for her to stomach?'

Beresford looked uncomfortable. 'It . . . er . . . it was the lad I sent off for a cup of tea who vomited, sir,' he admitted. 'He tried to restrain himself, but he just couldn't hold it in. He got as far from the crime scene as he could, before he threw up. Will he be in trouble?'

'Not if I have anythin' to do with it,' Woodend promised.

He crouched down to examine the corpse. The woman's skirt was a brown and white check; her blouse was white cotton. She was still wearing her heavy cloth coat, but her attacker had obviously ripped it open before he began his grisly work. Both her feet were naked, but her left shoe was lying beside her body.

'Any idea where her other shoe might be?' Woodend asked.

'It's over there, sir,' Beresford said, redirecting the beam of his torch for a moment to a spot a couple of yards distant.

So the attack had occurred where the body was found, Woodend thought. And when morning came, and it was light enough to do a proper search, they'd no doubt find the buttons from her coat.

He stretched forward and ran the edge of the woman's skirt through his thumb and forefinger.

Acceptable quality, he decided. Not too cheap, yet not too expensive.

There was nothing flashy about the clothes, which there certainly would have been if the woman had been on the game. In fact, it was quite a tasteful – almost restrained – outfit.

You couldn't tell *everything* from clothes, but Woodend was prepared to bet that when they did eventually learn the woman's identity, she would turn out to be a secretary or a clerk in a local government office.

'Do you think she's been raped, sir?' Beresford asked.

'Well, he didn't drag her knickers down so he could wipe his nose on them,' Woodend snapped.

And almost immediately he felt ashamed of himself, because this constable was a good lad, eager to learn his trade, and didn't deserve to be spoken to in that manner.

'I'd guess she's been raped, but you can never tell,' he said. 'We'll have to wait until the medical examiner's had a look at her.'

But raped or not, what had she been doing walking along a deserted towpath on a cold autumn evening? And if her attacker had been no more than a rapist, why had he reduced her face to a pulp after he had got what he wanted?

The last thing Whitebridge needed, the Chief Inspector thought, was a nutter on the loose.

He stood up again. 'Let me have another look at her face.'

Beresford shone his torch on the mess of blood, shattered bone and ripped flesh. 'It is a terrible sight, though, sir, isn't it?' he said.

'Yes, it is,' Woodend agreed.

He'd seen worse – much worse – but that still didn't make looking at this particular poor bloody woman any easier.

No one had been reported missing, Bob Rutter told Monika Paniatowski when she radioed through to headquarters. There had been the usual number of concerned citizens calling in, of course – the woman who claimed that her neighbours were sheltering Adolf Hitler, the man who swore blind that he had seen a flying saucer land behind the gas works – but none who claimed to have heard a scream coming from the direction of the canal, or who had seen a wild-looking feller carrying a blood-stained instrument.

It had, in other words, been a complete waste of time even going through the motions.

But then most police-work was a complete waste of time, Paniatowski thought – and any bobby not prepared to sift through one hell of a lot of chaff in the hope of finding one grain of wheat would be well advised to seek some other line of work.

From her vantage point on the bridge, she could just make out the shapes of the three men standing by the body. Even if the other two had not been wearing their pointed helmets, it would have been easy to pick out Woodend, because – as other officers, who were no midgets themselves, would tell you – the man was built like a brick shit-house.

Paniatowski watched Woodend lean down over the corpse. She should go and join him, she thought, but first she would have a cigarette.

As the smoke curled its way around her lungs, she found her mind returning to Bob Rutter's problems.

She should be happy about what was happening in Bob's marriage, she told herself. So why wasn't she?

Partly, she supposed, it was due to guilt. She liked Maria. She admired Maria. And what had she done? She had deliberately embarked on an affair with the woman's husband.

Which made her what?

A scarlet woman!

A home-breaker.

A callous bitch who was bringing further pain to a woman who had had more than her fair share of suffering.

Yet she was honest enough with herself to admit she could have ridden that out if she'd had to. Of course, the guilt – the deep shame – would go with her to her grave, but if she'd had Bob for herself, she would probably have been able to live with it.

But she wouldn't get Bob, would she? Not if Maria succeeded in taking his only child off him!

Oh, she could imagine what he'd say – 'It really isn't your fault I've lost the baby, Monika. I don't blame you at all.'

But it wouldn't be true!

Even if they moved in together after Maria had left him – even if they *married* once his divorce papers came through – the relationship would be poisoned, and, in the end, Bob would grow to hate her.

So what good could be rescued from the whole sad business?

None at all! Not one bloody thing!

Her fingers had been getting hotter and hotter, but she hadn't noticed it, and it was only now – when her cigarette had burned down so far that it had started to singe her flesh – that she cried out and dropped the bloody thing.

She reached into her pocket, took out a handkerchief, and wrapped it around the burned fingers. This wasn't pain, she told herself. Not real pain. *Real pain* was what she was feeling inside.

Woodend had stood up again, and appeared to be talking to the constables. She supposed she'd better go and join him, she thought. The murder would at least give her something to do – would focus her mind on something *solvable*.

Two

The Woodends lived in an old, stone handloom-weaver's cottage on the edge of the moors. Once there had been three of them, then Annie had grown up, and gone away to Manchester to study nursing.

So now there were just two, Woodend thought – as he lay in bed studying the patterns made by the overnight frost on the window – a middle-aged couple already sliding down the gentle slope to retirement. Charlie and Joan, soon to become *Darby* and Joan.

At least, he *hoped* that's what they were bloody well doing! But he couldn't be sure. The simple truth was that Joan's heart attack in Spain had scared the crap out of him. The doctors had assured him it was only a mild one, but that was no consolation at all, because that seemed to be almost on a par with being only a *little bit* dead.

He was doing all he could to ease the situation. He'd offered to employ a cleaner, but Joan had turned the idea down.

'If you think I'm havin' another woman doin' my jobs an' rummaging through my things, Charlie Woodend, you've got another think comin',' she'd told him.

He'd tried to do some of the work around the house himself, but by the time he got home, it had all been done.

'What do you expect me to do all day, while you're out catchin' criminals? Sit here twiddlin' my thumbs?' she'd demanded, when he'd remonstrated with her.

Still, at least he'd persuaded her to go and stay at her sister's house for a couple of weeks. At least she'd get some rest while she was there.

It must be terrible to lose your wife, he thought, as he swung his legs out of bed and felt the soles of his bare feet make contact with the cold linoleum.

Terrible?

It must feel like the end of the bloody world!

The frost had not come alone, but had brought ice with it for company, and the moorland roads which fed into Whitebridge were treacherous. Twice, Woodend was forced to slow to a virtual halt, and join the stream of traffic creeping past accidents caused by less prudent drivers. Once, he himself was nearly in a collision with some bloody idiot. The result of all this was, inevitably, that he arrived at the police car park a full twenty minutes later than he'd intended to.

Another black mark against me, he thought as he walked

across the car park towards the main entrance of the headquarters.

Another entry for Mr Marlowe's little black book, under
the heading, 'Things I've got against Charlie-bloody-
Woodend'.

Rutter and Paniatowski were where Woodend had expected
them to be – sitting at their desks in what Chief Constable
Marlowe liked, at press conferences, to refer to as 'the very
nerve centre of our murder investigation'.

The reality of the 'nerve centre' fell far short of the rheto-
ric. But then it was bound to. A dusty basement was a dusty
basement. However many desks were laid in a horseshoe shape
– however many extra phones were installed – no one was
ever going to mistake it for the plush FBI offices out of which
Hollywood B-picture cops always seemed to operate. Even
the blackboard – scrounged from somewhere or other, and set
up at the front of the room – failed to give the place the professional air that Mr Marlowe would have wished, and instead
merely reminded most people who saw it of their gladly relin-
quished schooldays.

Still, Woodend reflected, it at least made the Chief Constable
happy, and – to a certain extent – kept him off the backs of
the bobbies who were actually trying to solve the case.

Woodend himself had never cared for this way of working.
He liked to have a team backing him up, but he preferred it
to be a *small* team that he knew well – and would have trusted
with his life.

Nor was he one to sit around in a room all day – even if
it did have a blackboard with several different-coloured chalks
provided! Where he wanted to be was out and about. Immersing
himself in the atmosphere of the area in which the crime had
been committed. Collecting odd scraps of information which
he might – or might *not* – be later able to fit into the overall
picture. This was how *he* solved his cases. This was how he
gained his insights into who had committed the crimes and –
even more interestingly from his point of view – *why* they
had committed them.

17

He knew this habit of his – wearing out his boots almost as much as he wore out his brains – had earned him the nickname 'Cloggin'-it Charlie' back at the Yard, and that the nickname had followed him to Whitebridge. He knew, too, that though the name was never used to his face, it was used often enough behind his back. But it didn't bother him. In fact, he was quite proud of it. For while his method of working might make him a dinosaur in the eyes of some of his superiors, his arrest record also made it clear to them that at least he was a *successful* dinosaur.

Paniatowski and Rutter, who were both on the phone, didn't see him enter the room, and so he had time to examine them at leisure.

God, they both looked rough, he thought.

And not the kind of 'rough' that came from working up to eighteen hours a day for weeks on end. No, their 'rough', it seemed to him, came from an inner turmoil which had nothing to do with the job.

The two detectives hung up, so nearly at the same time that they might have been part of a synchronized phoning team.

'Has the handbag been found yet?' Woodend asked, sitting down opposite his two favourite police officers.

'No,' Rutter said. 'Nor has anything else which might have helped to identify the victim. In fact, there was nothing at all on the canal path which could be connected to the murder in any way, shape or form.'

Woodend sighed. 'We'll just have to go about it the hard way, then. Any reports of missin' persons?'

'None,' Rutter said.

'At least, none that have come in since last night,' Monika Paniatowski amplified.

'So what does that tell us?' the Chief Inspector asked.

'Well, if no one's noticed she isn't there, she probably lived alone,' Rutter said.

'Which means she's single,' Paniatowski added.

'Or divorced,' Woodend said.

'She's not been missed at work, either,' Rutter said. He

18

glanced up at the clock. 'Which either means that she doesn't – didn't – work factory hours or she didn't work at all.'

'You've both seen the body, have you?' Woodend asked, and when Rutter and Paniatowski nodded grimly, he said, 'What do you make of it?'

'The man's clearly a complete bloody lunatic,' Paniatowski said.

'Do you agree with that, Bob?' Woodend asked.

Rutter thought about it for a moment. 'Either that, or she'd done something that hurt him so much he just couldn't restrain himself from lashing out, even when she was dead,' he said finally.

Bloody hell fire, Woodend thought, I've known this lad since he was a fresh-faced young sergeant, wet behind both ears – an' I'd never have expected him to say anythin' like that!

'I'm not quite sure what you mean there, Bob,' he said, trying not to sound too troubled. 'Exactly what *kind* of thing do you think she might have done to hurt him?'

'I've no idea,' Rutter confessed. 'And I certainly don't condone what he's done—'

'Well, that *is* a relief,' Woodend interrupted.

'. . . but I can well imagine a man being driven to that degree of desperation,' Rutter persisted stubbornly.

'Can you indeed?' Woodend asked. 'Then I have to tell you, you've got a broader imagination than I possess.'

An awkward, uncomfortable silence descended over them. Half an eternity seemed to pass before Paniatowski said, 'Have we been sent the medical findings yet, sir?'

'No, we haven't,' Woodend answered gratefully. 'But I bet that if I pop down the morgue, the doc will give me at least her *preliminary* findings.'

The snap of cold weather had not deterred Dr Shastri from wearing her sari that morning – albeit, while she was outdoors at least, under her trademark sheepskin jacket. Seeing her now, Woodend was struck, not for the first time, by the contrast between the clinical coldness of the doctor's morgue and the vibrancy and colour of her attire.

'So what have you got for me, Doc?' he asked.

Dr Shastri clicked her tongue disapprovingly.

'I have only had the cadaver in question for a few hours, yet here you are already, demanding results,' she said. 'The trouble with you, Chief Inspector, is that you expect miracles.'

Woodend grinned. 'Why shouldn't I expect them, when you always deliver them?' he asked innocently. 'As I never stop tellin' people, you're the best police surgeon we've ever had.'

Dr Shastri smiled back. Her teeth were small, brilliantly white and even. 'You seem to think that flattery will get you everywhere,' she said.

'And won't it?'

'I am ashamed to admit that it will,' the doctor said, shaking her head as if amazed at her own gullibility.

She reached for a cardboard file which was lying on her desk, opened it and scanned the contents.

'I would say that your victim was twenty-eight or twenty-nine,' she said. 'Cause of death was strangulation.'

'Her knickers were around her ankles when she was found. Had she been raped?'

Dr Shastri frowned. 'Technically – and probably legally, as far as I know – I suppose she had been. I, myself, would prefer to think of it as violation.'

'Meaning what, exactly?'

'There had certainly been penetration – quite violent penetration, as a matter of fact – but the instrument used was not a penis.'

'Then what the bloody hell *was* it?'

'A fairly broad object without any sharp edges.'

'Like the handle of the axe he chopped up her face with?'

Dr Shastri shook her head. 'No. Anything wooden – even if it had been very smooth – would almost certainly have left splinters. Since there were none in evidence, I would have to conclude that it was either a bottle or some metal object.'

'Can't you be more specific?'

'Given time – and luck – I might be able to be more definite, but I would not hold your breath whilst you're waiting.'

'Was she already dead when he did this to her?'

'I'm afraid not.'

'Then why didn't she call out? Why didn't she scream?'

'She probably couldn't. There were traces of gum mixed in with the mush which was all that was left of her face. I would guess her killer had put some kind of adhesive tape over her mouth.' Dr Shastri paused in order to light up a long, thin, purple-coloured cigarette. 'I imagine your next question is, why she didn't struggle?' the doctor continued.

'It is,' Woodend agreed.

'She couldn't. Her hands were tied behind her back.'

'She could have lashed out with her legs.'

'Her ankles were bound together, too, though not so tightly as to make the penetration impossible.'

'Her wrists and ankles weren't tied when the body was discovered,' Woodend said.

'In which case the killer must have removed her bonds once he had finished his work.'

'Why?'

'You're the detective,' Dr Shastri said. 'You tell me.'

'Can you give me any idea of what she was tied up *with*? Was it some kind of rope or cord?'

'Almost certainly not. Like the instrument used for penetration, rope or cord would have left traces behind. And there were none.'

'So what the hell was it?'

'They are making ingenious use of plastics these days,' Dr Shastri said. 'My guess is that it would have been some kind of man-made bond. No doubt it will be found close to the scene of the crime.'

'We haven't turned up anythin' so far, which means that we probably never will.'

'In that case, I will give the matter more thought.' Dr Shastri flashed Woodend a meaningful look. '*When I have the time*.'

'Point taken, Doc,' Woodend said. 'Another question. I appreciate there was probably considerable vaginal damage, but were you still able to ascertain whether or not she was a virgin before she was attacked?'

Dr Shastri laughed. 'You can be so quaint and old-fashioned at times,' she said. 'This is the 1960s, my dear Chief Inspector. Twenty-nine-year-old virgins are as rare – and some would say as beautiful – as the Taj Mahal.'

'So she *wasn't* a virgin.'

'No, she wasn't.'

'What about the facial disfigurement? Was that done once she was already dead?'

'Yes, the poor woman was at least spared any knowledge of that.'

'What can you tell me about her while she was alive?'

Dr Shastri consulted her folder again, though, knowing her as he did, Woodend was sure that all the details were in her head.

'She was generally in good health,' the doctor said. 'She had never had a serious operation, nor had she ever been pregnant. Her fingernails are very well cared for and—'

'Any skin traces under them?' Woodend interrupted.

'I'm afraid not. As I said, her nails were in a very good condition, from which I would conclude both that she spent money on them and that she was not engaged in the kind of work likely to damage them. Her teeth are excellent. She has had recent dental work which, from its quality, I would say was done privately.'

'And locally?' Woodend asked hopefully.

'You really *do* expect miracles, don't you?' Dr Shastri said. 'There are certainly dental surgeons in Whitebridge capable of doing work to that standard of excellence, but she could just as easily have had it done in London. Or Edinburgh, for that matter.'

'Any scars of any kind?'

Dr Shastri laughed again. 'I thought you'd seen her face.'

'I meant, any scars prior to last night?'

'No.'

'Any other identifyin' marks?'

'You are hoping, I take it, that I will tell you of an unusual tattoo at the base of her spine – a tattoo which, furthermore, I happen to know could only be the work of one tattooist in the entire world. As an extra bonus, you would like me to tell you that he lives within a short driving distance of Whitebridge.'

'Within a short walkin' distance of this morbid bloody place would be even better,' Woodend said dryly. 'But you're not about to offer me such an easy solution to my problems, are you?'

'Unfortunately not,' Dr Shastri agreed. 'Your victim treated her skin – as she seemed to treat everything else about her – with a great deal of respect.'

'You've been a great help,' Woodend said.

'Of course,' Dr Shastri agreed, smiling again. 'I always am.' She paused, and her expression grew more serious. 'It's difficult to say for certain without doing at least some *basic* reconstructive surgery,' she continued, 'but I think she must have been a rather pretty girl.'

The phone rang just as Woodend was returning to his desk in the 'nerve centre', and Monika Paniatowski picked it up.

'Yes?' she said. 'Yes . . . Hardly misses a day . . . And if she does, she always let's you know . . . Have you tried . . . Oh, you have, and she's not answering . . . How old would she be? . . . Twenty-eight . . . And how would you describe her hair? . . . Thank you. We'll be in touch.'

She replaced the phone on its cradle.

'Well?' Woodend said.

'We may have a lead. A woman called Pamela Rainsford's failed to turn up for work this morning. She's normally very conscientious and—'

'Yes, yes, we could infer all that from your end of the conversation,' Woodend interrupted impatiently. 'Where does this woman work?'

'At New Horizons Enterprises, out on the industrial estate. It's a furniture company.'

'I know,' Woodend said. 'An' what's this Miss Rainsford's job out at New Horizons? She's not a French polisher or anythin' like that, is she?'

'Somebody who works with her hands,' Rutter explained, as if such clarification were necessary.

'No, she doesn't work with her hands,' Paniatowski said. 'At least, she doesn't do *heavy* work with her hands. She's a secretary.'

Secretaries in Whitebridge – a town more famed for its manual labour than its brain work – usually considered they had a position to keep up, Woodend thought. So dressing smartly – though not expensively – would just about fit the ticket.

He was virtually sure they'd found their victim, and he felt a certain sadness come over him – as it always did when the dead slab of meat he'd been examining took on a name and became a person in his eyes.

'Monika an' me'll drive out to New Horizons,' he told Rutter. 'You stay here an' hold the fort.'

Three

The commercial estate on which New Horizons Enterprises was located had been described in the local press as representing 'the industrial renaissance of manufacturing in Whitebridge'. Woodend, reading the words, had assumed that this was just a poncy way of saying that as old industries declined, new ones sprang up to take their place. Still, there was no doubt that the estate had breathed new life into the town, or that New Horizons had been one of the pioneers in the process.

The estate lay to the west of Whitebridge, about three miles from the town centre. Given traffic speeds at that time of day, it gave Woodend ample opportunity, during the journey, to talk to Monika Paniatowski about what exactly was bothering her. But he wasn't sure that he wanted to – or rather, he wasn't sure that *she* would want him to – so instead he decided to stick to the case.

'Got any New Horizons furniture in that flat of yours, Monika?' he asked, as he pulled out of the police headquarters' car park.

'Not that I'm aware of,' Paniatowski replied.

'Oh, you'd be well aware of it, if you did have any of their stuff. An' *I'd* be worried.'

'Worried? Why?'

'Because I'd be forced to ask myself how somebody on your salary could afford it.'

'It's expensive, then?'

'Horrendously. But I have to say, it's probably worth it. They use machinery for the basic jobs, but most of the finishin' is done by hand.'

Paniatowski lit a cigarette. 'I wouldn't have thought there'd be much call for that kind of thing in Whitebridge.'

'Nor is there,' Woodend agreed. 'Most of the stuff's shipped off to London, or else sent abroad.'

'It's not like you to know about things like expensive furniture, sir' Paniatowski said. 'Have we had dealings, in an official capacity, with the company before?'

'Not as far as I'm aware,' Woodend said. 'But I happen to know the boss of the place slightly.'

Paniatowski pulled a face. 'Oh, you are moving up in the world. You'll be joining the Freemasons next.'

'It's not like that,' Woodend told her. 'I know Derek Higson because I went to school with him.'

'So he's quite old, then,' Paniatowski said, teasingly.

'Watch it!' Woodend said, with mock severity. 'It's not a

sergeant's place to pass comment on the advanced age of her boss, even if he has got one foot in the grave.'

'One foot?' Paniatowski repeated. 'It's as little as that, is it?'

Anyone hearing the conversation would imagine it was the normal banter which had developed between two people who worked so closely together, Woodend thought. But he knew better. The words might be the right ones, but the tone wasn't. Monika was forcing it.

'Are you havin' any problems in your personal life?' he asked, abandoning his earlier resolve.

The air inside the car was suddenly chillier by several degrees.

'Problems?' Paniatowski said. 'Why should I have problems? My whole life's like a dream come true.'

So that had told him, hadn't it? Woodend thought.

New Horizons Enterprises was an impressive building by any standards. It was much larger than any of the other units on the estate. And it was much more adventurous in its concept. While the rest of the buildings had opted for a modified-cotton-mill frontage, New Horizons' architect had clearly been given licence to go wild with futuristic glass and steel.

A slim young man in a smart suit, and sporting a smart haircut, was waiting for them in the car park.

'Tom Blaine,' he said, shaking Woodend's hand, and then – almost as an afterthought – shaking Paniatowski's. 'I'm the Personnel Manager here at New Horizons. Do you really think this horrible thing could have happened to one of our employees?'

One of our employees! Woodend thought.

Was that any way to refer to a young woman who had been viciously butchered?

'Death can strike anywhere, at anybody, an' at any time,' he said. 'Unless, of course, workin' for New Horizons gives your staff a special immunity I know nothin' about.'

'I'm not sure I'm following you,' Blaine said.

Then you shouldn't be workin' with *people*, Woodend thought. But aloud, he contented himself with saying, 'Is there a big room available inside? A canteen or somethin' of that nature?'

'Yes, we do have a canteen,' Blaine said uncertainly.

'Good, then I'd like you to usher all your clerical staff in there, so I can talk to them.'

Blaine glanced down at his wristwatch. 'Conveniently enough, they are due to have their break in about half an hour,' he said.

'Well, that is convenient,' Woodend agreed. 'Except that I'd like to talk to them five minutes from now.'

'But—'

'Don't argue, lad,' Woodend snarled. 'Just bloody do it! An' there's one more thing.'

'Yes?'

'I'm used to dealin' with the organ-grinder, not his monkey, so I'd be grateful if you'd make sure your boss is there when I talk to his people.'

Blaine looked ready to express his outrage at the insult, then, noting how much Woodend towered over him, decided that a sullen demeanour might be a wiser option.

'Mr Higson isn't here at the moment,' he said. 'He's away on a business trip in Europe.'

'Nice work if you can get it,' Woodend said. 'It'll have to be his Number Two then. An' don't try tellin' me *you're* his Number Two, because I know Derek Higson well enough to be sure he'd never leave a bloody fool like you in charge of the place.'

Blaine sniffed. 'I'll see if *Mrs* Higson is in the building,' he said.

'Aye,' Woodend agreed. 'Why don't you do just that?'

The canteen was all chrome and glass, and while Woodend could see the advantages of using such materials from a hygienic point of view, he *couldn't* see how it would do anyone's digestion any good to eat their dinner in a space-ship.

27

The twenty clerical staff, most of them women, had been assembled as per instructions, and were sitting at the tables, looking at him with expressions which displayed a mixture of dread, excitement, and morbid curiosity.

'You'll all have heard the news this mornin', an' I expect a bright lot like you will have worked out what this is all about,' Woodend said. 'Our bein' here is proof of nothin' – there's any number of reasons why Miss Rainsford might not have turned up – but police work is a process of elimination. And that's what we're doin' – eliminatin'.' He paused, to let his words sink in. 'In a minute, my sergeant's goin' to be handin' out photographs of the murder victim. I wouldn't look at the face, if I was you – you'd not be able to recognize your own mother if this had been done to her – so just have a look at the clothes.'

Paniatowski walked along the table, handing out the photographs. She'd not distributed more than half of them when one the women started crying.

'It's her!' the woman sobbed. 'I know it's her!'

'How can you be so sure?' Woodend asked.

'This . . . this skirt and blouse. I was with her when she bought them. She . . . she was w. . .wearing them at work, yesterday.'

Soon, several other voices were shouting – or even screaming – that yes, this was definitely the outfit Pamela had been wearing the previous day.

'Calm down!' Woodend ordered. 'I know this is a distressin' experience, but if you want to help us find your friend's killer, you're just goin' to have to calm down.'

Gradually the noise subsided, until it was reduced to a few muffled sobs.

'That's better,' Woodend said. 'Now we're goin' to have to talk to all of you, but it'd help us if, when my sergeant takes your name, you'd try to let us know how well you knew Pamela, so we'll be able to decide who to see first.'

It was as Paniatowski produced her notebook that Woodend noticed the woman standing at the back of the room. She was around thirty, he estimated, and she had an athlete's build and stunning blonde hair which cascaded down over her shoulders.

Even from a distance, it was possible to guess that the suit she was wearing had probably cost her more than any of the clerical staff earned in a month. But it wasn't just money which made her look the way she did. Dress any of the secretaries or typists in those clothes, and they just wouldn't be able to carry it off. On the other hand, dress this woman in a sack, and she'd still look good.

Woodend made his way to the back of the room. The woman made no move to meet him half-way, but instead watched his advance with interest. As he got closer, he could see that she'd been crying, but even that only seemed to enhance her beauty.

'Poor bloody Pamela,' she said, when he was close enough to hear.

'I'm Chief Inspector Woodend,' he said.

'I know you are.'

'And you are . . .?'

'Lucy Higson. The Personnel Manager said you wanted me to be here.'

Lucy Higson! Derek's wife! But he must be a good twenty years older than her.

A slight smile came to the woman's face. 'It's not the age of a man that counts,' she said. 'It's the man himself.'

'Bloody hell, was I that obvious?' Woodend asked.

'Probably not to most people. But I know what signs to look for. God knows, I've had enough practice looking at them since I married Derek. Half the men we meet wonder how he ever got to be such a lucky bastard, and the other half just assume I married him for his money.'

'An' did you?' Woodend asked, before he could stop himself.

Lucy Higson did not take offence. 'I'd have married him if he'd been living in the gutter,' she said. 'How can I help you with your investigation?'

'Mainly by not doin' anythin' to obstruct it,' Woodend said. 'Your Personnel Manager seemed to find it most inconvenient that I should want to talk your staff outside their normal break time.'

'That little prick!' Lucy Higson said with a vehemence that surprised him. 'I told Derek we should never employ Tom Blaine. But my husband's like so many men who've raised themselves through hard work and ability – far too impressed by other people's paper qualifications.'

She reached into her pocket for a packet of cigarettes and offered it to Woodend.

'I don't smoke cork-tipped,' Woodend said.

'Quite right, too,' Lucy Higson said. 'It's not a man's cigarette.' She placed one of the cigarettes between her lips, and without waiting for Woodend to offer her a light, produced a gold lighter out of her pocket. She lit the cigarette, and inhaled deeply. 'Don't you worry about young master Blaine,' she continued. 'I'll keep him in order.'

'What can you tell me about Pamela Rainsford?' Woodend asked.

Lucy Higson took another drag of her cigarette. 'She's been my husband's secretary for about three years. She was a nice girl. Not an outstanding personality or overly bright, but very conscientious. I knew she'd just suit Derek. That's why I hired her.'

'You hired her? Not Blaine?'

'This was back in the days before Derek thought we needed a Personnel Manager. I'm very much looking forward to those days returning in the not-too-distant future.'

'Do you think they ever will?'

Lucy Higson smiled again. 'Oh yes. I usually get my own way – in the end,' she said.

I'm sure you bloody do, Woodend thought. 'What can you tell me about Pamela's personal life?' he asked.

'Very little,' Lucy Higson admitted. 'She was quite a pretty girl, so I assume she had boyfriends. But she never told me about them, and I never asked. This is very much a *businesslike* business. We treat our employees well – far better than most of the companies around here – but we've never pretended we're all part of one big happy family. I could probably find out something about her, if you wanted me to, but after what's happened I assume you'd prefer to do that yourself.'

'Aye, I would,' Woodend agreed.

'I'll arrange for a room to be put at your disposal then,' Lucy Higson said crisply. 'Anything you want – people *or* resources – you only have to ask. The canteen does a pretty decent meal, so if you want anything to eat, simply pick up the internal phone and I'll see it's brought to you straight away.'

'You're very kind,' Woodend said.

For a moment, the remark seemed to puzzle Lucy Higson. 'It's funny, you know, but I've never thought of myself as kind. Fair, yes – I pride myself on being fair – but never *kind*.' A tear appeared in the corner of her right eye. 'I said earlier that we've never thought of our employees as part of the family.'

'I remember,' Woodend replied.

'So why do I feel as if I've just lost one of my family now?' Lucy Higson wondered.

Four

Jenny Thomas – the woman whose sobs had been the first confirmation that the dead woman actually was Pamela Rainsford – sat opposite Woodend and Paniatowski in the office that Lucy Higson had provided for them.

She was, Woodend guessed, about the same age as Pamela had been. There was no wedding ring on her finger, so it seemed likely that she, like the dead woman, was unmarried.

He glanced down at the picture of Pamela which the personnel office had given him from her record, and then looked back up at Jenny. It seemed to him that the age-old tradition of the very pretty girl choosing a best friend who was – at best – plain, had clearly been followed in this case. Pamela, with her auburn hair, green eyes, pert nose and slim figure, had undoubtedly been what, in his day, would have been called a real looker. Jenny, on the other hand, had a dumpy shape and poor complexion, and would be very lucky to turn *any* heads when she walked down the street.

Jenny sniffed into the large white handkerchief she'd been holding on her lap. She had calmed down a little in the previous half-hour, but she was still very clearly distressed.

'I understand that this is painful for you, but there are questions we have to ask,' Woodend said soothingly.

Jenny Thomas managed a slight nod. 'I know that.'

'What can you tell us about Pamela?' Paniatowski asked.

The other woman looked bewildered. 'Tell you about her? I don't know where to start,' she confessed.

'Let's begin with when you first met her,' Woodend suggested.

'That would be when she first began working here, which was just over three years ago.'

'Do you know where she'd been employed before that?'

'She wasn't. She was studying at secretarial college in Bradford.' Jenny Thomas sniffed again, and this time Woodend thought he detected a sign of disdain. 'It was a very *good* secretarial college,' she continued. 'That's why Pamela started out as Mr Higson's secretary, instead of having to work her way up from the typing pool, like everybody else.'

She had the better looks and the better job, Woodend thought – and even *best* friends can sometimes be envious.

'She was rather old to be going to secretarial college, wasn't she?' Paniatowski asked.

'She called it her second chance,' Jenny Thomas said. 'She was lucky there. Not all of us get one.'

No, Paniatowski thought, we don't.

'Do you know what she was doing before she went to secretarial college?' the sergeant asked.

'She was married.'

'She must have been almost a child bride.'

'She was. Got married as soon as she left school.'

'But it didn't last?'

'No, it didn't. She divorced the swine for desertion – which was no more than he deserved!'

'You knew him, did you?' Paniatowski asked.

'No,' Jenny Thomas admitted. 'But you know what men are like.'

Paniatowski shot Woodend a warning look, then said, 'Oh yes, I know what men are like, all right. Do you happen to know if Pamela had any contact with her husband after the divorce?'

'She told me she hadn't heard a word from him since the day he walked out of the door for a packet of cigarettes – and never came back.'

'So what about the other men in her life?' Paniatowski asked.

'She's had boyfriends, but they never lasted,' Jenny said, and the hint of resentfulness was back.

'Could you give us their names?'

'I would if I knew them, but she was very secretive about them. Wouldn't tell me who they were – or even where they worked – however much I asked.'

And I'll bet you asked *a lot*, Woodend thought.

'If you know so little about the relationships, how do you know they didn't last long?' Paniatowski wondered.

'Because when they were over, she'd come back to me. I mean . . .'

'Yes?'

'We'd start knocking about together again. Going to the Saturday night dances at the Whitebridge Palais. Things like that.'

She sounded almost like a jealous lover, Woodend thought, but he was sure that had never been her intention.

What she *had* meant – even though she would not express it in those terms herself – was that when Pamela was unattached, she could bask in the reflected glory. Or to put it in it's crudest terms, the ugly girl could always rely on a date with the ugly friend of the handsome young man who wanted to get off with Pamela.

'Have you been going out to the Palais together recently?' Paniatowski asked.

'No,' Jenny Thomas admitted. 'Not recently.'

'When was the last time you did?'

'Must have been about a year ago.'

'So her current boyfriend would appear to be more serious.'

Jenny Thomas stuck her chin out defiantly. 'It won't last,' she said, with all the conviction of a woman who really *wanted* to believe her own words. 'It *never* lasts.' And suddenly her chin began to wobble and fresh tears appeared in her eyes. 'What am I saying?' she asked no one in particular. 'It *can't* last, can it? Because Pamela's dead!'

Maria Rutter ran her hand along the arm of the chair in which she was sitting.

Leather, she thought. Soft, expensive leather, both from the touch and the smell.

It was a pretty safe bet that any solicitor who invested in chairs like these was going to put in a pretty hefty bill for any work he did, but she didn't mind that. She wanted the best, because when you were starting out with the disadvantage of being blind, you needed whatever edge you could get.

'As I understand it, Mrs Rutter, you're contemplating leaving your husband,' the solicitor said, in a rich voice which blended in well with the chairs.

'That's correct,' Maria agreed.

'It's a big step, you know,' the solicitor cautioned. 'Something of a leap in the dark.' He paused for a moment, and she could imagine the horrified expression which had come to his face. 'I'm sorry,' he continued. 'I didn't mean . . .'

'That's all right,' Maria assured him.

'Is it . . .?' the solicitor began. He paused again. 'I don't know quite how to put this.'

'Were you going to ask if my husband has been less attentive to me since I've gone blind?' Maria wondered.

'Well, yes.'

'I was blind when I married him. That's not the problem.'

The problem wasn't even Monika, she thought. The problem was that Bob had not only loved Monika, but that he *still* loved her.

'It's not my place to advise you on anything other than strictly legal matters,' the solicitor said. He laughed uncomfortably. 'After all, I'm not a marriage guidance councillor.'

'But . . . ?' Maria asked.

'But I think that in your special situation, you should think carefully before instituting legal proceedings.'

'You mean that since I'm blind, I should be grateful for what I've got, however miserable my existence might be?'

'No, no,' the solicitor said hastily. 'I wouldn't quite put it like that.'

'Then how *would* you put it?'

'I'd just say that your life doesn't need any more complications than it already has.'

Maria stood up. 'Thank you for your time,' she said, feeling in front of her with her white stick.

'Please sit down again, until I can call someone to lead you out, Mrs Rutter, the solicitor said.

'I can manage,' Maria replied, negotiating her way around the chair.

'The door's—'

'I know where the door is,' Maria said sharply. 'It's only a few minutes since I came in through it.'

'I know, but—'

'I'm blind, not stupid.'

'Quite,' the solicitor agreed uneasily. He cleared his throat. 'There is . . . er . . . a question of my fee.'

A mocking smile came to Maria's lips. 'You'd take money

off a poor blind woman, would you?' she asked. 'A woman who is so pathetic that you expect her to stay with her husband however bad things get.'

'I . . .er . . . sympathize with your predicament, but you must understand that business is business.'

'Of course,' Maria said. 'Send me your bill.'

'I'll see it's posted today,' the solicitor said.

Maria's smile broadened. 'I wouldn't have thought you could have prepared it so quickly.'

'Oh, this is a very efficient office,' the solicitor assured her.

'And you have the right kind of typewriter, do you?'

'The *right* kind of typewriter?'

'Yes. You may not quite have come to appreciate this yet, but one of the disadvantages of being blind is that you can't see. So if you want your bill paid, you'd better send it in Braille.'

Five

'Got any contacts in the Bradford Police, Monika?' Woodend asked, when Jenny Thomas had snuffled and shuffled her way out of the room.

'Yes, as a matter of fact, I have,' Paniatowski replied. 'There's a sergeant there who I met on a course last year.'

'Did you get on well?'

'Very. We liked each other from the start. It might have developed into something if . . .'

She didn't say any more, but she didn't need to.

It might have developed into somethin' if she hadn't still been desperately in love with Bob Rutter, Woodend thought, filling in the space.

There was an awkward pause – life seemed to be full of awkward pauses between them recently – then Woodend said, 'It might be a good idea to get on to this mate of yours.'

Paniatowski nodded, rang Bradford Central, and asked to be connected to Sergeant Bill Conner.

'I knew you couldn't resist my charms for ever,' Conner said, when he came on to the line.

'Don't flatter yourself, Sweet William,' Paniatowski said lightly. 'I'm only ringing because I want something.'

'Of course you are,' Conner agreed, happily enough. 'That's the way the women in my life always treat me. So what can I do for you, Monika?'

'I was wondering if you had any records on a Pamela Rainsford,' Paniatowski said.

'Why? What's she done?' Conner asked.

'You sound as if you know her.'

'I do. Or at least, I did before she moved away. She was married to a mate of mine – Constable Tony Rainsford.'

'And he deserted her, didn't he? Walked out one morning and never came back?'

There was a pause on the other end of the line, then Conner said, 'Who's been spinnin' you that line?'

'It isn't true? He didn't walk out?'

'He did not. Tony *moved* out, but right up until the day she left Bradford, she always knew where she could find him.'

'*Why* did he move out?'

'Why does anybody leave their wife?'

'There's dozens of reasons. What was his?'

Another pause. 'To tell you the truth, I'm not really sure,' Conner admitted. 'When most men are bein' given grief by their womenfolk, it's usually impossible to make them shut up about it. But not Tony. He never said a word. But we could tell somethin' was wrong, anyway.'

'How?'

'The last couple of years they were together, he'd come on duty lookin' so rough you'd swear he'd been dragged through a hedge backwards.'

'Was that because he was drinking heavily?'

'Definitely not. Not at that time, anyway.'

'Then what *was* his problem?'

'Like I said, he didn't talk about it. But if you ask me, I'd have to guess that there was somethin' wrong in the bedroom department.'

'That's right, blame it on the woman!' Paniatowski said, not quite sure whether Conner's comment had amused her or angered her. 'Women are such frigid bitches, aren't they? They'll never give a man what he really wants – what he really needs.'

It was anger, she decided, as she heard herself speak the last few words. Definitely anger.

'I think you've got hold of the wrong end of the stick, Monika,' Conner said. 'I think it was *him* what was havin' problems keepin' up with *her*.'

'So she was sleeping around?'

'I don't think so. If she had have been, we'd probably have known about it down at the station. An' if that *had* been the case, I imagine he'd have cited it in the divorce proceedin's.'

'So he was the one who divorced her?'

'That's right.'

'And what grounds?'

'I believe it was mental cruelty.'

'I'd like to speak to him,' Paniatowski said.

'I'm afraid you're a bit late for that.'

'What do you mean?'

'He's dead. Killed in a car crash a few months after Pamela left, poor bugger. It was the drink that got him, of course. He went from virtually teetotal to bein' a ravin' dipso in no time at all. I think that despite it all – whatever the "all" actually bloody was – he must have still loved her.'

'You're sure it was drink that caused the crash?'

'Absolutely certain. I examined the wreck of his car myself. It smelled like a bloody distillery.'

Paniatowski sighed. 'Well, thanks for your help anyway, Bill,' she said.

'You never did get around to tellin' me why you were askin' about her,' Connor pointed out.

'She was murdered last night.'

'Oh,' Connor said.

'You don't sound at all surprised,' Paniatowski told him.

'How can you say that! I'm right shocked!' Conner protested. 'Honestly I am.' He paused for a second time. 'But you're not far off the mark, in a way,' he admitted. 'I never imagined she'd end up like that, but I'm not really surprised that she has, if you know what I mean.'

'No, I'm not sure that I do,' Paniatowski admitted.

'Well, there was always somethin' a little bit *dangerous* about Pamela,' Conner explained. 'I couldn't put my finger on it exactly, but she always gave the impression she was livin' on the edge.'

A procession of other young women and girls streamed through the office to be questioned by Woodend and Paniatowski. They varied from the very pretty to the downright unattractive, from the clearly quick and intelligent to the plainly dull and plodding. Some showed their obvious distress, while others were very subdued. And there were even a few, Woodend thought, who were secretly – and guiltily – thrilled to be involved even peripherally in a sensational murder. The only thing they *all* had in common was that they had very little to add to what Jenny Thomas had already said.

'Pamela never talked much about her private life,' a blonde invoice clerk said.

'Wasn't that unusual?' Woodend asked.

'I suppose it was, now I think about it.'

'But it never occurred to you before?'

'Well, no,' the invoice clerk admitted. 'Pamela wasn't like most of the girls who work here, you see. She seemed to have her own set of rules.'

'I think this latest boyfriend of hers was something special,' said a brunette shorthand-typist who wore her hair in an elaborate beehive.

39

'What makes you say that?' Paniatowski asked.

'Sometimes she'd start getting very edgy when it got near to clocking-off time. You know the sort of thing. She didn't seem to be able to concentrate properly, and couldn't stay in any one place for more than a few seconds.'

'And what did you think that meant?'

'Well, that this boyfriend – whoever he was – was taking her somewhere special – somewhere expensive.'

Or somewhere *exciting*, Paniatowski thought – though she had no idea why that particular idea had popped into her head.

Neither Woodend nor Paniatowski thought to order lunch, but at one o'clock it duly arrived, delivered on two dull tin trays by a couple of the office juniors. Woodend, deep in thought, only started to appreciate just how good the meat and two veg was when he'd almost finished it.

The trays were taken away, and the questioning continued along much the same lines as it had before lunch.

'I *liked* Pamela, but I couldn't say I really *knew* her,' confessed a wages' clerk who – being older than most of the other women – was starting to go grey. 'It's Jenny Thomas you should really be talking to. She was Pamela's best friend.'

Woodend pictured the look in Jenny Thomas's eyes when she'd been explaining how Pamela would quickly drop her when she'd taken up with another man.

With friends like her, he thought, who needs enemies?

Six

It was half-past five when Bob Rutter, standing next to the blackboard in the 'nerve centre', announced to his team that while he expected them to carry on with their inquiries for at least two or three more hours, he had other matters to attend to, and was going home.

'Going home, sir?' repeated one of them, an eager young detective constable called Bates.

'Yes! Have you any objection to that, *Chief Superintendent* Bates?' Rutter demanded aggressively.

'No, sir, but . . .'

'But what?'

'But nothin', sir.'

But it's not like you to shirk your duty, sir, Rutter supplied silently, on Bates's behalf. It's not like you to leave up to others work that you should be doing yourself.

True enough. It *wasn't* like him. But his life was falling apart, and it was much more important to make one last effort to save it than it was to catch whoever had killed Pamela Rainsford.

It only took him ten minutes to drive from the centre of Whitebridge to the new suburb in which his family – for the moment, at least – lived. He was close to home when he saw the illuminated billboard, and though he'd been expecting it, he still frowned.

Welcome to Phase Two of the Croft Estate
Two hundred exciting new executive houses
Show-house now open
Prices reduced

'Phase Two!' he said disgustedly.

There had *been* no Phase Two – or even any talk of one – when he had bought his house in Elm Croft a couple of years earlier. One of the things which had attracted him to that particular property was that it was on the edge of the estate, with an uninterrupted view of the moors.

'And there's no chance there'll be any more building in front of it, is there?' he'd asked the estate agent, before handing over his deposit.

'There's *always* a chance,' the agent had replied, in the

41

exaggeratedly frank way that such agents had. 'When you think about it, Mr Rutter, there's always a *chance* you'll be struck by a meteorite or win a couple of hundred thousand quid on the football pools. But it's not something you can spend your life worrying about, now is it?'

'Even so——' Rutter had said doubtfully.

'You soon learn *never* to say "never" in my line of work,' the agent interrupted, 'but as far as I know, all that land beyond the estate is owned by an old farmer who'd rather cut off his own leg than sell a square inch of it.'

The old farmer's determination to hold on to his land – if such determination had ever actually existed – crumbled little more than a year after the Rutters had moved in, and the bull-dozers arrived less than a week after that.

Furious, Rutter had gone to the Croft Estate office and demanded to know what they hell was going on.

The *new* plan, he was told, was to build three more 'crofts' – Birch Croft, Sycamore Croft and Ash Croft.

'But you need have no worries about feeling hemmed in,' Mr Sexton, the building manager, assured him. He pointed to a plan on the wall of his office. 'The next row of houses will be facing the other way, so the bottom of your garden will be touching the bottom of the garden of the corresponding house in Birch Croft. And it'll be a *big* garden, Mr Rutter.' He laughed. 'You'd almost need to mount an expedition to get from the Birch Croft house to yours.'

Rutter failed to see the humour. 'When does work on Birch Croft actually start?' he'd asked.

'Oh, not for a while yet.'

'But the bulldozers are already there.'

'Ah, I see what you mean. It's Ash Croft – what you might call the outer ring of houses – which we'll be building first.'

'And why might that be?'

'Because they'll be the easiest ones to sell. Because they'll be the ones with the . . .'

He stopped suddenly, as if he'd said more than he'd intended to.

'The ones with the uninterrupted view of the moors,' Rutter said, finishing the sentence off for him.

'Well, yes, that's right,' Sexton admitted.

'Just like I had, when your agent sold me my house.'

Sexton shrugged. 'What can I tell you, Mr Rutter? Times change. Things move on. It's the way of the world.'

'So because you want to sell the houses on Ash Croft first, I'll be forced to live next to a building site for at least a year?'

'You'll soon get used to it,' Sexton said, with the indifference of a man who held all the cards. 'Besides, it probably won't be anything like as noisy as you seem to think it will.'

Now, nine months later, Ash Croft was completed – though the houses had not been selling half as quickly as Mr Sexton had clearly anticipated. And soon – out of the morass the builder had created while constructing it – Birch Croft and Sycamore Croft would begin to rise.

Rutter had gradually come to terms with the situation. Sexton had been right about the fact that the large gardens would mean there was a considerable distance between the two rows of houses, he told himself. And anyway, an uninterrupted view of the moors was not something a man on a detective inspector's salary could reasonably expect.

But now, driving home on a day in which his world seemed to be unravelling like a ball of string, he began to take a darker view again. In his mind, the Croft Estate was now symbolic of his whole approach to life – proof that when he had two courses of action open to him, he would always choose the wrong one.

Maria was on the hall phone when Rutter entered the house through the back door. Standing in the kitchen, he couldn't distinguish the words. But he could tell that she was speaking Spanish, so it was more than likely that she was talking to one of her parents.

He opened the kitchen door and stepped into the hallway just as Maria was replacing the phone on its cradle. He coughed, as he always did, to let her know that it was him, and not some intruder.

'What time is it?' she asked.

'Just after six.'

'Then why are you home so early? I thought you had a new murder case to investigate.'

'We do. It's some poor bloody woman who—'

'I am not Monika Paniatowski,' Maria said cuttingly. 'I get no pleasure from hearing the grisly details of your work. My only interest is to wonder how you could bear to drag yourself away from your precious investigation.'

God, what a bloody mess he'd made of things! Rutter thought. What a bloody, bloody mess.

'I came home early because I'd already instructed the team on exactly what to do, and—' he began.

'I told you, I have no interest in your work,' Maria interrupted.

'I know that. I was just explaining to you how I came to be free for the rest of the day.'

'But why should you even *want* to be free for the rest of the day?'

'I thought we might spend some time together. I thought we might try to talk things through.'

'There is nothing to talk about,' Maria said coldly. 'Besides, how do you know I'm not busy myself?'

'I'm sorry?'

'Oh, I see how your mind works. Why should the poor blind woman have any plans of her own? Isn't she just supposed to stay quietly at home until her lord and master deigns to return?'

'I've never seen things in that way,' Rutter protested. 'You know I haven't, darling.'

'I *thought* I knew many things,' Maria said, 'but it seems that I was wrong about *most* of them. And as it happens, I *do* have plans of my own – plans which require your absence – and so I would appreciate it if you would return to your precious work.'

There might not be any right things to say in this situation, Rutter thought, but there were certainly wrong ones. And the *worst* thing he could possibly do, he felt instinctively, would be to ask her about her phone call.

'What were you talking to your parents about?' he was horrified to hear himself say.

'What has that got to do with you?' Maria countered.

'They're my in-laws.'

'That is certainly true – for the moment at least. But that still does not give you the right to question me about my private conversations.'

'Are you planning to go and visit them?'

'Perhaps.'

'For how long?'

'That has not been decided yet.'

'A week?' Rutter asked frantically. 'Two weeks?'

'That is my business.'

'It's not *just* your business. Not if you're planning to take my daughter with you.'

'It's your fault that this is happening, Bob,' Maria said, sounding a little more like her old self again. 'Not mine! Yours!'

'I know,' Rutter admitted miserably.

'Could you do one thing for me before you go out again?' Maria asked.

'What?' Rutter replied. And when she had told him, he said, 'Why should you want me to do that?'

'Just for once, can't you do what I ask without asking questions?' Maria countered.

'You're expecting a visitor, aren't you?' Rutter demanded.

'Since I've already said I want you out of the house, I should have thought that was obvious.'

'Who is it? Who's coming round?'

'After what you've done, you really have no right to ask.'

She was spot on, Rutter thought. He *did* have no right to ask. Absolutely no right at all!

*   *   *

At seven o'clock – when Woodend and Paniatowski had interviewed so many young women that they'd scarcely have noticed if they had finally reached the end of the line and started again – Lucy Higson appeared at the door.

God, but she was a striking woman, Woodend thought, and wondered how Derek Higson – a man of his own age, for God's sake! – had managed not only to pull her but to hold on to her.

'It's past clocking-off time, but I've talked to the staff and told them they're to stay here for as long as you want them to,' Lucy said.

Woodend forced a weak grin. 'I shouldn't have imagined they would have liked that very much.'

'They didn't,' Mrs Higson agreed, returning his smile. 'At least, they didn't like it until I informed them they could book it down as overtime. If there's one thing that Derek and I have learned in this business, it's that if you need to put an immediate stop to grumbling, just offer double pay.'

The woman was a real cracker, Woodend told himself – and not just in the looks department.

But though she'd gone to a lot of trouble to make it possible, even the thought of interviewing anyone else that day was enough to make his head start throbbing.

'You've been very helpful, Mrs Higson, but I think you can tell your staff they can all go home now,' he said.

'So you've finished here?'

'I wish we had,' Woodend admitted. 'But I'm afraid we'll be back again first thing in the morning, to begin afresh. We haven't even started on the shop-floor staff yet.'

'You're going to question all our craftsmen and apprentices, are you?' Lucy Higson asked, sounding surprised.

'Any reason why we shouldn't?'

Lucy Higson shrugged. And she managed to make even *that* gesture seem elegant.

'There's no reason at all why you shouldn't talk to them,' she said. 'I just think it would be a waste of time.'

'Why's that?'

For a moment, Lucy Higson seemed unsure of how to answer.

'I don't wish to appear to be speaking ill of the dead,' she said finally, 'but there's a certain tendency among the girls who work in the office to think that they're somehow *better* than the men with jobs on the shop floor. What they fail to realize, of course, is that it's the craftsmen who are the real heart of the enterprise. Without them, and the superb work they do, we'd have nothing to sell. Without them, we'd all go hungry.'

'So what you're really sayin' is that Pamela was a bit of a snob?'

'I wouldn't put it quite as strongly as that,' Lucy Higson replied, sounding slightly uncomfortable. 'Let's just say that she chose to keep something of a distance between herself and those who, quite unfairly, she might have seen as mere *manual* labourers.'

When a girl does that, it can hurt, Woodend thought, especially when it's a *pretty* girl who you'd like to impress. And sometimes, faced with rejection, admiration can turn into loathing. Sometimes it can even make normally decent-enough men feel a strong urge to punish.

Seven

It had been dark for some time when Woodend and Paniatowski finally emerged from the offices of New Horizons Enterprises, and with the darkness had come a chill which promised another cold night. It wouldn't be long now before early-morning windscreens were covered with a thick layer of frost, and engines stuttered in response to the demands of starter motors, Woodend thought.

47

The two detectives climbed into Woodend's Wolseley, both lighting up cigarettes as they did so.

'I get heartily sick of all the people who ask how there can be a God when there's so much sufferin' in the world,' Woodend said, as he pulled away. 'Fortunately, bein' a serious student of theology, I've got a rebuttal right at my fingertips. And what I say to them is this – "If there is no God, then who the bloody hell created pubs?"'

'Sorry, sir, what was that again?' Monika Paniatowski asked.

Woodend sighed. 'It wasn't *that* funny a line the first time round, so it certainly wouldn't improve with repetition,' he said.

'What wouldn't?'

'I was just indicatin' – in my own bumblin', fumblin' way – that at the end of a day like this, it's a bloody good thing there's a pint waitin' for us.'

'If you don't mind, sir, I think I'd rather give the pub a miss tonight,' Monika said.

Woodend raised a surprised right eyebrow. 'What's the matter? Not feelin' well?'

'I'm all right,' Monika said, unconvincingly. 'I'd just rather go home and get my head down. You *don't* mind, do you?'

Of course he minded. Some of their best work had been done in the public bar of the Drum and Monkey. There were cases which would have gone unsolved but for the inspirations which came from lubricating their brains with ample supplies of best bitter and double vodka. Besides, business apart, he rather enjoyed having a drink with his team.

'I don't mind at all if you don't come,' he lied. 'Where would you like me to drop you off? At the station?'

'Yes, please,' Monika replied.

The public bar of the Drum and Monkey was crowded, but the landlord – bless his little cotton socks – had made sure that the team's usual table was kept free. Except that there didn't seem to be any reason to reserve it that night, because Monika had gone home, and there was no sign of Bob Rutter.

'DI Rutter's not happened to have been in tonight, has he, Jack?' Woodend asked.

'Not that I've seen,' the landlord replied. He pointed to the phone behind the bar. 'Do you want to call the station, an' see if he's still there?'

'Not at the moment,' Woodend said, because, after all, he didn't want the Inspector to think that he was *chasing* him – that he was *desperate* for the man's company.

Sitting at his usual table, pint of best bitter in front of him, he waited for new ideas to start flooding into his head. But none came. He needed stimulating, he told himself. He needed the input that only Bob Rutter and Monika Paniatowski could provide.

He tried to remember what it was like working without them, and found he couldn't. Though Bob Rutter had only been with him for six years – and Monika Paniatowski for considerably less – closing a case without their help now seemed almost inconceivable.

'Phone call for you, Mr Woodend,' the landlord called out across the busy room.

Woodend did his best not to look too eager as he stood up and walked over to the bar, but there was still a definite spring in his step.

'Where are you, Bob?' he asked into the mouthpiece.

'It's not Bob, Charlie,' said a female voice with the slightest hint of a foreign accent.

'Maria?' Woodend asked.

'I'm so glad I found you there, Charlie,' Maria Rutter said. She sounded like she'd been crying, Woodend thought.

'Is somethin' the matter, lass?' he asked.

'A great deal's the matter, Charlie,' Maria said. 'Can you come to the house?'

'When? Now?'

'No, not now. Give me half an hour or so to get things a bit straighter.'

To get *yourself* a bit straighter, more like, Woodend thought.

'Is Bob with you?' he asked.

'No, he isn't.'

'Do you want me to see if I can find him?'

'No!' Maria said – almost screamed.

'Is he—'

'I'd rather you came alone, Charlie. Please!'

'All right, if that's what you want,' Woodend agreed. 'Do you still want me to leave it for half an hour?'

'I . . . Yes, that would be best. Finish the pint you're drinking now, have another one, and then come to see me.'

'Listen, if you'd rather . . .' Woodend began.

But he was only talking to the dialling tone.

Maria placed the phone back on its cradle, then made her way down the hall to the kitchen. She walked confidently because, in her own domain, everything had a place and there was no danger of any inanimate object lurking in ambush for her.

There were two radios in the kitchen, one tuned permanently to the Home Service and the other to the Third Programme. She clicked the switch on one of them, and found herself listening to Wagner's 'Ride of the Valkyries'.

Charlie would like a cup of tea when he arrived, she thought. And chocolate biscuits – he was always very partial to chocolate biscuits. She reached up to the cupboard, located the handle, and opened the door.

If anybody could tell her what to do about the mess she was in, it was Charlie Woodend, she told herself. True, he was Bob's boss. But he was also her friend – a man she trusted, a man she respected. Yet even Charlie Woodend would be pushed to create any sort of order out of this confusion – even the great magician himself would have trouble pulling off this particular trick.

Her fingers had located the biscuits, and she carefully took them down.

The music on the radio was reaching its climax – swelling to fill the whole kitchen. It was so loud that it completely masked the sound coming from the living room – a sound which, if she had heard it, would have told her the catch on the French windows was being forced.

Woodend finished his pint, and then ordered another one, just as Maria had instructed him to. As a result, he did not leave the Drum and Monkey until twenty minutes after the phone call.

Later, he would try to tell himself that while Maria had seemed upset, there had been no real urgency in her voice. He would point out – as he defended himself in the case which he himself was also prosecuting – that Maria had specifically said he should wait half an hour. If he'd ignored her instructions and left immediately, he would argue, it would have made no difference. Because even if he'd been driving a racing car – and even if there'd been no other traffic on the road – he *still* wouldn't have got there in time.

Yes, he would tell himself all this – and there were others who would argue his case even more strongly than he did himself. But it didn't make any difference.

No bloody difference at all!

Eight

There were lights burning in most of the windows on Elm Croft, but the Rutter house was in darkness. Which told him two things, thought Charlie Woodend – the perpetual detective, the *compulsive* detective – as he pulled his Wolseley up at the edge of the curb. The first of those things was that Bob had not returned home yet – but from his earlier conversation with Maria, he had rather suspected that would be the case. The second thing was that the baby must be asleep.

So why should Maria waste electricity? Why turn on the lights when, however brightly the house might be illuminated, she would continue to move around in a world which was eternally dark?

Woodend switched off the engine, opened the car door, and stepped out into the chill night air. The street was deserted, but that was hardly surprising. The residents of the Crofts Estate would be safely indoors by now, their eyes glued to the flickering magic box which brought all the wonders of the world into the corner of their living rooms.

He was already on the Rutters' path – making his way along the side of the house – when the unimaginable occurred.

The blinding flash – like a thousand suddenly flaring matches – came first. The deep angry boom and the scream of shattering glass followed almost immediately after it.

For a moment Woodend was back in war-time France: landing on that Normandy beach under heavy enemy fire; seeing his closest comrades fall all around him; hearing the angry roar of the guns; smelling the stench of blood, fear and desperation.

The past receded as quickly as it had arrived. His ears were ringing, his eyes were finding it hard to focus, but he knew where he was – and what must have happened.

He sprinted down the path to the kitchen door. The window panes had gone – he could hear the glass from them crunching under his feet – and through what was now no more than a hole in the wall, he could see that the whole of the kitchen was on fire.

He'd never get into the house that way, he told himself. If he tried, his eyeballs would fry before he'd even crossed the threshold.

He retreated back to the front of the house. He didn't test the front door to see whether or not it was open – there was no time for such refinements – but just lashed out at the lock with his boot. The door groaned, but didn't give. He kicked again, and this time it burst open.

A wave of hot air hit him. The hallway was thick with smoke, and beyond it he could just see the flickering flames.

How's the fire managed to spread so fast? he wondered. How the bloody hell has it managed to get so far so quickly?

He lowered his head and plunged into the house. His eyes began to smart almost immediately, and he could feel the thick black smoke snaking its way to his lungs. As he made his way along the hallway, he forced himself to take much shallower breaths.

And all the time he was thinking, 'If Maria was in the kitchen when the explosion happened, then she's already dead! If the baby was with her, then she's dead as well!'

So why was he wasting his time even *heading* for the kitchen? he asked himself angrily.

If Maria was still alive she'd be somewhere else in the house – probably huddling terrified in a corner, probably clutching her poor frightened little child tightly to her!

He would not have believed how hard it was to turn round – how simply rotating himself in thickening smoke could be one of the most difficult things he'd had to attempt in his entire life.

The lounge/diner was to his right, near the front entrance. He opened the door and screamed hoarsely, 'Maria! Maria! Are you in there? For God's sake tell me if you're in there!'

Some light was seeping into the room from the street lamps outside, but he didn't need that light to see – because the fire had already found its way through the serving hatch and was licking hungrily at the French window curtains and the three-piece suite.

There was no one in the room, but that didn't mean there was no one anywhere else in the house. Woodend's stomach churned as he realized that there was nothing for it but to go upstairs.

He flicked the switch at the top of the hallway, and through streaming eyes saw the landing light come on. The fire was already spreading up the hall – why *was* that happening? – and once he got upstairs there was absolutely no guarantee he'd ever be able to get down again. He stuck his head through the front doorway, sucked in a gulp of the largely unpolluted air outside, then ran up the stairs two at a time.

The master bedroom was empty. So was the spare room. The baby's cot stood in the centre of the nursery, but there was no sign of the baby herself. When he found nothing in the bathroom either, he understood that the whole dangerous exercise had been a complete waste of time.

He heard the sound of a fire engine siren wailing in the distance, and thought, 'God, they've been quick!'

But not quick enough. Nowhere near quick enough!

Moments before the air upstairs had seemed perfectly fresh, but now he was finding it difficult to breathe again.

'Must be a reason for that,' he thought hazily. 'Has to be a reason . . . a very good reason.'

He staggered – why was he staggering, he wondered? – out on to the landing again, to discover that the fire had pursued him, and now the whole of the staircase was ablaze.

Shouldn't have spread so fast, he thought for the fifth or sixth time. No reason why it should have spread so fast.

He returned to the master bedroom, and opened the window. Above his head the light fizzled, and then the room was plunged into darkness.

A crowd had gathered outside.

Bloody nosy parkers! he thought. What's the matter with you? Nothin' good on the telly at this time of night?

The fire engine was just pulling on to the street, its lights flashing, its siren still howling. Woodend wondered idly how long it would take the firemen to get the ladder up to him. If they were as good as they claimed to be, it shouldn't take much time at all. On the other hand, if they *weren't* that good he wouldn't be around to take the piss out of them for it, because he'd be bloody well dead!

He hoisted himself up on to the window ledge.

'Somebody's up there!' a woman's voice screamed below. 'He's going to jump!'

Well, of course I'm goin' to bloody jump! Woodend thought. What else do you expect me to do? Stay here and roast?

Rutter's prize flower patch was just below him, he noticed.

Bob always said that even if Maria couldn't actually see the flowers, at least she could bloody well smell them.

'Jump!' several voices urged from below.

Bugger you, I'll jump in my own time, Woodend thought.

'Jump!' the voices screamed again.

In fact, if it means destroying Bob's prize flower bed, I might not jump at all, Woodend thought. It's only a few weeks to Christmas. I might just stay here until Santa Claus comes to call, then I can leave on his sled.

You've gone loopy, Charlie Woodend, he told himself. You *have* to bloody jump.

In the event, it was more of a half-jump and a half-collapse-forward. Several people on the ground screamed as he fell, but by that point he had very little interest in anything save for the swirling images inside his head.

He was lying on his back, staring up at rows of white tiles.

White tiles?

Staring *up* at them?

How could he be staring up at them. Did that mean that he was hanging from the bloody ceiling?

He closed his eyes again, and when he opened them once more, it all started to make more sense. The tiles were *on* the ceiling, he was on a bed. Put the two together, and he was almost certain that meant he was in a hospital.

But why? Had all that greasy food, washed down with pints of best bitter and rounded off with a cigarette, finally brought on the heart attack that Joan had been warning him of for so long?

No, Joan was the one who'd had the heart attack – while they'd been on holiday in Spain.

So just what *was* going on?

He turned his head to one side, and saw the man in blue uniform who was sitting next to his bed.

'So what's it all about, Constable?' he asked.

And then he remembered. The sudden explosion. The shattering glass. The flames. The smoke.

'Maria?' he said.

The constable coughed awkwardly. 'One body has been recovered from the kitchen of the house, sir. It was fairly badly burned, but the general feeling is that it has to be Mrs Rutter.'

'And the baby? What's happened to the baby, man?'

'Mrs Rutter's child was not in the house at the time of the explosion, sir. She's quite safe.'

'And . . . and Bob?'

'Are you talking about *Inspector* Rutter, sir?'

'Well of course I'm talking about *Inspector* Rutter, you bloody fool! Who else could I be talkin' about?'

'Mr Rutter's in a state of shock. I believe that he's been quite heavily sedated.'

Woodend swung his legs over towards the edge of the bed, and was surprised to discover that he seemed to have acquired a number of fairly painful aches.

'I'll go an' see Bob anyway,' he told the constable. 'I've no doubt he'll be wantin' to talk to me.'

The other man placed a restraining hand on his shoulder. 'It wouldn't do any good, sir.'

'I'm your boss, you jumped-up little turd,' Woodend said angrily. 'So don't go tryin' to tell me what would an' what wouldn't do any good.'

The constable's hand continued to press down on him. 'Mr Rutter's probably still unconscious, sir. And even if he isn't, he wouldn't even recognize you, given the state he's in.'

'If he doesn't recognize me, then he doesn't recognize me,' Woodend said, wondering why he was finding it so difficult to shake off the constable's hand. 'But whether or not, I'm going to see him anyway.'

'Oh no, you're not,' said a new voice from the doorway.

'Oh no, you're not. Oh yes, I am,' Woodend said. 'What is this? A rehearsal for the bloody Christmas pantomime?'

'Quite apart from the injuries you sustained in your fall, you inhaled a lot of smoke,' the doctor said.

'After puffin' on Capstan Full Strength for nearly thirty years, it was a doddle,' Woodend countered.

But even to his own ears, his words lacked conviction.

'You could have died,' the doctor said.

'But I didn't.'

'No, and, as it happens, apart from some heavy bruising I don't think any serious damage has been done. But I'm still keeping you in for observation overnight.'

'In a pig's arse you are!' Woodend said angrily. 'You doctors might think you can act like God Almighty, but I'm a bobby, an' I know the law.'

'You should try to rest now,' the doctor said soothingly.

'An' the law says you can't keep me here against my will,' Woodend continued. He turned his head slightly to look at the constable again, and unleashed on himself a fresh wave of pain. 'You heard all that, did you?' he asked.

The constable nodded. 'Yes, sir.'

'Then fetch me my clothes, and we'll be leavin'.'

'But, sir—'

'Don't "but sir" me. Get me my bloody clothes.'

Perhaps the constable argued some more. Woodend wouldn't have known if he had, because when he woke up again it was already morning.

Nine

It was ten o'clock by the time Woodend fully realized where he was, half past ten before he had mustered sufficient energy to demand to be released. The paperwork took another twenty minutes, and – since the formidable matron refused to give him his clothes until the process was completed – it was not until a little before eleven that he was able to leave the hospital.

The uniformed constable waiting at the door of his room had a familiar look about him.

'Beresford, isn't it?' Woodend asked.

'That's right, sir.'

'An' you're here to take me to headquarters, are you?'

'I'm not sure, sir,' the constable confessed. 'I rather *think* the idea was to drive you home.'

'I don't know whose idea it was, but it's a very bad one,' Woodend said. 'Headquarters in the place I need to be.'

'The doctor said—'

'The doctor said I'm fine,' Woodend lied, and then winced as he felt a sudden pain shoot across his back. 'You take me to headquarters, lad, an' if anybody gives you any grief over it, you can say that – against all good sense – I insisted.' The pain had moved to the base of his neck, but he could live with it. 'But there's one thing we have to do before we leave,' he continued, 'an' that's to go an' see how Inspector Rutter's gettin' on.'

Beresford's eyes flickered for an instant. 'Mr Rutter isn't here any longer, sir. He left with a couple of other officers, half an hour ago.'

'An' I suppose they tried to take *him* home, as well, did they?'

The moment the words were out of his mouth, Woodend felt sick. Of course the officer hadn't tried to take Bob home, he thought. Bob didn't *have* a home any longer.

How could he ever even have said that? he asked himself. What kind of mindless, insensitive clod – what kind of *gutter rat* – was he?

'You mustn't feel guilty, sir,' Beresford said, reading the expression on his face correctly. 'You've been through a lot in the last few hours. It's perfectly understandable you'd get a bit confused.'

'Aye, you're right,' Woodend agreed, partly forgiving himself. 'So where did they take Mr Rutter?'

'To the station, sir.'

'I wouldn't have thought they have made him do the

paperwork so soon after his bereavement,' Woodend said. 'But perhaps that's what he wanted.'

'Perhaps so,' Beresford said, noncommittally.

'Well, we're doin' no good standin' around here,' Woodend said. 'Time we got our skates on.'

'Yes, sir,' Beresford said compliantly.

It was only as Beresford was driving him towards the centre of Whitebridge that the grief really hit Woodend, but when it did, it came with the force of a landslide.

Maria was dead! Beautiful, wonderful Maria was dead!

Images of the past flashed through his mind.

He remembered the first time he had met her, back in London. Bob had only recently become his sergeant then, and had been on pins about how they'd get on. But he need have had no worries, because the middle-aged English detective and the young Spanish research student had hit it off right from the start.

He recalled going to see her in hospital, just after the eye surgeon had told her she would never recover her sight, and he – who had faced death in North Africa and Normandy – had marvelled that anyone could show such courage.

He pictured her walking down the aisle on her wedding day, radiating happiness and moving with all the assurance of a woman who could actually see where she was going.

And she *had* seen where she was going! Woodend thought. In her mind's eye there'd been a clear vision of her future as Bob's wife and the loving mother of his children.

How could it have ended like this? Why did she have to die in a stupid accident?

Perhaps a sighted person would have known that something was wrong, and got out of the house before the explosion occurred, he thought. And if that were the case, then life, which had already cursed her by striking her blind, had been doubly cruel in making that blindness the cause of her death.

'Are you all right, sir?' Beresford asked.

'Of course I'm not bloody all right!' Woodend snapped. 'I've just lost someone I loved.'

They were approaching the Grapes when he saw a woman entering it. She was wearing a smart suit – with the skirt just short enough to reveal her excellent legs – and had long black hair which fell down over her shoulders.

Woodend's grief receded, and was replaced by a lake of bubbling volcanic anger.

So Elizabeth Driver was back in Whitebridge, he thought. He should have expected that from a woman who was not so much a crime reporter as a ghoul feeding off the misery of others.

'Stop the car!' he said.

'Pardon, sir?'

'Stop the bloody car.'

'But I thought—'

'You're not paid to think, Constable. You're paid to do as you're bloody well told.'

Beresford signalled, and pulled over to the curb. 'Do you want me to—' he began.

'You just wait here until I come back,' Woodend said, climbing out of the car.

He had been too restrained in the past, he told himself as he walked towards the pub door. He had let Elizabeth Driver get away with all kinds of things, because he had not wanted to soil his hands by coming into contact with a louse like her. Well, those days were gone. He would finally tell her exactly what he thought of her. He would pull no punches, because she merited no such consideration.

He knew that what was about to follow really had nothing to do with Driver – that his rage was directed at the rotten world in general, rather than at a rotten reporter in particular. But he didn't care. He needed to hit out – and Elizabeth Driver was the perfect target.

He pushed the swing door open. Elizabeth Driver was already standing at the bar, and he heard her order a gin and tonic.

Under normal circumstances, perhaps, he might have noticed the shake in her voice. But these were not normal circumstances.

He walked up to the bar, and tapped her on the shoulder. 'Nice to see you again, Miss Driver,' he said sarcastically.

The look on Elizabeth Driver's face, when she turned round, came as something of a shock.

He thought he'd seen her whole repertoire of expressions – her defiance when he'd caught her trying to pull a fast one on him and his investigation; the mixture of sullenness and anger when he'd thwarted her plans to distort the truth; the cunning expression which crept into her eyes when she was about to offer him some kind of deal; the way that expression turned sultry when she had decided that – since all else had failed – she might as well offer him her body again, because maybe this time he just might succumb.

Yes, he'd thought he'd seen them all. But never – never – had he seen her so haggard and nervous.

For a moment he was almost inclined to hold off on his attack, but she'd never shown anyone mercy in the past, and so she had no right to expect it from him now.

'How'd you get up here, Miss Driver?' he asked. 'Overnight train? First-class sleeper, as befits a reporter of your obvious calibre?'

Elizabeth Driver looked confused. 'N. . . no!' she said.

Had she stuttered? Woodend asked himself incredulously. Had this woman, with nerves of steel and ice running through her veins, actually *stuttered*?

'I've . . . I've been here for a few days,' she continued.

'Why?' Woodend asked.

She should have told him to mind his own business – the old Elizabeth Driver would have done just that – but instead she looked down at the floor and said, 'It was a private matter.'

'But now you're here, you thought you might as well stay and cover the murder?'

'Yes.'

'An' why not? It's got all elements that a journalist of your stature can really get her fangs into, hasn't it? A single defenceless woman, viciously killed. Blood and gore all over the place.

61

If you push it, you might even to be able to bring in the sex angle. It's just up your street. Handle it right – as you always do – an' your paper's circulation should go through the roof.'

'It's not like that this time,' Elizabeth Driver said, almost pathetically.

'Isn't it?' Woodend asked, unrelentingly. 'Then what *is* it like?'

'I want to see justice done,' Elizabeth Driver said – and for once she really *did* sound sincere.

'Whatever for?' Woodend wondered. 'Why should you give a toss about Pamela Rainsford?'

Elizabeth Driver looked at him blankly. 'Who?' she asked.

'Pamela Rainsford! The murder victim!'

'Oh, her,' Elizabeth Driver said.

'What do you mean? Oh her? Who else could we be talking about?'

'Maria Rutter.'

'But that was an accident, for God's sake!'

'You haven't been told, have you?' Elizabeth Driver said, shocked.

'Haven't been told what?'

'It wasn't the explosion – or the fire – that killed her. She was already dead by then.'

'How could you possibly know that?' Woodend asked.

But he already knew the answer to his question. Dr Shastri would never leak her findings to the press in exchange for a few pounds, but there were plenty of people connected with the morgue who would.

'The initial findings suggest that she was killed by a blow to the back of the head,' Elizabeth Driver said flatly.

'But she hadn't got an enemy in the world,' Woodend said, still unable to believe it. 'Who'd have had any reason to kill her?'

'Who do *you* think?' Elizabeth Driver asked. 'Who *usually* has a motive in domestic murders?'

'You're not sayin' . . .' Woodend gasped. 'You can't be sayin' . . .'

62

'And who do you think it was who was taken straight from the hospital to the interrogation room in police headquarters?' Elizabeth Driver asked.

Ten

The man who entered the interview room and sat down opposite Bob Rutter was around forty-six years old. His head was bullet-shaped, and he had darting eyes. Between his large nose and thin-lipped mouth rested a short, overly clipped moustache.

'DCI Evans,' he announced.

'I know who you are,' Rutter answered.

More to the point, he knew *what* Evans was. The DCI, based in Preston rather than Whitebridge, had a formidable reputation as a hatchet man – an officer more than willing to do the unpalatable jobs that none of his colleagues wanted to touch.

It was Evans who had been brought in to try to fit up Cloggin'-it Charlie on corruption charges during the Dugdale's Farm murder. And though he had not been successful on that occasion, he had a good track record otherwise, and had left a trail of destroyed careers in his wake all over Central Lancashire.

'I have a series of questions which I'd like to put to you, Mr Rutter,' Evans said flatly.

'You do know that my wife's just died in an awful tragic accident, don't you?' Rutter asked. 'That I'm totally devastated by it? That I've got a young child to take care of?'

'I'm fully aware of everything connected with the incident,' DCI Evans replied.

'The *incident*!' Bob Rutter said aghast.

'And you should be well aware that in circumstances like these, there are certain formalities which have to be gone through,' Evans continued.

'I'm perfectly willing to go through the procedures, but does it have to be right now?'

'Yes.'

'Look, I'm not an ordinary member of the general public. I'm on the Force. I would have thought that entitled me to a little leeway.'

'I'm afraid it doesn't. Once we start bending the rules for our own people, it isn't long before we start bending the rules for others. And that's when the rot really starts to set in.'

'Surely a few hours wouldn't make any difference.'

'We all have our jobs to do,' DCI Evans said sternly. 'And mine is to ask you a few questions.'

'And when I've answered them, can I go?'

'We'll see about that.'

Rutter sighed. 'Ask your questions,' he said.

'Could you account for your movements yesterday?'

'*All* of yesterday?'

'From about six o'clock in the evening onwards should be more than sufficient.'

'We're working on a case,' Rutter said. 'A woman who was murdered down by the canal. My boss, Mr Woodend, was asking questions at the factory where the woman worked. I was in charge of the house-to-house questioning in the area where the dead woman had lived.'

'And this house-to-house questioning went on until . . . ?'

'I don't know exactly.'

'*Why* don't you know exactly? Didn't you look at your watch when the investigations were concluded for the day? Didn't you jot the time down in your notebook?'

'I wasn't actually there when the house-to-house questioning finished,' Rutter admitted.

'Now that is interesting,' Evans said. 'You were in charge of the team, yet you abandoned them.'

'I didn't *abandon* them. I *left* them to get on with it. They're a good team. I trust them. Besides . . .'

'Yes?'

'I was tired. I was finding it difficult to concentrate on the job, and I didn't want to make any mistakes.'

'You were tired,' Evans said, nodding. 'So I assume that you went home to rest?'

'You know I bloody didn't!' Rutter said angrily. 'If I'd gone home, I'd have been dead as well.'

'So what did you do?'

'I drove around.'

'Interesting,' Evans said. 'You say that you were tired, but you drove around.'

'Maybe "tired" is the wrong word to use,' Rutter said exasperatedly. 'I was *tense*! All right! Are you happy with that? I was tense – and *when* I'm tense I find driving around relaxes me.'

'Where did you go?'

'What's this all about?' Rutter demanded.

'You've been a policeman long enough to be able to work it out for yourself,' Evans said coldly. 'But just in case you haven't, I'll be more explicit. What it's *about*, Mr Rutter, is my asking questions and you answering them.'

Rutter nodded, acknowledging that, unpalatable as it might be, what the other man had said was true.

'I don't *know* where I drove,' he admitted. 'I had a lot on my mind. I wasn't paying attention.'

'What a very dangerous state to be in when you're behind the wheel,' Evans said. 'How long were you away on this drive of yours?'

'I left the house at about half past six. I got back just after nine, when it was . . . when it was all over.'

'Do you remember stopping anywhere on this drive of yours? For petrol, perhaps? Or for a cup of tea?'

'I filled up the petrol tank yesterday morning. And I wasn't thirsty, so I didn't stop for a drink.'

'That's very strange,' Evans mused. 'Whenever I'm feeling nervous, I always have a *terrible* thirst.'

'I didn't say I was nervous,' Rutter protested.

'No, you didn't,' Evans agreed. 'You said you were tense. You said you were worried you'd make mistakes because you couldn't concentrate properly. But you never said you were nervous.'

He paused. Most men would have taken the opportunity to light up a cigarette, but DCI Evans didn't smoke. He didn't drink, either.

'Did anyone see you on this drive of yours?'

'Not to my knowledge.'

'Pity. If you'd been involved in a minor collision, or been given a speeding ticket, you'd have had just the alibi you needed.'

'*Do* I need an alibi?' Rutter asked. 'What do I need an alibi *for*?'

'There's a patch of unused land behind your house, isn't there?' Evans asked, ignoring the question.

'There's a *building site* behind my house, to be strictly accurate,' Rutter corrected him. 'It's going to be the next phase of the estate development.'

'Patch of unused land or building site, it doesn't really make much difference,' Evans said carelessly. 'The point is that anyone wishing to approach your house would not necessarily have to do it from the front. It would be perfectly possible to park on the street at the other edge of the land, cut across, climb over the back fence, and enter your house through the French windows. In the dark, it's likely the intruder could make the whole journey without anyone seeing him. He could even, if he had a mind to do so, leave the same way.'

'What intruder?' Rutter asked. 'Who are we talking about?'

'Who indeed? Would you say that you and your wife had a happy marriage, Inspector?'

'It had its ups and downs,' Rutter said.

'And how would you describe the state it was in just before your wife's death? Up? Or down?'

'It was fine.'

'No problems?'

'None at all.'

'And if were to ask your friends and neighbours that same question, would I get the same answer?'

'Yes.'

'You're sure? Because it would look bad if that didn't turn out to be the case.'

'Ask *who* you like *what* you like,' Rutter said defiantly.

'Oh, I shall,' Evans said. 'Rest assured, I shall. The reason your child was spared from the explosion last night was that she was at a neighbour's house. Is that correct?'

'Yes.'

'Did she spend a lot of her time in other people's houses? And *if* she did, was that because your wife – being blind – was unable to look after her as she should have done?'

'How dare you!' Rutter said furiously.

'How dare I what?'

'How dare you suggest that my wife couldn't look after our baby properly?'

'I'm merely considering the facts, Mr Rutter.'

'It wasn't as easy for Maria as it would have been for a woman who could see, but she made up for that by trying harder. She had more guts and determination than any other woman I've ever met.'

'So she was a determined woman?'

'Haven't I just said so?'

'And once she's made her mind up on something, there was no way you – or anybody else – could change it?'

'I didn't say she was inflexible. I never suggested she wasn't capable of persuasion.'

'Let's return to the question of your child,' Evans suggested. 'Did your wife farm her out to the neighbours a great deal?'

'No, she bloody didn't!'

'But she did leave the baby with neighbours last night?'

'Yes.'

'Was it, in fact, *she* who left the baby with them. Or was it, perhaps, someone else?'

67

'Are you asking that question because you don't know the answer – or because you *do*?'

'Whichever is the case, it should not affect your reply.'

'*I* took the baby to the neighbours',' Rutter said wearily.

'And when might this have been exactly? After you'd finished driving around?'

'No, you bastard! Before I *started* driving around!'

'Let me assure you that personal abuse will get you nowhere with me,' Evans said rebukingly.

'I'm . . . I'm sorry,' Rutter said. 'You have to understand the pressure that I'm under.'

'So you took the child to the neighbours' between the time you abandoned your team and the time you started driving?'

'Yes.'

'Which must mean that you went home.'

'Well, of course it means that I went home!'

'Did you record that fact in your notebook?'

'No.'

'Why not?'

'Bobbies nip home for a few minutes all the time,' Rutter said. 'It's something that's always turned a blind eye to.'

'Not by me,' Evans told him. 'Never by me. Who's idea was it to take the baby round to the neighbours'?'

'Maria's.'

Evans raised a surprised eyebrow. 'I thought you said your wife was a very conscientious mother.'

'I don't remember using that exact word, but yes, she was.'

'And yet she abandoned the baby.'

'Abandoned her? For God's sake, she asked the neighbours to look after the baby for a few hours. She'd have done the same for them.'

'If they'd felt they were able to entrusted their children to the care of a *blind* woman.'

'You really *are* a bastard, aren't you?' Rutter said.

'At any rate, it was not she who asked the neighbours to look after the child. It was you.'

'Yes.'

'Why?'

'Maria said she wasn't feeling very well.'

'Physically? Or psychologically?'

'Physically.'

'Do you have any witnesses to this conversation?'

'Of course not. We were alone in the house.'

'How convenient. So your wife wasn't feeling well. In which case I fail to understand why you chose to drive around, instead of staying with her. Unless, of course . . .'

'I told you, I had a lot on my mind. I needed some thinking space.'

'. . . unless, of course, you were away for a much shorter time than you now claim you were.'

'When I got back to the house, the place was a burned-out shell, and the ambulance . . . the ambulance had already taken my wife away.' Rutter stood up. 'I've answered all your questions, now I have to be going.'

'Sit down, Inspector!' Evans said.

'I have my daughter to consider.'

'Your daughter is in good hands. The Social Services Department is looking after her.'

'I don't *want* the Social Services looking after her.'

'I'm sure that's true. It's probably one of the very few things you've said during the course of this interview that *is* true.'

'What's that supposed to mean? Are you calling me a liar?'

'If you do not sit down, Inspector, I will call for assistance to *make* you sit down,' Evans said.

Rutter sank defeatedly back into his chair. 'What am I supposed to have done?' he asked.

'You *know* what you're supposed to have done. You're supposed to have killed your wife.'

'Are you seriously suggesting that I rigged up the explosion that killed her?'

'No, I am suggesting that you struck her on the back of the head with a blunt instrument.'

Rutter's mouth fell open, but though he struggled for words, none would come out.

'A most impressive show,' Evans said. 'But not quite convincing enough in the face of the facts we already have – and the ones we will no doubt collect during the course of the investigation. You thought you were totally unobserved when you sneaked back to your house, but that is what people like you *always* think. Experience should tell you that some-one will have spotted you – or at least spotted your car – and that is really all we'll need.'

'I didn't kill my wife,' Rutter said, finally finding his voice.

'You probably thought the fire would destroy all the evidence of your vicious attack, but, unluckily for you, it didn't.'

'Are you charging me?' Rutter asked.

'Not yet,' Evans told him. 'But I'd be surprised if we hadn't by the end of the day.'

Eleven

Chief Constable Henry Marlowe was very happy with his position in life. He liked drawing the large salary which went with his job, and being driven around in an official car by a uniformed driver. He relished the power he had to make and break careers, and the attitude that power engendered towards him in others. He took pleasure from the fact that as Chief Constable he was always right – even when he, and everyone else, knew that he was wrong. Yet even in the most perfect of existences, there were still a few flies in the ointment – a couple of wasps buzzing around to spoil the picnic. And the biggest of these, he had long ago decided, was Chief Inspector Charlie Woodend.

Woodend refused to be impressed by his title. Woodend simply would not see that the main aim of any investigation carried out in Central Lancashire was to enhance the reputation of its Chief Constable. And worst of all, there had been occasions when Woodend had made him look a complete fool.

He'd tried to get rid of the bloody man a number of times – putting him in impossible situations, handing him cases which ought never to have been solved. But, like some malevolent rubber ball, Woodend had always bounced back – making the impossible possible, solving the unsolvable.

But not this time! Marlowe promised himself. This time he would *not* get away with it. This time, he would overstep the bounds in an effort to help a man who – it would soon be plain to everyone else – was beyond help.

And the true beauty of it was that Marlowe would have to do nothing himself to achieve this most favourable result. He had merely to sit back and let the Chief Inspector destroy himself.

It was these thoughts which caused him to smile when he heard the ruckus in his outer office, and allowed the smile to grow even broader as – above the vocal protests of his secretary – an unseen hand turned his inner office door knob.

By the time the door had been flung open, to reveal the big man in the hairy sports coat, the Chief Constable's smile had been replaced by a grave expression.

'I see that while your short spell in hospital may have mended whatever damage was done to your body, it's singularly failed to mend your manners, Chief Inspector Woodend,' he said.

He liked the line. It sounded even better now than it had when he had privately rehearsed it earlier.

'I've been told Bob Rutter's been arrested,' Woodend said.

'Then you appear to have been misinformed. Inspector Rutter is merely being *questioned*.'

'You can't really believe he killed Maria.'

'I don't know whether he's guilty or not,' Marlowe said. 'Because, unlike you, Chief Inspector, I would never presume to prejudge the results of a colleague's investigation.'

'What colleague's this?' Woodend demanded.

'DCI Evans.'

'That's bastard's no colleague of mine.'

'Ah, but he is. You're brother officers, whether you like it or not. But why are we even discussing Mr Evans? I would have thought you'd have your mind on other concerns.'

'Other concerns?' Woodend said, momentarily mystified.

Marlowe shook his head sadly, as if this merely confirmed a long-held suspicion.

'There is the small matter of the murder of Pamela Rainsford which you should be investigating,' he said. 'Or had you forgotten that?'

'Take me off that case,' Woodend said. 'Put me on the Maria Rutter killing instead.'

'I can't do that.'

'Why not?'

'Firstly, because it would be damaging to the Rainsford case to change senior officers at this stage in the proceedings. And secondly – and possibly more importantly – because you lack the objectivity to take over the Rutter investigation.'

'Bollocks!'

'It is far from bollocks, as you choose to put it. I've commented before on the fact that you seem to develop an unhealthily close relationship with the officers you have working under you, and—'

'We operate as a tight team. That's how we get cases solved,' Woodend interrupted.

'. . . and, as a result of that, I would be most unwilling to have you investigate one of your own direct subordinates.'

'I don't see what you're gettin' at.'

'Then to be blunt, Chief Inspector, I think your main aim, if you were in charge of the Maria Rutter investigation, would be to prove that her husband *could not* be the guilty party.'

'Are you sayin' that if I was given the opportunity, I'd doctor the evidence?' Woodend demanded.

'I'm saying you might not be objective enough to see all the facts in their proper light.'

'An' DCI Evans is?'

'Exactly.'

'I want the case,' Woodend said.

'And I'm telling you that you can't have it.' Marlowe gave a practised frown. 'In fact, I'm no longer sure that you're currently stable enough to handle even the Rainsford case. Perhaps you should consider taking some leave. I certainly wouldn't block that.'

It was a tempting idea, Woodend thought. Being on leave would give him the free time he needed to investigate Maria's murder privately. But it would also deny him access to the resources of police headquarters – and cut him off completely from whatever snippets of information he could pick up on the case from talk in the canteen and in the corridors.

'I'm quite prepared to continue working on the Rainsford investigation, sir,' he said.

'Whereas, I'm no longer sure that it's—'

'As you pointed out yourself, it might damage the investigation to change the senior officer in charge now.'

Marlowe pretended to think about it. 'You do realize that I will expect you to keep yourself completely detached from the Rutter investigation, don't you, Chief Inspector?' he said.

'Yes, sir,' Woodend agreed, but he was thinking: You can *expect* what you like. It doesn't mean you'll *get* it.

'And that failure to remain detached would have to be considered a very serious infraction of discipline?'

'Yes, sir,' Woodend replied, adding silently: But you'll have to catch me at it, first.

'And that such a *serious* infraction would almost certainly be considered a resigning matter?'

'Understood.'

'I shall require a definite undertaking from you that you feel capable of handling the Rainsford case while keeping yourself completely away from the Rutter case.'

'You've got it.'

'In writing, Chief Inspector. I shall need it *in writing*.'

'It'll be on your desk within half an hour.'

'Very well, Chief Inspector,' Marlowe said gravely. 'Given that proviso, you may keep the Rainsford case.'

'Thank you, sir,' Woodend said, forcing the words out – and hoping they didn't bring his stomach lining with them.

Once the Chief Inspector had left, Marlowe allowed the smile to creep back on to his face.

Woodend had not only offered himself up as the sacrificial goat, he thought – the bloody fool had even offered to pull his own entrails out.

As Woodend was walking slowly down the steps to the basement, he could feel the air of despondency from the officers working on the Pamela Rainsford case rising up to meet him.

But then that was only to be expected, he thought, because Bob Rutter was a popular inspector, and nobody would like what was happening to him.

Monika Paniatowski had moved her desk to the far corner of the room, well away from any of the other officers. At that moment she had the phone in her left hand and was making notes with her right.

Woodend was surprised to see her there – and if she felt anything like as bad as she looked, it was a miracle that she'd managed to find the strength to turn up at all.

She forced a tired smile to her face as Woodend sat down beside her. 'Good to have you back, sir,' she said. 'How are you feeling?'

'I fell out of an upstairs window, an' I've got bruises on parts of my body I didn't even know I had,' Woodend said. 'Other than that, I'm feelin' grand. What have *you* been doin' while I was away?'

'I've been trying to reconstruct Inspector Rutter's movements from the notes he made,' Paniatowski said.

Good old Monika! Woodend thought. I knew I could rely on you.

'You might not have found anythin' quite yet that'll blow the case apart,' he said, in a low but encouraging voice, 'but just keep pluggin' away at it, an' I'm sure you very soon will.'

A puzzled look came to Monika's face. 'I'm not sure that I quite understand you, sir,' she said.

'What is there not to understand?' Woodend asked. 'You've been reconstructing Bob's movements. Isn't that right?'

'Yes, sir.'

'An' you've been doin' it so that you can prove he was nowhere near his house at the time Maria was killed, haven't you?'

'No, sir.'

'Then *I* don't understand.'

'I've been trying to work out what he did yesterday on the Rainsford case, so that we can pick up the threads where he left off.'

'An' what about Maria's murder?'

'I thought you'd have been told, sir. That's already being investigated by another officer.'

'Another officer!' Woodend exploded. 'It's bein' investigated by that bloody hatchet man DCI Evans!'

'Yes. I know.'

'The man who tried his damnedest to fit me up in the Dugdale's Farm murder case!'

'He *didn't* try to fit you up,' Paniatowski contradicted him.

'Didn't he? Well it certainly felt like it at the time.'

'What he *did* do was fail to understand the nature of the conspiracy which had been set up to bring you down. But he played no part in that conspiracy himself.'

'No, he didn't,' Woodend admitted. 'But we had to do all his work for him. An' that's all I'm suggestin' this time – that we do his work for him.'

'We have another case to investigate, sir,' Monika Paniatowski said.

'I don't believe this,' Woodend told her. The words came out louder than he'd intended them to, and several of the other officers looked up. 'I really don't believe this,' he continued, more quietly. 'Are you so obsessed with your own precious career that you'll just ignore the mess that Bob's in?'

'That's not fair!' Paniatowski hissed angrily.

'Isn't it?' Woodend asked. 'My, but appearances can be deceptive, can't they? I thought you used to have some feelings for him, but apparently I was quite wrong.'

'I still have feelings for him,' Paniatowski said, even angrier now. 'I *love* him! I tried to put it all behind me after we broke up, but I couldn't. All right? Are you satisfied now you've got me to admit it?'

'Then I don't see why you won't help me.'

Paniatowski slammed her palm down hard on the desk. 'God, but you can be so thick sometimes,' she said.

'You've lost me again.'

'The great Chief Inspector Charlie Woodend!' Paniatowski sneered. 'Cloggin-it Charlie – the man who they say has an instinct for knowing just how other people think! How they feel! And you still don't see it, do you?'

'See what?'

'It's *because* I still love Bob so much that I don't want any part in the investigation. It's *because* I love him that I don't want to be the one who finds the piece of evidence which finally seals his fate.'

'You think he did it!' Woodend said, astounded.

'Well, of course I think he did it!' Paniatowski said, as the tears filled her eyes. 'Who else would have killed a blind woman, and then tried to make it look like an accident?'

Twelve

If Monika really believed that Bob was guilty of Maria's murder, Woodend told himself, then there was nothing he could do or say to change her mind. And if that belief led her on to a further one – that there was no point in her looking for evidence which might clear Bob, because no such evidence existed – then he should respect her decision not to become involved.

So, in the light of that reasoning, there was no justification for the feelings of revulsion and betrayal he experienced when he looked at her. None at all!

But they were there, whether he willed them or not.

The feelings would pass. He was sure of that. Whether he could save Bob or whether he could not, a time would come when he would regain his affection and respect for Monika – when he would not only understand her position (as he already did), but *accept* it (as he most certainly did not).

Yes, that time would come, but for the moment he felt so much animosity towards her that he judged it better that they worked separately. Thus, whilst he drove to the New Horizons' factory – a part of his mind on the Pamela Rainsford case, but most of it working on what he could do to help Bob Rutter – Monika set off in the other direction, to conduct the house-to-house inquiries in the area where Pamela had lived.

Woodend noticed the Rolls-Royce Phantom V the moment he pulled on to the New Horizons' car park.

Noticed it? his brain mocked him. *Noticed* it! He could hardly have bloody *missed* it!

The Roller stood out from all the cars around it as a diamond would have stood out if it had been resting on a bed of cultured pearls. It positively *gleamed* in the weak autumn sunlight, as if even the sun itself had picked out *this* car as something special.

So Derek Higson was back in Whitebridge, Woodend thought.

Higson's dad had ridden to work on a squeaky old push-bike he'd rescued from the scrap heap – a bike that even other *poor* people laughed at. The son, on the other hand, had become such a flashy bugger that he rode around in a car which must have cost as much as the whole street on which he grew up.

'What am I thinking?' Woodend asked himself, shocked at the ideas which he found crossing his mind – and, even more, the sour juices with which they were larded.

He didn't give a bugger whether Derek Higson had a Rolls-Royce or not. But even that wasn't *strictly* true. He was *glad* that Derek had a Roller – if that's what made him happy. The man had come from nothing – less than nothing – and had worked his backside off to get where he was today. Now he employed hundreds of people and, according to what Woodend had heard from several sources, treated them extremely well. So wasn't he *entitled* to a flashy car?

Woodend climbed out of his Wolseley, and stopped to light up a cigarette. The thoughts he'd just *almost* had about Derek Higson were a warning to him, he decided – a clear indication that what had happened to Bob and Maria was making him see the *whole world* from a jaundiced perspective.

The door to the administration block opened, and a man walked out. He was about Woodend's age, though slightly heavier around the middle, and with a little less hair. Even from a distance, it was possible to tell that the suit he was wearing had been purchased from somewhere much more exclusive and expensive than the tailors' shops on Whitebridge High Street.

The man had been heading towards the main factory door, but then he noticed Woodend and immediately changed direction.

'Good to see you, Charlie, but I wish it could have been under different circumstances,' he said, holding out his hand.

'Good to see you, too, Derek,' Woodend said, shaking the hand.

But he was thinking: Take away the flashy suit, an' you're just an ordinary middle-aged bloke like me. So how the hell did you manage to pull a woman like Lucy?

'I've just got back,' Higson said.

'Aye, I assumed that,' Woodend told him. 'Where've you been?'

'Holland. The fat burghers of Amsterdam have got a lot of money burning a hole in their pockets, and they recognize quality when they see it. That makes them a very good market for us.' Higson's expression clouded over. 'Listen to me, talking like a salesman at a time like this,' he continued. 'Have you come to interview some of my staff?'

'That's my intention,' Woodend replied. 'But I wouldn't mind a short chat with you, if you could spare the time.'

'But of course I can spare the time,' Higson said. 'If it will help you to catch Pamela's killer, you can have all the time you want.'

They adjourned to the nearest pub, which was called the Golden Partridge. It had plush seating and thick carpets, and most of the customers were carrying leather briefcases. It was not Woodend's sort of place at all, but Derek Higson seemed perfectly at home in it.

'What can you tell me about Pamela Rainsford?' Woodend asked, when they'd bought their drinks and taken them over to a corner table.

Higson looked vaguely troubled. 'Not as much as I'd like to,' he confessed. 'The truth is, Charlie, I could tell you more about her work than I could about her as a person.'

'Well, that'd be a start,' Woodend said encouragingly.

'Pamela was efficient in her way,' Higson said, 'but she was a little too timid for my tastes.'

'How do you mean?'

'My old secretary, Gloria, was a real battleaxe. She used to bully me into doing the things I *should* be doing, rather than the things I *wanted* to do. Pamela was the complete opposite. She had neither the confidence or the initiative to step into Gloria's shoes.'

'So why didn't you replace her with someone who had?'

Higson smiled awkwardly. 'My wife appointed her,' he said.

'So what?'

'Ever since we got married, I've been encouraging Lucy to take a more active part in the business, partly because I thought she'd enjoy it, and partly, I suppose, as a kind of self-defence mechanism.'

'Self-defence mechanism?'

'If she's heavily committed to the firm, she can't really complain that I am, too. Lucy never complains when I have to work late, because she's right there working beside me.'

'I see.'

'But one of the drawbacks to this policy of mine is that I have to be very careful not to undermine her – very careful not to seem as if I'm questioning her judgement. And if I'd moved Pamela to another part of the business, and taken on a new secretary who was much more like Gloria, that's exactly what I would have been doing.' Higson laughed. 'Besides, it's done me no harm to discipline myself, rather than relying on my secretary to do it.'

'You have no idea what Pamela was doing on the canal bank the night she was killed?' Woodend asked.

'None at all. I don't even know whether she lived near the canal, or right on the other side of town. I suppose you think that's rather remiss of me.'

'It's not for me to—' Woodend began.

'Derek, you old reprobate!' said a new voice. 'So you're finally back from your travels, are you?'

Woodend and Higson looked up. The man who had spoken was in his late forties and, like Higson, was wearing a very expensive suit.

'Good to see you, Clive,' Derek Higson said.

'I've got a little business I might be able to put your way,' the other man continued, his tone both matey and confidential. 'A bit of business that will do *neither of us* any harm.'

'That's great,' Derek Higson said, without much conviction. 'The thing is, Clive, I'm rather busy just at the moment. So why don't you ring up my sec— . . . my office . . . and we'll arrange a meeting?'

'Fair enough,' the other man said, and made his way over to the bar.

'To tell you the truth, I think it's pretty remiss myself that I know so little about *most* of my staff,' Higson said to Woodend. 'It wasn't like that in the old days, when I was starting out. But then the company got bigger, you see, and as the public face of it – the one the customers want to see – I spend so much time travelling these days that I doubt I could even *name* half our work-force.'

'What's botherin' you that you're not tellin' me about, Derek?' Woodend asked.

Higson looked startled. 'However did you know there *was* something bothering me?'

Woodend grinned. 'We were in the same class from the time we started school at five until we left it at fourteen.'

'True, but—'

'I've always been a nosy bugger. I think that's why I became a bobby. I watch people – an' I remember what I've seen.'

'Doesn't everyone?'

'Not like me. There was a girl in our class who you used to fancy. I can't recall her name at the minute, but—'

Higson laughed. 'Good God!' he said. 'You're talking about Martha Crockton, aren't you?'

'That's right,' Woodend agreed. 'Martha Crockton. You were in love with her.'

'I don't know about that,' Higson said, slightly awkwardly. Then he grinned. 'It may not have been love, but just think-ing about her was enough to make me mess my pants.'

'Then it's close enough,' Woodend said. 'When you were five, you used to talk to her about snails an' snakes. When you were fourteen, you'd talk to her about the latest film that was playin' at the Alhambra. But what you always *wanted* to say – right from the beginnin' – was that you'd be over the moon if she'd agree to come for a walk in the woods with you. You never did say that – but it was always on your mind. I could see it was – just like I can see that there's somethin' in your mind right now. So why don't you tell me what it is?'

'I'd like to,' Higson admitted. 'But there are a couple of obstacles standing in my way, and I'm not sure how to deal with them.'

'What about dealin' with them one at a time?' Woodend suggested.

'All right,' Derek Higson agreed. 'The first one is that I can't really say what I want to say without putting us both in an embarrassing position.'

'This *is* about the murder, is it?'

'Yes, it is.'

'Then I would have thought that our embarrassment would be the least of your concerns. Unless, of course, it involves a third party.'

'It does.'

'In what way?'

'I know things that I probably shouldn't know as a member of the general public. That's where the third party comes in.'

'Oh, I get it now,' Woodend said. 'You've got friends among the top brass in the Whitebridge Police.'

'We do tend to move in the same social circles,' Higson said, almost apologetically.

'An' they sometimes feed you the juicer details of the cases we're involved it?'

'It's not something I've ever asked them to do,' Higson said. 'But the plain fact is that I couldn't shut them up if I wanted to. They're a bit like bookies and stockbrokers, who insist on giving you tips. They think they're doing you a favour. They think you'll like them for it.'

'An' do you?' Woodend wondered.

'I wouldn't be human if I didn't relish knowing things that are being kept from other people,' Higson confessed. 'But that doesn't mean I think it's right. And that doesn't mean I didn't feel ashamed of myself after I made my telephone call to police headquarters this morning.'

'You wanted to know the details of Pamela Rainsford's murder,' Woodend said.

'That's right. But I think – I honestly do believe – that I

didn't do it for any prurient reason. That the only reason I wanted those details was because it might put me in a better position to see if I could help.'

'An' who supplied the details?'

'That, I'd rather not say.'

'I'd be willin' to put my money on Mr Marlowe.'

'And you'd be perfectly entitled to do so. But I'm neither going to deny or confirm it.'

'So the first thing holdin' you back was that you didn't see how you could let me know how much you'd learned about the murder without compromisin' your mates in the Whitebridge aristocracy,' Woodend said. 'What was the second thing?'

'The second thing is that I'm not a policeman. I don't know how your minds work, and I don't know how murderers' minds work. So when I have a thought – as I did this morning – I'm not sure if I should keep it to myself or not. You see, it might help you to have the perspective of someone who is not a professional like you are. On the other hand, my idea might both be totally wrong *and* sound just plausible enough to skew your view of the case. And I'm not sure I'm prepared to take such a responsibility on myself.'

'I have to listen to laymen's opinions all the time,' Woodend said. 'I think you can trust me to distinguish between what might be of use an' what's a complete waste of time.'

'Very well,' Derek Higson said. He took a deep breath. 'From what Henry Marl— . . . from what my source in the Force said, I take it that poor Pamela was sexually assaulted before she was killed.'

'That's right.'

'But she wasn't . . . how can I put this? . . . she wasn't assaulted in the way we would normally assume a woman would be assaulted.'

'She was penetrated by some kind of instrument, rather than by a penis, if that's what you mean.'

Derek Higson was growing quite flushed. 'Yes, that's what I mean,' he said, mopping his brow with his handkerchief.

'But have you asked yourself why such an instrument was used?'

'There are a range of possibilities. I just haven't decided which one fits this particular case yet.'

'But a range of possibilities *do* exist?'

'Yes. I've just said as much, haven't I?'

'Would you mind listing some of them?'

'Well, for a start, her killer could have been impotent,' Woodend said. 'Or he could have decided that his sexual organ wasn't up to the job of violating her as she deserved to be violated.'

'*Deserved* to be violated?' Derek Higson repeated, looking almost sick.

'Deserved from *his* point of view,' Woodend explained. 'What he did to her didn't give him sexual pleasure – or if it did, it was a sexual pleasure far beyond my comprehension. What it really was, as far as I can see, was a *punishment.*'

'So her killer *knew* her?'

'Not necessarily. At least, he didn't have to know her as she really was. She might have symbolized his mother to him. Or the wife who humiliated him by running off with another man.'

'I see,' Derek Higson said thoughtfully.

'You still haven't told me your ideas on the matter,' Woodend pointed out.

'After hearing what you've just said, I'm not sure I want to,' Higson confessed. 'You speak with so much assurance about a world I'm completely ignorant of. I'm sure my ideas will be laughable to you.'

'Try them out anyway,' Woodend encouraged.

'Well, you say that he might have been impotent, or he might have been punishing her – or women in general – but there seems to be one big question that you haven't even stopped to ask yourself at all,' Higson said.

'And what might that be?'

'How do you know it's a man *at all*? Why couldn't the killer just as easily have been a *woman*?'

Thirteen

The call came through on the police radio just as Woodend was returning to the New Horizons' factory with Derek Higson.

'DCI Evans would like to speak to you, sir,' the officer on the switchboard said.

'When?' Woodend asked.

'As soon as you can get back to headquarters, sir.'

'Well, God alone knows when that will be,' Woodend said. 'I'll be as quick as I can, but tell him not to hold his breath, because I'm workin' on a murder case of my own.'

The switchboard officer coughed embarrassedly. 'I don't think that's quite what the message meant, sir,' he said.

'Then what did it mean?'

'That you are to drop whatever line of inquiry you're following, and return to headquarters immediately.'

'You're sure it means that?' Woodend asked.

'Almost certain, sir,' the switchboard operator told him. 'We've all just had a memo circulated from the Chief Constable's office. He says, an' I'm quotin' here, sir, "DCI Evans's inquiries are to take precedence over all other investigations. All officers – of whatever rank – are to regard Mr Evans's priorities as their own, and are to make the necessary adjustments in their own schedules in accordance with his needs." In other words, sir—'

'In other words, when DCI Evans says "Jump", the only question we should be askin' is "How high?" Have I got that right?'

'I rather think you have, sir,' the switchboard operator said.

Woodend kept himself under control while he was signing off, but once he had hung the microphone up he hit his dashboard with such force that the whole car seemed to rattle.

'They're bastards!' he said to the world in general, and no one in particular. 'They're a pair of bloody bastards.'

The table in the interview room had always stood squarely in the centre of the floor space, with the interviewee's seat facing the door, Now, Woodend noted, it had been moved so that it was much closer to the wall. Part of the reason might have been to accommodate the huge reel-to-reel tape recorder which DCI Evans must have brought with him from Preston, but there was also an element of the DCI wanting to make his own mark on his newly colonized territory.

Evans himself was already sitting when Woodend entered the room. Almost any other officer on the Force would have stood up and held out his hand. Evans merely gave the new arrival a dead stare and said, 'You are Chief Inspector Woodend?'

'You know bloody well I am,' Woodend replied.

'And you know – *quite* well – that I'm obliged to ask anyway, for the purposes of the record,' said Evans, pointing to the tape recorder, which was already humming away menacingly.

'I'm DCI Woodend,' Woodend confirmed.

'Then please take a seat.'

Woodend lowered himself into the chair opposite the other man. It wasn't standard Whitebridge police issue, and it creaked as he put his weight on it. He was prepared to bet that Evans had brought it with him from his own station, that – like the massive tape recorder – he saw it as just one more prop in his travelling inquisitorial show.

Woodend looked into the other man's eyes – an experience not unlike staring into the eyes of a dead fish. The last time they'd met – the last time they'd *clashed* – Evans had not only spectacularly failed to make the charges stick, but had seen his case proved to be a fabrication from start to finish. That would have been enough to make any other man feel slightly uncomfortable about this new confrontation, but Evans showed not the slightest sign of either embarrassment or remorse.

'You arrived at the Rutters' house shortly after the explosion,' Evans said. 'Is that correct?'

'No, it isn't. I arrived just *before* the explosion. If I'd been any earlier, I wouldn't have been here to talk to you now.'

Evans's lips twitched slightly, as if he were relishing the thought of Woodend being blown into several pieces.

'You went into the house,' he said.

'Of course I went into the house.'

'Why?'

'I thought runnin' the risk of gettin' burned to death might make a bit of a change.'

'Your sarcasm is not appreciated,' Evans said.

'Then stop askin' such bloody daft questions.'

'I'll ask you again. Why did you go into the house?'

'I thought there might be a chance of savin' Maria an' the baby.'

'Though, as it happened, your schoolboy heroics were unnecessary.'

'That's right,' Woodend agreed heavily. 'The baby wasn't there – an' Maria was already dead.'

'The fire spread quite quickly, didn't it?'

'Aye,' Woodend agreed. 'A damn sight *too* quickly.'

'Did you ask yourself why that was?'

'Not at the time. I had other things on my mind.'

'And now you've had time to think about it?'

'I suppose it was *helped* to spread.'

'That's correct. The murderer had laid a trail of paraffin from the kitchen to other parts of the house. His intention was probably to destroy all the evidence, but his actions had quite the opposite effect. If he'd confined the fire to the kitchen, it would have been much more intense, and all we would have had to give to the medical examiner would have been a few cinders. As it was, the cadaver was really in quite an acceptable condition.'

Woodend shuddered. The 'cadaver' was Maria, he reminded himself. And he didn't even want to think about what 'acceptable condition' meant.

'What I still don't see is why you had any reason to visit the Rutter house at all,' Evans said.

'You make it sound as if I'd never been there before. Bob Rutter is a colleague—'

'And he was in the house, was he? Or, at least, he had been there recently, and you just missed him?'

'No. Bob was out workin' on the current investigation.'

'So you didn't expect to find him there?'

'No.'

'Then I return to my original question, Chief Inspector. What were you doing there?'

'I went to see Maria.'

'Indeed?'

'Indeed! Maria is – or was – a close personal friend.'

'Despite the difference in your ages?'

Woodend shook his head, almost despairingly. 'You really have no notion of what friendship *is*, do you, Mr Evans?'

'Perhaps not, at least in your terms. So why don't you explain this friendship to me.'

'We were friends because I liked her – right from the start – and she liked me. It wasn't that we had any *particular* interest in common, like model railways or whippets. It was an instinctive thing.'

'How close *was* this friendship of yours?'

'Oh, I see the direction that nasty little mind of yours is goin' in,' Woodend said. 'Maria an' I were lovers, were we? Then Bob found out about it, an' killed her in a fit of jealousy?'

'It's a possibility. *Were* you lovers?'

'No, we weren't. But if we had been, it wouldn't have been Maria that Bob went after – it would have been me!'

'Even though you're much bigger and stronger than she was? Even though *you* can see?'

'How could somebody who knows as little about people as you do ever get to be a DCI?' Woodend wondered. 'Some of the stuff I've scraped off the sole of my boot would have made a better bobby than you are.'

'I see now where Inspector Rutter learned his offensive attitude from,' Evans said. 'And I'll tell you the same thing I told him. You will gain nothing from being abusive.'

'Oh, I don't know about that,' Woodend said. 'I feel better already for havin' told you what I think of you.'

'Why did you go to see Mrs Rutter?' asked Evans, showing the first signs of getting rattled.

'Why shouldn't I have?'

'Because you were in the middle of an investigation.'

'Life can't stop just because you're investigatin' a murder,' Woodend said. 'You have to eat an' drink,' he paused, 'an' *fart*,' he continued with emphasis, 'just like you would on any other day. An' sometimes, occasionally, you can even find time to visit a friend.'

'Did you seriously think that using such a crude term as "fart" would throw me off my stride?' Evans asked.

Not really, Woodend admitted to himself. But then we can always live in hope.

'You're holding back on me,' Evans said accusingly.

Too bloody right, I am, Woodend thought. I'm not about to throw one of my children to the wolves, just because the chief wolf has a warrant card.

'I would have expected more co-operation from a man in your position,' Evans said.

'Aye, an' maybe if this wasn't so much of a witch hunt, you'd get it,' Woodend replied.

'Need I remind you that all this is being recorded?'

'No. But it's a two-edged weapon, is a tape recorder. You might think you're puttin' on a good show, but until you hear it played back, you'll never really know *which* one of us sounds like an officious prat.'

'Was there any specific reason why you visited Maria Rutter when you did?' Evans asked.

Woodend hesitated. There was only so much he could do to protect Bob, he told himself. Because when push came to shove, the bastard sitting opposite him was right – and he had to put his duty as a policeman first.

'Maria rang me,' he said. 'She *asked* me to go round.'

'Did she give you a reason?'

'No.'

'And you didn't ask for one? Just dropped everything and rushed to her house?'

'There wasn't much to drop. I was only havin' a pint at the time. Besides,' he continued reluctantly, 'she sounded upset.'

'And what did you think had upset her?'

'It could have one of any number of things.'

'But what was the first of those things that came into *your* head?'

Woodend sighed. 'Some time ago, Bob Rutter had an affair,' he said. 'It's been over for more than a year, but my first thought was that Maria might have found out about it.'

'And you think *that's* why she rang you?'

'It's certainly a possibility.'

'Did she ring you as a friend? Or was it because you're Inspector Rutter's superior?'

'It may have been a bit of both.'

'Or is there yet *another* possibility? That she rang you because not only did Rutter work for you, but the woman he had an affair with did, as well?'

He was playing cat and mouse, Woodend thought. That was only natural. All policemen did it. But did the bastard have to enjoy it so much?

'Bob Rutter's affair was with one of my sergeants,' he said.

Evans was having so much fun that he even permitted a ghost of a smile to appear for a moment on his thin lips. 'One of your sergeants,' he repeated. 'Was it a homosexual affair?'

'No.'

'So it was a female sergeant who he was betraying his sacred marriage vows with?'

'Obviously!'

'And how many female sergeants do you have working under you, Mr Woodend?'

'One. My bagman.'

'That would be Sergeant Paniatowski?'

'You know bloody well it would be Sergeant Paniatowski.'

'So to sum up: Inspector Rutter had an affair with Sergeant Paniatowski. His wife found out about it. She rang you because she wished to discuss it with you. And when you got there, someone with an urgent motive to get her out of the way had already killed her.'

'I didn't say she knew about the affair – only that she *might* have done,' Woodend protested. 'Look, Bob Rutter's an experienced bobby. He's investigated hundreds of crimes in his time – a fair number of them murders. If he had been plannin' to kill his wife, he'd have done it in such a way that the finger of suspicion would never have pointed at him.'

'You would think so, certainly,' Evans agreed. 'But I suppose that desperate times call for desperate measures. And desperate measures sometimes lead to carelessness.'

'What *desperate times*, for God's sake?'

'You were wise to tell me the truth, however reluctantly you may have done so,' Evans said, glancing at the tape recorder again. 'Because much of what you have told us, we already knew. And as for the rest, it would not have taken long to uncover it.'

'*What* desperate times?' Woodend repeated.

'Did you know that Mrs Rutter had only recently paid a visit to her solicitor?'

'Concernin' what?'

'We don't know yet, though we have a fairly good idea. And did you also know that Mrs Rutter rang her parents in London?'

'I should imagine she did that quite regularly. She was very fond of her mum an' dad. Were *you* very fond of your mum an' dad, Chief Inspector Evans? Or do you have no idea what I'm talkin' about?'

'It is Mrs Rutter's parents we are discussing,' Evans said. 'And according to her father – who I spoke to just half an hour ago – she made a very specific request during her last call to him.'

'You should have left the poor man alone!' Woodend said angrily. 'Hasn't he suffered enough already?'

'I am investigating a murder,' Evans reminded him. 'In my place, you would have done exactly the same thing.'

Woodend bowed his head. 'You're right,' he admitted. 'I forgot myself for a minute.'

'Am I to take that as an apology?'

'Yes,' Woodend said. 'It's an apology. You were only doin' your job, an' I should never have criticized you for it.'

'Apology accepted,' Evans said, with a slight smirk. 'Perhaps we can now get back to the matter in hand.'

'What matter in hand?'

'Don't you want me to tell you what Mrs Rutter's father said?'

'I suppose so.'

'Mrs Rutter asked if she and her daughter could come and stay with him,' Evans said. 'He naturally enough wanted to know how *long* she intended to stay. She said she couldn't be sure, but it might be for quite a while. "Until I've worked out what I'm going to do next," were her precise words. Do you see where all this is leading, Mr Woodend?'

'No.'

'Then I'll have to spell it out for you. Mrs Rutter was planning to leave her husband, and take his only child with her to London. He didn't want to lose the child, but—'

'He wouldn't have wanted to lose Maria, either.'

'Why would that have bothered him? He must have tired of her already – or he would never have embarked on his affair.'

'It's not that simple,' Woodend groaned.

But he was starting to see that, to a cold fish like Evans, it probably *was* that simple.

'As I was saying, he didn't want to lose the child, but he must have recognized the fact that once she was in London, there would be little chance of ever getting her back. On the other hand, were his wife to meet with a fatal accident, he could have both his child *and* his paramour. The best of all worlds. But he had to make sure that a convenient accident actually happened, didn't he? And there wasn't a lot of time. So he botched the job of covering his tracks, and now we have him.'

It made sense, Woodend thought. Certainly enough sense to convince a jury, and probably enough sense to convince most of the people who knew Bob personally. And as much as he was trying to fight off the feeling, he was not at all sure that it wasn't starting to make sense to him!

Fourteen

Monika Paniatowski stood in the entrance foyer of the town hall.

She wished that she was dead – as dead as Maria Rutter.

She wished that she was dead *instead of* Maria Rutter.

But slowly the old instinct for survival began to reassert itself. It had sustained her when she and her mother had been on the run in war-torn Europe, she reminded herself. It had allowed her to endure what she'd been forced to endure in the home of her stepfather. And it would not let her down now. She was alive, and she had a job to do. And she would do it far better than anyone else could – because that was the only reason for doing it at all.

It was the end of the working day for those employed in the council offices, and slowly the foyer began to fill with people trying to look as if they were not actually *rushing* home.

The lead which had brought her to the town hall had been provided by a shopkeeper whose business was located quite close to where Pamela Rainsford had lived.

'Yes, I did see her knockin' about with a young feller, but that was quite a while ago now,' the man had said.

'Can you describe him?' Paniatowski had asked.

'I can do better than that. I can tell you his name.'

'So he's local, is he?'

'Not as far as I'm aware.'

'Then how do you know his name?'

'Ah, I see what you're gettin' at. I had a bit of trouble with the Council. They're always sayin' they want to encourage small businesses, but once you start one up you soon discover how bloody-minded they can be about enforcin' their petty rules an' regulations. An' let me tell you, Sergeant, there's more red tape involved in local government than—'

'He's connected with the Council, is he?' Paniatowski interrupted.

'What? Oh yes, that's the point, you see. When I went to the town hall to try an' get everythin' sorted out, he was the feller who interviewed me. I mentioned that I'd seen him with Pamela. I thought that might sort of melt the ice a bit – make him see me as more of a human bein' an' less of a problem – but it had the reverse effect. He went all cold on me, as a matter of fact. Still, he was helpful enough when we did get down to business, an'—'

'His name!' Paniatowski said. 'Can you give me his name?'

'Well, of course I can, lass. You only had to ask.'

'The chap you're lookin' for is just comin' out of the lift now,' the town hall doorman said, pointing for Paniatowski's benefit.

94

The man in question was around twenty-six or twenty-seven, she guessed. He had a neat haircut and a suit which, while not expensive, was smart and well-cared for. He looked exactly like what he was – a clerical officer who had hopes of one day becoming a head of department.

She took a step forward, to block the man's path. 'Mr Tewson?' she asked. 'Mr Peter Tewson?'

'Yes,' Tewson said, suddenly looking worried.

Paniatowski produced her warrant card. 'CID. I'd like to ask you some questions, if you don't mind.'

'What about?'

'Pamela Rainsford.'

'How did you . . . I mean, who told you that . . . ?'

'That you used to go out with her?'

'Yes.'

'Does it really matter how we got on to you? Your name came up in our inquiries, that's all.'

'It was a long time ago.'

'It was less than three years ago.'

'I haven't seen her for ages.'

'And does that mean you have no wish to see Pamela's killer brought to justice?'

'No, of course it doesn't mean that.'

'Then I'd greatly appreciate it if you could spare me half an hour or so of your time.'

'Will it take as long as that?'

'It might do. Let's just see how it goes, shall we?'

Tewson glanced nervously around him, looking at the other clerks who were leaving the office.

One of them smiled at him and said, 'You'd better hope Daphne doesn't find out about this.'

Tewson paled. 'She's . . . this is a police officer. She's making inquiries about a neighbour of mine.'

The other man's smile broadened. 'You can tell that to the marines,' he said. 'Police officer! She doesn't look like any police officer I've ever met. But don't worry, your secret's safe with me.'

The moment he'd gone, Tewson turned back to Paniatowski and said, 'Look, do we have to talk *here*?'

'Not necessarily,' Paniatowski replied. 'Anywhere will do. Where do you suggest?'

'There's a café just around the corner from here. We sometimes go there at lunchtime, but there'll be nobody I know in it now. We could meet there in five minutes.'

'You will be there, won't you?'

'Oh, I'll be there,' Tewson assured her. 'Believe me, I want to get this over just as much as you do. Probably more.'

The café was called Ye Olde Copper Kettle. It smelled of toasting teacakes and bubbling coffee. Most of the afternoon shoppers had already gone home, and Paniatowski pretty much had her choice of tables. She had only been sitting there for a couple of minutes when Peter Tewson entered, and, after quickly surveying the room, joined her.

'You seem a little nervous,' Paniatowski said.

'The secret of getting on at the town hall is being able to fit in,' Peter Tewson said. 'And it's not a sign of fitting in to be seen talking to a plainclothes policewoman.'

'Or to have gone out with a murder victim,' Paniatowski said.

'Or that,' Tewson agreed gloomily.

'Who's Daphne?' Paniatowski asked.

'What?' Tewson said, jumping as if he'd just been administered an electric shock.

'Your friend said he wouldn't tell Daphne. I was just wondering who Daphne was.'

'Oh, I see,' Tewson said, relaxing a little. 'Daphne's my fiancée. We're getting married next spring. We've already got the honeymoon in Bournemouth booked.'

'I take it that if Pamela had lived, she wouldn't have been one of the guests at the wedding,' Paniatowski said.

Tewson shuddered. 'No, she bloody wouldn't.'

'Why not?'

'Like I said, she belongs in the past. Very much so. I haven't seen her for over two years.'

'Was it a bitter break-up?'

Tewson considered the question. 'Not bitter, exactly,' he said finally. 'But I certainly wouldn't have called it very pleasant.'

'Who ended it?'

'Me.'

'And why was that?'

Tewson should have been expecting the question, but it still seemed to floor him. 'You know how it is,' he said.

'No, I don't,' Paniatowski replied. 'But I imagine I will when you've told me.'

Tewson shrugged. 'I just got fed up with her. That's all.'

He'd built a shell of caution around himself, Paniatowski thought, and if she was going to get anywhere, she needed to break through it. She decided to go for where he was probably most vulnerable – for where most men of his age were most vulnerable – his masculine pride.

'I expect Pamela was two-timing you, was she?' she asked.

'No!' Tewson said, stung, just as she'd intended he would be. 'No, I've never had a girl two-time me.'

'Ah, I see what it must have been, then,' Paniatowski said airily. 'There was something wrong with your sex life, was there? Whose fault was that? Couldn't you satisfy her?'

Tewson looked at her oddly. 'Are you quite sure that you're a policewoman?' he asked.

'You've seen my warrant card, haven't you?'

'Yes, but . . .'

'But what?'

'These questions you're asking. They're not the sort I'd expect a policewoman to ask. They're a bit *personal*, aren't they?'

'I'm working on behalf of the victim,' Paniatowski said. 'She took being murdered very personally indeed.'

'I mean, I've never been asked questions like these before.'

'This is the 1960s, in case you haven't noticed,' Paniatowski said. 'Not all women are quite as shy and retiring as they used to be. Of course, that may not have been your experience.'

'What are you suggesting?'

'It's obvious. I see it all now. Pamela *was* one of those shy and retiring girls. And the reason you chucked her is that while she had no objection to the odd bit of slap and tickle, you weren't as persuasive as some other men are at getting your girlfriend to go as far as you wanted her to.'

Tewson didn't want to laugh – not when he was talking to a policewoman, not when they were discussing another woman who had been *murdered* – but he just couldn't help himself.

'Have I said something funny?' Paniatowski wondered.

All signs of amusement drained from Tewson's face.

'Look, I told you I'm getting married soon, didn't I?' he said.

'Yes?'

'Well, my fiancée *is* a bit prim, if the truth be told. I wouldn't like her to know some of the things I got up to before I met her. And I certainly wouldn't want to be in any trouble with the police.'

'Why should you be in any trouble with the police?'

'Maybe you can advise me on the law,' Tewson said cautiously – feeling his way as he went. 'Can you be charged with public indecency if there's been no actual complaint from the public?'

'What?!' Paniatowski asked.

'I mean, is it indecent just to *do* it, or do you have to be *seen* to do it? And even if you're *seen*, is it still indecent if the people who see it think it's just a bit of a joke?'

'If you're a flasher, then I'd advise you to seek urgent medical help,' Paniatowski said. 'But I'm certainly not going to arrest you for something you've done in the past.'

'A flasher!' Tewson repeated. 'Exposing myself in public! Is that what you think I'm talking about?'

'Isn't it?'

'No, it bloody well isn't!'
'Then tell me what you *do* mean.'

The first time, Tewson explained, was when they'd been going out together for a couple of weeks. Up to that point, Pamela had allowed him to stick his tongue in her mouth and give her breasts the occasional squeeze, which he'd considered to be very satisfactory progress for a few dates.

That evening, they were out for a drive in the country, and had been going down a quiet lane when the engine of his Morris Minor had started to miss. He'd coaxed it on for another hundred yards, then it had finally died on him.

'So what do we do know?' Pamela had asked. 'Can you fix it?'

'Not me,' Tewson had replied. 'I know nothing about cars. But there's a phone box about half a mile back down the road. You wait here, and I'll go and call the AA.'

The Automobile Association had told him that it was a busy night, but they could probably get a breakdown truck to him within the hour. He walked back to the car, and gave Pamela the news.

'The point is, she could have started right then,' Tewson explained to Paniatowski. 'But she didn't. She waited for at least half an hour before she began making her moves.'

'I think I'm beginning to get the picture,' Monika Paniatowski said.

'Have you ever made love in the back of this car?' Pamela asked.

'Made love?' Tewson repeated stupidly. 'What do you mean?'

'What do you think I mean? Have you ever done it. Have you ever gone the whole way?'

'Well, no.'

'It'll be a bit cramped back there, but that should make it all the more interesting.'

He noticed her use of tenses. 'It'll' not 'It'd'. 'When?' he asked.

'Now!'

He tried to calculate how long it was since he'd made his phone call. 'But the breakdown van will be here soon,' he said.

'So what? We'll see its headlights long before it arrives, and have plenty of time to adjust our clothing.'

'But it's not only the breakdown truck that could come,' he said, panicking. 'There might be other cars. For all I know, this lane could be on the route of a police patrol car.'

'Don't be such a chicken. We're in the middle of the country-side,' Pamela said contemptuously.

'Or walkers!' Tewson said. 'If somebody was walking down this lane, we wouldn't see them until they were right on top of us.'

'But by then you'll be right on top of me. *Don't you think it's worth the risk?'*

'I don't know.'

'Well, if you don't fancy me enough to take a little chance like that, maybe we should stop seeing each other.'

'There'll be other opportunities,' he said.

'No, there won't,' Pamela replied firmly. 'It's now or never.'

He was young. His hormones were raging. It was now.

'Even then, she seemed to hold back,' Tewson explained to Paniatowski. 'It wasn't . . . it wasn't until we saw the head-lights of the AA van, that she really got going. That she really began moving her . . .'

'There's no need to paint me the full picture,' Paniatowski said.

'We tried to act normally when the mechanic arrived. But he could tell what had been going on. I could see it in his eyes.'

'It wasn't a one-off, was it?' Paniatowski asked.

'No,' Tewson admitted.

*   *   *

It was far from a one-off. A few days later Pamela wanted to do it again, this time in the car park behind the cinema, just minutes before the picture was about to end. And as time passed, her demands became increasingly dangerous. They did it in the church yard. They did it on some rough ground within spitting distance of the police station. They did it in the multi-storey car park.

It was a Bank Holiday Monday that was the final straw. They were in the woods when Pamela made the suggestion, and this time she insisted they take all their clothes off.

'There's loads of people around,' Tewson had protested. 'Picnickers and such like.'

'I'm not saying we should do it on the path,' Pamela said scornfully. 'We could go deeper into the woods.'

'I don't fancy it.'

'Then maybe I'd better start looking for a new boyfriend.'

They had done it, shedding all their clothes, as Pamela had wished. And this time, finally, their luck had run out. As he had approached his climax Tewson had heard the sound of whistles and catcalls behind him, and turning his head, was horrified to see that they were being observed by a group of young men holding bottles of beer in their hands.

He and Pamela had picked up their clothes and fled, to the accompaniment of more ribald comments. But even at the time, it had occurred to him that Pamela's desire to escape had not been half as strong as his was.

When they had put some distance between themselves and their watchers, they came to a halt and dressed.

'Well, that's the last time we try that,' Tewson had said firmly, as he struggled into his trousers.

'Why?' Pamela had asked.

'Because we got caught,' he told her, hardly able to believe that she had even needed to ask the question.

'So we got caught,' she said calmly. 'It was bound to happen sooner or later.'

'*You* liked *it, didn't you?*' he said accusingly.

'*I didn't* mind *it,*' Pamela replied.

'*Well, I did,*' Tewson said. '*And we're not doing it any more.*'

'*Aren't we?*' Pamela asked, and he noticed a dangerous edge creeping into her voice.

'*No, we're not,*' he said. '*There's no need to. You've got a flat. We could do it there.*'

'*If we can't do it where I want to, then we're not doing it at all,*' Pamela said.

'I work for the town hall,' Tewson told Paniatowski. 'Some of the bosses there are very conservative. If word had got out about what I'd been doing, my chances of promotion would have gone right down the tubes.'

'So you broke it off,' Paniatowski said.

With his confession over, Tewson was starting to relax, and now he even risked a grin. 'No, *she* nearly broke it off,' he said. 'Several times! She might have been a bit weird, but she was certainly very energetic.' A wistful look crossed his face. 'Despite all the worry it involved, I don't think I'll ever enjoy sex quite as much again.'

'Do you think that was why she was on the canal bank?' Paniatowski asked. 'Was she doing more of what she'd done with you?'

'That did occur to me,' Tewson said seriously. 'Poor Pamela. I was shocked when I heard what had happened to her, but I can't say I was surprised, if you know what I mean.'

'I know what you mean,' Paniatowski agreed.

'She was like a drug addict, wanting a bigger fix all the time,' Tewson said. 'Something was just bound to go terribly wrong eventually.'

102

Fifteen

'Where the hell's Cloggin'-it Charlie?' Monika Paniatowski wondered, as she sat alone at the team's usual table in the public bar of the Drum and Monkey. 'If he's coming, he should be here by now.'

It couldn't be pressure of work that was keeping him away, she thought, because when the pressure was really on, this place was where Woodend *did* most of his work.

So it had to be *her*, didn't it? *She* had to be the reason that he hadn't turned up.

Instead of understanding why she would find it difficult to help him in his attempt to clear Bob's name, Woodend had taken it as a personal insult – and possibly as a betrayal!

Well, if that was his attitude, she told herself angrily, he could go screw himself!

But even as the thought ran through her mind, she knew she didn't mean it. Charlie Woodend was her rock – her one certainty in an uncertain world. When she was in trouble, he helped her. When she needed encouragement, he provided it. She couldn't even begin to imagine how she could manage without him.

'It's a crying shame to see a pretty girl sitting there all alone,' said a voice somewhere above her head.

She looked up. The man was a stranger to her – which meant that he was a stranger to the public bar of the Drum and Monkey. He was around thirty, with heavily slicked-back black hair. He was wearing a check jacket – which, for all its garishness, hadn't been cheap – cavalry twill trousers and suede shoes. A sales rep of some kind, Paniatowski decided – a man whose stock in trade was that he believed he could talk anybody into anything.

103

'I don't want company,' she said.

A lie! She wanted company all right – just not his.

'What experience has taught me about pretty girls is that they don't know *what* they want until they've tried it,' the man said. 'What are you drinking? Gin and tonic, is it?'

'Vodka and tonic.'

'Oh, I say! A lady with exotic tastes indeed. Please do me the honour of letting me buy you another one.'

'I've hardly started this one.'

'Never mind that. There's no harm in having a fresh one lined up, now is there?'

The man glanced down at his gold watch.

She could read his mind, she thought. *It's getting late*, he was telling himself, *so I'll give this bird one more try, and if I'm not getting anywhere, I'll go and see what else I can pull.*

He was everything she disliked about men, Paniatowski decided. Crude, manipulative and insincere. Selfish, insensitive and arrogant. Though Charlie Woodend and Bob Rutter were so different to each other in so many ways, they almost looked like twins when contrasted to this loathsome creature.

'So what do you say, darling?' he asked. 'Can I sit down, or what?'

'It's a free country,' Paniatowski told him, 'but I think you'd be making a mistake.'

A smile of triumph flashed across his thin lips and was gone again in little more than a second. 'Making a mistake, am I?' he asked. 'Well, why don't you let me be the judge of that?'

Ash Croft – the latest phase in the Crofts Estate development – was in a state of transition, Woodend thought, as he coaxed his car over the bumps and potholes of the as-yet-unmetalled road. The first houses he passed were little more than shells, while those in the next section lacked doors and window frames. Only the last few houses, at the end of the row, had been fully completed – and even of these, only two or three actually looked as if they were being lived in.

He pulled up in front of one of the houses which *was* inhabited. There was no garden to speak of yet, but that had not deterred its owner from installing at least half a dozen leering garden gnomes.

Woodend walked up to the door and rang the bell. The man who opened the door had a pinched face and a thinning thatch of mousy brown hair.

'You're that detective,' he said, making it sound like an accusation. 'I've seen you at the factory.'

'That's right,' Woodend agreed. He looked around him. 'You don't seem to have many neighbours as yet, Mr Bascombe.'

The other man scowled. 'There are those who can afford to keep two establishments running, but I'm not one of them,' he said. 'The wife didn't like it, but as soon as the house was ready, we moved in.'

'I don't blame you,' Woodend told him. 'I'd have done the same, in your position. Any sensible man would.'

'There's too much money around these days,' Bascombe complained.

'And the problem is, most of it's in the wrong hands,' Woodend chimed in obediently.

'You're right about that,' Bascombe agreed. 'So . . . er . . . what can I do for you?'

'If you don't mind, I'd like a bit of a chat,' Woodend said.

'What? Now?'

No, not now, Woodend thought. I've driven all the way out here just to tell you I'd like a chat *tomorrow*.

'Now would be best, if that's convenient for you,' he said aloud.

'Well, I suppose—' Bascombe began.

'Excellent,' Woodend said, taking a step forward, and thus obliging the other man to take a step back, so that before Bascombe knew what was happening, they were both inside the house.

Bascombe reluctantly led him into the living room. It was

neat and tidy, and totally antiseptic – the sort of room which people who don't know any better think will impress their visitors.

'I suppose you'd better take a seat,' Bascombe said ungraciously.

Woodend sat down on the mock-velvet sofa; Bascombe lowered himself into the armchair on the opposite side of the coffee table.

'This really is very good of you,' Woodend said ingratiatingly.

'What I don't see is why, if you wanted to talk to me about Miss Rainsford's murder, you couldn't have done it at New Horizons, like you did with all the others,' Bascombe complained.

Because *the others* don't live on the same estate as Bob Rutter, Woodend thought. Because *the others* don't have houses which are only separated from Bob's by a strip of empty land.

'There simply isn't time to talk to everyone during the course of the working day, Mr Bascombe,' he said. 'So what we have to do in that situation is make choices.'

'Choices?'

He was a vain, self-important little man, Woodend decided, the kind of man who always thinks that only *he* could do *his* job, whereas everything that goes on around him could easily be accomplished by a team of trained monkeys.

'In police work, we generally find that we have to deal with two kinds of people,' he said gravely. 'There are those who we can see right away will have little of use to tell us, and we rush through them while we're on the site.' He paused. 'On the other hand, those people we think might be able to make a significant contribution to our investigation we leave till later, so we can talk to them at leisure.'

'You think *I* could make a significant contribution to your investigation?' Bascombe asked, half-alarmed, half-flattered.

'Indeed I do,' Woodend said.

'I can't think why.'

Woodend laughed. 'You would if you thought about it,' he

promised. 'Look at it this way, Mr Bascombe. Most of the women I talked to are little more than teenagers, with their minds too fixed on their love lives to notice much of anything else.'

Bascombe chuckled. 'You're right about that.'

'As for the men, well, I don't mean to be rude, but . . .'

'Go on,' Bascombe said eagerly.

'. . . but experience has taught me that men who work with their hands are far less observant than those who work with their brains.' Woodend paused again, even more weightily this time. 'What did you say was your position again, Mr Bascombe?'

'Assistant dispatch manager,' the other man said, with some pride.

'Exactly. A man who works with his *brain*. That's why it's worth my while to make a special effort to see you. Do you understand what I'm sayin'?'

Bascombe puffed out his chest a little. 'Well, when you put it like that, I suppose I do,' he said.

'I want to find out what Pamela Rainsford was like as a person,' Woodend continued. 'What her interests were, for example. Who she was friendly with. I've talked to Mr Higson, but I have to admit I didn't find what he had to tell me very helpful. I'm not saying it wasn't accurate, you understand, just that it didn't give me any leads.'

Bascombe's chest puffed out a little further. 'Well, of course, he's not in the factory all that often. Travels around a lot. So I think you're right. I think that those of us who spend more time at New Horizons – *and* use our brains – will probably be in a better position to help you.'

'Mr Higson seems to think that Pamela was a rather quiet girl,' Woodend said.

Bascombe chuckled again. 'Mr Higson would think that,' he said. 'Pamela was quiet enough when she was with him, but when he wasn't there she was a completely different person.'

'Completely different? In what way?'

'Very sure of herself. Cocky, even. And though I have

no wish to speak ill of the dead, I have to say that I found her attitude to some of my colleagues a little too free-and-easy.'

'Are you sayin' that she flirted with them?'

'Well, yes, I suppose I am.'

'But it was just a *harmless* flirtation, wasn't it?'

'I wouldn't know about that,' Bascombe said darkly.

'She never tried it on with you, did she?'

Bascombe folded his arms. 'She did *not*. She wouldn't have dared.'

'So she was always respectful to you?'

'Not as respectful as I would have liked, but at least she didn't throw herself at me.'

'Maybe the reason she was so quiet with Mr Higson was because she was afraid of him, too,' Woodend suggested.

'Afraid of *him*!' Bascombe said, mildly contemptuous. 'If you think that, you can't know Mr Higson very well.'

'I don't,' Woodend agreed. 'That's why I'm asking *your* opinion.'

'Mr Higson doesn't want people to be afraid of him. He likes to be *liked*. And I suppose,' Bascombe added grudgingly, 'he generally is.'

'So if she wasn't afraid of him, why didn't she flirt with Mr Higson?'

'Because a woman like she was couldn't take rejection,' Bascombe said, speaking solemnly as if he were revealing a great truth which lesser men might well have missed. 'She wanted all the men around her to be enchanted with her. And she knew Mr Higson never would be.'

'Because of his wife?'

'Of course it was because of his wife. Mr Higson likes the best. He drives a Rolls-Royce, and he's got a Rolls-Royce of a wife.' Bascombe smirked. 'So why should he go chasing after a cheap, flashy model that so many other men have already had a ride in?'

The mention of cars was too good an opening to miss, and Woodend seized his chance with both hands. 'Did you happen to notice any strange vehicles parked on this street last night?' he asked.

'There was a *fire engine* parked on the road over there,' Bascombe said, pointing through the picture window into the darkness. 'But I've no doubt you'll have heard all about that.'

'I have,' Woodend said patiently. 'But I was asking about cars parked on *this* road, especially ones which left shortly before the fire engine arrived.'

'What's this got to do with Miss Rainsford's murder?' Bascombe asked suspiciously.

'Nothing at all,' Woodend admitted. 'But it might have a great deal to do with Maria Rutter's murder.'

'I thought some other policemen were investigating that,' Bascombe said. 'The ones who came round to talk to my wife while I was out at work.'

'You haven't talked to them yourself, have you?' Woodend asked.

'No. Like I said, I wasn't here.'

If they'd missed him earlier, they should have paid a second visit by now, Woodend thought. But Evans's team probably hadn't considered that necessary – because they were convinced they had their man, and there was no point in busting a gut collecting any more evidence.

It was sloppy police work, Woodend thought. He hated that at any time, but he hated it even more when the fate of Bob Rutter depended on the investigation being conducted properly.

'The reason I brought the matter up is because I'm doing a favour for the lads who were round earlier,' Woodend lied. 'If you tell me what you know, they won't have to come back, will they? So *did* you see any strange cars?'

'As a matter of fact, there was one of those new Ford Cortina GTs parked just down the road, about half an hour before the fire engine arrived,' Bascombe said.

'You're sure that's what it was?'

'Positive. I went to have a good look at it, because I'm

thinking of buying one myself. It's different to last year's GT, you see, because the grille's wider and there's a new panel for the auxiliary instruments in the middle of the—'

'This car couldn't have belonged to one of your neighbours, could it?' Woodend interrupted

Bascombe shook his head. 'No, they'd soon have let me know about it if *they'd* bought one. Besides, it wasn't parked in front of any of the houses that people are actually living in. It was next to one of the shells down the road.'

'What colour was it?' Woodend asked.

'It was green,' Bascombe said. 'But then most of them are.'

Sixteen

Woodend was driving towards the Drum and Monkey almost on automatic pilot when it suddenly struck him that it was the last place on earth he wanted to be.

The reasons for this change of heart were obvious enough, he thought.

The first was Bob Rutter wouldn't be there, and his very absence would serve as a silent rebuke to the man who should have been able to get him out of gaol – and was far from certain that he could.

The second was that while there would be no Bob, there probably *would* be Monika, and he just couldn't face the thought of being with her on that particular evening.

So where should he do his drinking? he wondered.

There was a pub called the Bluebell straight ahead of him. That seemed as good a place as any.

The last time Woodend had been in the Bluebell, it had been a traditional pub like the Drum and Monkey, with a number of smallish rooms, each catering to a different mood and clientele. It wasn't like that now. Some smart alec at the brewery – a man who obviously thought he knew more about pubs than the people who actually used them – had set his evil plans in motion, and modernized the place.

Woodend gazed around the vast cavern of a room which had been created, and almost walked out. Then, remembering the Bluebell served one of the best pints of bitter in the whole of Central Lancashire, he walked across to the bar and ordered himself a drink.

'Well, if it isn't Charlie Woodend,' said a woman's voice immediately to his left. 'How you doin', Charlie?'

Woodend turned. Perched precariously on a very high bar stool was the obviously drunk Elizabeth Driver.

'I'm not givin' any interviews to the press at the moment, Miss Driver,' he said. 'An' even if I was, I wouldn't be givin' one to you.'

'Don't want an interview,' Elizabeth Driver slurred. 'Want . . . want to talk to my old pal Charlie.'

The barman placed his pint on the counter.

'Lemme . . . lemme pay for that,' Elizabeth Driver said.

'I'll buy my own,' Woodend told her, sliding some coins across the bar.

He was about to take his drink over to a table when Elizabeth Driver reached across and grabbed his arm. 'Please!' she said 'Please! I need to talk.'

As much as he disliked and mistrusted her, there was something in her voice that prevented him from brushing her hand aside immediately.

'If you want to talk, make it quick,' he said gruffly.

'Do you . . . do you believe in hell?' Elizabeth Driver said.

'I believe there are people who can make *life* hell for other folk,' Woodend replied.

'And I'm one of them?' Elizabeth Driver asked.

'An' you're one of them,' Woodend confirmed.

Elizabeth Driver shook her head, though not in denial. 'I've done some terrible, terrible things to get a good story,' she said.

'You don't need to tell me that.'

'I've broken up marriages. I've made people lose their jobs. But this is the worst I've ever done, and I'll burn in hell for it.'

'What have you done?' Woodend asked.

'Don't you know?' Elizabeth Driver asked, with some of her hectoring old self back in her voice. 'Can't you work it out?'

'You're drunk, Miss Driver,' Woodend said. 'Your best plan is to get back to your hotel an' try to sleep it off.'

'There's a . . . there's a saying in my trade,' Elizabeth Driver told him. '"I'll kill for a story." That's what we say. Only we're not suppos . . . supposed to mean it, you see. It's only fig . . . figurative. Nobody's . . . nobody's ever intended to take it literally.'

'You're makin' no sense, you know,' Woodend said.

'I'm a killer. Don't you understand that? I'm a bloody killer. I should be arrested.' Elizabeth Driver held her hands out in front of her. 'Come on, Charlie, put the cuffs on me.'

Given the state she was in, and where she was sitting, she should never have tried such a complicated manoeuvre. As she thrust her hands forward, her body swayed and she lost her balance completely. If Woodend hadn't caught her, she would have fallen right to the floor.

'Call a taxi,' Woodend told the barman.

Cradled in his arms, Elizabeth Driver moaned softly.

At first, the taxi driver was dubious about managing the drunken journalist all on his own, but when Woodend dangled the possibility of a large tip in front of him, his attitude suddenly changed and he agreed that it would no problem at all.

Woodend watched the taxi pull away, then wondered what he should do next. He could go back into the Bluebell, he supposed, but it wasn't the pub it used to be, and anyway, his encounter with Elizabeth Driver had soured the place for him.

Much better then, to try somewhere else completely. The Wheatsheaf was just up the road. He didn't use the place very often, and the chances of running into someone he didn't want to talk to were practically nil.

Yes, he decided. He'd go to the Wheatsheaf, have a couple of quiet pints on his own, and then call it a night.

His theory that there would be no one he knew in the pub was shot to pieces the moment he crossed the threshold. To get to the public bar, it was necessary to walk down the corridor, which entailed passing the best room. And sitting in the best room, he saw, were Lucy and Derek Higson.

If the couple hadn't noticed him, Woodend would probably have continued on until he reached his natural habitat. But Derek Higson *did* notice him. Worse, he looked delighted to see him.

For a second, Woodend contemplated ignoring Derek's energetic waving, then decided that would be churlish. There really was no alternative but to go and join the Higsons.

Woodend sighed heavily.

First Elizabeth Driver, and now the Higsons. It just wasn't turning out to be his night, was it?

Paniatowski and the man, who said his name was Teddy, were walking along the canal towpath. Twice Teddy had tried to grab hold of her hand, and twice Paniatowski had rejected it. Now Teddy stopped, and looked at his watch with the flame provided by his lighter.

'It's getting late,' he said.

'Is it?' Paniatowski asked.

'I'll have to be going back to my hotel soon,' Teddy said. 'I've got a busy day ahead of me tomorrow.'

'You could head back now,' Paniatowski suggested.

'I'm not in *that* much of a rush,' Teddy protested. 'I was thinking. It's quite a mild night for autumn, isn't it?'

'There's a bit of a nip in the air,' Paniatowski said.

'We wouldn't notice that if we cuddled up together on the bank over there. We could lie on my coat.'

Paniatowski took several steps back from him. 'No!' she said.

'What do you mean, no?'

'I should have thought it was plain enough.'

'I've bought you three vodka and tonics!' Teddy said, with just a hint of outrage in his voice.

'I never asked you to,' Paniatowski reminded him. 'In fact, if I remember rightly, I refused all three times. But you insisted.'

'It didn't stop you from drinking them, though.' Teddy paused for a second, as if considering what approach to try next. 'Why did you come down here with me in the first place, if you didn't fancy a bit of how's-your-father?' he asked.

'Do you want the truth?'

'I most certainly do! I think I'm *entitled* to the bloody truth.'

'You're entitled to nothing, but I'll tell you anyway,' Monika Paniatowski said. 'We're here because I wanted to give you the opportunity to prove that – contrary to all appearances – you could behave in a decent and dignified manner if the occasion calls for it.'

'And what's that supposed to mean.'

'It means that when I say "no", you accept it with good grace.'

'Like hell I will,' Teddy said angrily. 'Not after you've been leading me on, like you have.'

'I haven't been leading you on,' Paniatowski said firmly. 'I promised you nothing – and you're getting nothing.'

'Look, I don't want to get rough with you—' Teddy began.

'Good,' Paniatowski interrupted. 'Because I really wouldn't advise it.'

'. . . but after all the time and money I've spent on you I'm entitled to a little something. And I'm going to take it.'

'Don't make me hurt you,' Paniatowski said.

Teddy laughed. '*You* hurt *me*? You must be joking. You might be quite fit for a lass, but you're no match for me.'

Two seconds later, when he was kneeling on the canal bank, holding his nose and moaning softly, he realized he might have been wrong about that.

Seventeen

'I didn't realize that you drank in pubs, just like us ordinary mortals,' Woodend said, with forced joviality, as he sat down at the Higsons' table.

'But I *am* an ordinary mortal,' Derek Higson said.

And though he'd said the words with a mock seriousness which invited dismissal, Woodend suspected he really *did* believe them.

'It's true I'm probably the only one from our old class who can afford to ride around in a Rolls-Royce,' Higson continued, 'but that's only skin deep. You won't have to scratch very far below the surface before you uncover the Sudbury Street Elementary School kid with a runny nose and his socks round his ankles.'

'You *never* had a runny nose,' Woodend said scornfully. 'If memory serves me well, you were sent out every mornin' with a freshly ironed Irish linen hankie. An' I know for a fact that your mum stitched together the best black elastic stockin' garters in the area.'

'Aye, she was a grand woman, was my mam,' Higson said, slipping easily back into the vernacular he had used as a child. He hesitated before he spoke again. 'Listen, you must have thought it terrible of me not to mention what happened to your inspector's wife this morning, but I'd only just got back, and I hadn't even heard about it.'

'Do you think the husband did it?' Lucy Higson asked.

'It doesn't matter whether he did it or not,' Derek Higson said, in a voice which was *almost* a rebuke. 'Guilty or innocent, Charlie will have taken it hard, because that's the way he is.'

115

Lucy Higson frowned. 'I'm not sure I understand,' she confessed.

Higson laughed, taking the edge off his earlier implied criticism. 'You wouldn't,' he said. 'You'd have to have been at Sudbury Street Elementary, instead of at your posh prep school, to really understand. Charlie here has always had what you might call a protective instinct. He took any number of younger lads under his wing in his time. And I was one of them.'

Oh, you most certainly were, Woodend thought.

He tried to remember the name of the boy who made Derek Higson's life a misery for quite a while.

Terry Dawes! *Foxy* Dawes! That was it!

There were those who said that Dawes had earned his nickname because of his red hair, but others – who knew – said it was because he was a cunning, ruthless little bastard.

As a copper-knob, Foxy should have been the natural object of the playground bullies, but he'd avoided that fate by becoming the leader of the bullies himself.

He'd been very good at it, Woodend thought. He'd had a natural talent for picking out the best targets – for honing in on the boys it would be most satisfying to persecute. And one of his chief victims had been Derek Higson.

The thing that made Derek so vulnerable was that his family was poor, even by the standards of Sudbury Street Elementary. Derek's clothes were always beautifully clean, but he wore second-hand short trousers all the time he was at school, and his grey socks were more darning than they were socks.

Little Charlie Woodend had ignored the bullying at first, believing then – as he still did now – that if you were ever to grow to be a man, you had to learn to fight your own battles. But the incident in the lavatories had changed all that.

The boys' lavatories are at the end of the school yard. They are not a place Charlie ever goes to by choice – they are freezing in winter and stink in the summer heat – but some-times the call of nature cannot be resisted.

On this particular day, he hears all the shouting and scream-ing as he is walking towards the door, but it is only when he gets inside that he realizes what is happening.

Foxy Dawes's gang is crowded around a prone figure on the floor. That figure is Derek Higson. His short trousers are around his ankles, and he is crying his heart out.

'Look at him, Charlie!' Foxy Dawes says gleefully, point-ing at Derek's crotch area.

Charlie, to his own eternal shame, does look, then says, 'I think you should leave him alone.'

'Look at him!' Foxy chants. 'Look at him, look at him, look at him!'

'Let him go,' Charlie says.

Foxy should take warning from his tone, but he is having too good a time to even notice.

'Look at him, look at him, look at him!'

Charlie lashes out with his fist. He will get six strokes of the cane for it later, but Foxy loses three teeth and his gang will never bother Derek Higson again.

'You seem miles away,' the much older, much richer, Derek Higson said, cutting into Woodend's memories of his childhood.

'What?' the Chief Inspector asked, startled.

'You seemed miles away. I was just saying that you stuck up for me in the old days, and I bet you've stuck up for this Inspector Rutter of yours in just the same way.'

'I'd rather not discuss it, if you don't mind,' Woodend said.

'Of course you'd rather not,' Higson said, looking abashed. 'I'm sorry that I ever brought the matter up. I get rather carried away with my own curiosity, sometimes.'

'Sometimes? You *always* get carried away,' his wife said adoringly. 'You have a real interest in people, Derek. That's what makes you so good at your job.' She stood up. 'I hope you gentlemen will excuse me for a second,' she continued, before turning and heading towards the toilets.

Woodend found himself admiring her retreating rear, then instantly felt guilty about it.

'How did we manage to get so out of touch with each other after we left school, Charlie?' Derek Higson wondered.

It happened long *before* we ever left school, Woodend thought. I think it happened that day in the lavatory, when it became plain to both of us that you needed me more than I needed you. We should have been equals, but we weren't – and neither of us was ever really comfortable with that. 'People *do* just drift apart,' he said aloud. 'When we left school, we set off on such different paths. Then there was the war. Then I moved down to London. It was inevitable.'

'I suppose it was,' Higson said reflectively.

Woodend tried to remember just how much he *did* know about Higson since their school days together. It was a very incomplete picture at best. Derek entered the furniture business as an apprentice cabinetmaker, that much he was sure of. And he had married even before he came out of his time.

'Your first wife died, didn't she?' he said, then realized with horror that he had spoken what he had meant only to be thinking.

'Yes, she did,' Higson replied. 'It was cancer that took my Jane. It was a tragedy. She was barely into her thirties.'

'I'm really sorry, Derek. I never should have mentioned it,' Woodend said contritely.

'It's all right,' Higson assured him. 'It was a terrible cross to bear at first. I thought it would kill *me* as well. But eventually, everything settled down to a mild numbness, and memories of her only flared up to haunt me occasionally. I never thought I'd marry again. I was quite content – though that's not exactly the right word – to live on my own for the rest of my life. Then I met Lucy, and it was like being given a huge electric shock. She'll never replace Jane, of course, and it would be wrong to think she should. What I have with Lucy is different to what I had with Jane, but in a way it's just as wonderful.'

118

'You're a lucky man,' Woodend said.

'Yes,' Higson agreed seriously. 'In so many ways, I suppose I *have* been lucky.'

'I've been thinkin' over what you said about Pamela Rainsford's killer possibly bein' a woman,' Woodend said.

Higson looked shocked. 'Oh God, the last thing I wanted to do was to influence you in any way,' he said. 'What do I know about criminal investigation? I'm just a furniture sales-man with a smooth line in patter. I wouldn't recognize a murderer if he hit me on the head.' He laughed, then looked ashamed of himself. 'Sorry, that wasn't a very tasteful thing to say in view of what happened to your inspector's wife, now was it?'

'The thing is, why shouldn't it be a woman?' Woodend persisted. 'She'd have to be quite strong, but then a lot of women are nowadays. It was a particularly vicious attack, but if we've learned anythin' over the last few years, it's that women can be just as vicious as men. An' once we open ourselves to the possibility that a woman could have killed . . .'

He paused, aware that, despite his sober intentions, Derek Higson was on the verge of laughing again.

'What have I said that's so funny?' he asked.

'Nothing really,' Higson said. 'I was just wondering if you always discussed your cases with members of the general public.'

By God, he's right, Woodend thought. That's *exactly* what I was doing! Derek's more than just a feller I met in a pub, but he's not *a lot* more.

'I think I must be losin' my marbles,' he said aloud.

'I think all us kids from Sudbury Street Elementary are,' Derek Higson said. 'It's called "growing old".'

A young – and somewhat flushed – waiter approached the table. 'Are you Mr Woodend?' he asked, almost breathlessly. 'I mean, are you *Chief Inspector* Woodend!'

'That's right,' Woodend agreed.

'The famous detective,' Derek Higson said, for good – and, to Woodend's mind, *unnecessary* – measure.

119

'I thought I recognized you from your picture in the papers, only I couldn't be sure,' the waiter said.

Woodend sighed. This kind of thing happened from time to time, and usually he could deal with it good-naturedly. But on a night like this, it was the last thing he needed.

'Look, lad, I'm not a film star or summat like that,' he said. 'I'm just an ordinary bobby who's tryin' to wind down a bit after a hard day's work. So if you wouldn't mind—'

'I'm sorry. Didn't I say?'

'Say what?'

'There's a phone call for you, Mr Woodend,' the waiter told him. Then he added, almost with reverence, 'It's police headquarters.'

'This had better not be a joke, lad,' Woodend said in a voice which was almost a growl.

'It isn't.'

'But how the bloody hell did "police headquarters" happen to know that I was here?'

'It didn't.' The waiter frowned. 'Or do I mean *they* didn't? Anyway, they've been ringing round all the pubs, hoping to find you at one of them. They say it's very important you go to the station right away. It must be something to do with the murders.'

'Maybe it's a new lead,' Derek Higson, catching the waiter's enthusiasm. 'Maybe it's just the break you've been waiting for to close the case.'

Both of them were talking like extras in a bad television police drama, Woodend thought. And in Derek's case, he himself was to blame for it.

He should never have discussed the investigation with Higson, he told himself. And nor would he have done – nor would he have *needed* to have done – if he'd felt able to talk about it to Monika Paniatowski.

'Is the feller who rang up still on the line?' Woodend asked the waiter.

'Yes, sir. The landlord told him to hang on while I went to see if I could find you.'

'Then before I go rushin' off to "police headquarters", I supposed I'd better check it's not just some crank call,' Woodend said.

'If it does turn out to be genuine, would you like me to drive you down to the station?' Higson asked, with growing excitement.

'Funnily enough, Derek, I happen to have wheels of my own,' Woodend said gruffly.

Derek Higson looked dropped on. 'I'm sorry,' he said. 'I wasn't trying to . . . I only thought . . .'

'I appreciate the offer,' Woodend said, in a gentler tone. 'But I don't think it would do my image as a honest bobby any good to be seen arrivin' at the police station in a Rolls-Royce.'

'Oh, we're not in the Roller,' Higson said. 'That's just for business. When we're out for pleasure, we use Lucy's car which is a much more unassuming vehicle. So if you'd rather we drove you . . .'

'Thanks anyway, but I can manage,' Woodend said, standing up.

'Of course. But if you do need help at any time . . .'

'I'll let you know,' Woodend promised.

But he was thinking to himself that if there was one thing worse than bloody amateurs like Marlowe, who wore the uniform, it was bloody amateurs like Higson, who didn't.

The landlord stood behind the counter in the public bar, holding out the telephone. Woodend took it off him, and said an irritable, 'Yes?'

'Duty Sergeant here, sir,' said the man on the other end of the line. 'I think you'd better get down here as soon as possible.'

'Is this somethin' to do with the Pamela Rainsford investigation?' Woodend asked.

'Not exactly, sir,' the duty sergeant replied.

Then he told him what it *was* exactly about.

Woodend handed the phone back to the landlord. 'You don't happen to have the number of the Drum an' Monkey, do you?' he asked.

'Yes, I do,' the landlord replied. 'Would you like me to ring it for you, Mr Woodend?'

From the enthusiasm in his voice, it was obvious that he was another amateur mystery fan.

There was no wonder he did most of his drinking in the Drum, Woodend thought. At least there they saw enough of him to realize that there was very little glamour in his job.

'Yes, if you could ring the Drum an' Monkey, I *would* appreciate it,' he said aloud.

The connection was made, and the landlord of the Drum came on the line. 'What time are you plannin' to close tonight, Jack?' Woodend asked.

'Half past ten, Mr Woodend,' the landlord replied sanctimoniously. 'Just as the law requires that I do.'

'I'm not askin' you when you close your doors,' Woodend said. 'I'm askin' when you're likely to stop servin'.'

'Now, Mr Woodend—'

'An' don't give me any crap about the two bein' the same thing. Your pub is notorious for its lock-ins. An' I should know, because I've taken part in any number of them.'

'Sorry, Mr Woodend, I was forgettin' that you're one of my regular law-breakers,' Jack said, and from the tone of his voice Woodend could tell that he was grinning.

'So what time *are* you thinkin' of closin'?'

'On time. I fancied an early night for once. The regulars won't like it, but it *is* the landlord's prerogative.'

'Could you do me a favour?'

'If it's within my power.'

'Kick the customers out when you feel like it, but don't go to bed until I get back.'

'Any particular reason for that, Mr Woodend?'

'Aye, there is,' Woodend said. 'I'm just off down to headquarters, an' when I get there I'm goin' to be up to my neck in shit. So when I *have* finally cleaned the mess up, I'd rather like to wash away the taste of it in a place where I can feel comfortable.'

'Will you be alone?' Jack asked.

'That depends on just how good a shit-cleaner I turn out to be,' Woodend replied.

Eighteen

The corridors of police headquarters seemed so hollow when the place was nearly empty, Woodend thought, listening to the echo of his own footsteps as he approached the Duty Sergeant's desk.

The Duty Sergeant looked up. 'What a bloody mess, sir,' he said without preamble.

'It certainly doesn't get much bloodier,' Woodend agreed. 'What happened *exactly*?'

'Sergeant Paniatowski brought this feller in about an hour ago. He was mumblin' somethin' about her havin' tried to kill him. I took him straight to the sick room. When I'd got him settled in there, I put a call through to Doc Shastri, then escorted DS Paniatowski to the holdin' cells.'

'Did she offer you any explanation for what had happened?'

'Didn't say a dickie bird. To tell you the truth, she seemed to be almost in a daze.'

'An' she's still in the holdin' cells now, is she?'

'Yes, sir. Do you want to see her?'

'Later maybe,' Woodend said. 'I've other fish to fry first. Has she been charged yet?'

'No, sir. Given that she's one of our own, I thought it best to leave it until a rankin' officer like yourself arrived.'

'Quite right,' Woodend agreed. 'Where's the complainant?'

'He's still in the sick room, sir.'

'When was the last time you spoke to him?'

'It must have been round about ten minutes ago, sir. I took him a cup of tea through.'

'An' what sort of mood is he in?'

'What sort of mood would you *expect* him to be in, sir? He's the sort of feller who'd be an awkward bugger at the best of times – an' this isn't one of them. As far as he's concerned, he's had some of his own blood spilt, an' now he'd rather like to see some of Paniatowski's follow it.'

'Does he know she's a policewoman?'

'I couldn't say, sir.'

'What did you call her when they arrived?'

'Monika. Like I always do.'

'An' did you, at any point, call her Sergeant Paniatowski, or give any indication that she might be on the Force?'

'Not that I can recall, sir. The need for it never seemed to come up.'

'Well, that's somethin', anyway,' Woodend said. 'What can you tell me about the man?'

'His name's Edward Allcard. He's thirty-one, lives in Leeds, but he travels all over the North sellin' machine parts. He comes to Whitebridge about once a month on average.'

'Give me some statement forms, will you?' Woodend said.

The Sergeant reached into the drawer and produced the required forms. 'Will you want somebody in there with you, or are you goin' to take the statement yourself, sir? he asked.

'I'm rather hopin' there won't be any statement to be taken,' Woodend replied.

'I wouldn't get my hopes up *too* high, sir,' the sergeant cautioned. 'Allcard's itchin' to get it all down on paper.'

'I'm sure he is,' Woodend agreed. 'For the moment!'

Woodend had always thought that the 'sick room' was rather a grandiose title for a place that contained no more than an examination table, a sink and a desk, but given Chief Constable Marlowe's penchant for giving the most ordinary of things the most extravagant of titles, he supposed he should be grateful it hadn't already been renamed the 'Medical Response and Recuperation Unit'.

He knocked and opened the door. The man he'd come to see was sitting on the edge of the examination table. His nose was heavily bandaged, and there were blood stains on his shirt.

'Mr Allcard?' he asked.

'Yes,' the travelling salesman said aggressively. 'And who the bloody hell are you?'

'Chief Inspector Woodend.'

The title seemed to somewhat mollify Allcard.

'Well, it's about time that somebody in authority came to see me,' he said. 'When all's said and done, I'm the victim here. I shouldn't have been kept waiting like this.'

'I'm afraid these things *do* take time, sir,' Woodend said sympathetically, crossing the room and sitting behind the desk.

'That's all very well, but I need my beauty sleep,' Allcard replied. 'I've got an important business meeting arranged in a few hours' time and . . .'

A looked of horror passed over what was visible of his face. He raised his right hand to it, though he was very careful not to touch his nose.

'How can I go to my meeting looking like this?' he asked miserably.

'You could say you fell over,' Woodend suggested. 'Or better yet, say you hurt yourself rescuin' a poor little doggie from the canal. Most people are suckers for stories like that.'

'Do you think it's funny, Chief Inspector?' Allcard demanded angrily. 'Because, let me assure you I bloody don't. I've been attacked, and I want to see justice done.'

'Quite so,' Woodend said soothingly.

'I mean, it was a very *serious* attack. That nigger doctor said my nose was *broken*.'

'Dr Shastri is an Indian,' Woodend said mildly.

'That *wog* doctor, then,' Allcard said impatiently. 'Why should it make any difference what jungle she's crawled out of? She's seen my nose, and she says it's broken.'

125

'Where did you meet your attacker?' Woodend asked. 'On the canal towpath?'

'No, of course I didn't.'

'Then where?'

'I met her in a pub – a seedy little dive called the Drum and Monkey.'

'A seedy little dive,' Woodend repeated thoughtfully. 'An' why did you go into this *dive* in the first place?'

'I would have thought a senior police officer like you should be able to work that out for himself,' Allcard said scornfully. 'I went in there for a drink! When you work as hard as I do, you're entitled to a few bevvies before you finally turn in for the night.'

'But why go into a *dive*?' Woodend wondered.

'It was convenient,' Allcard said.

Woodend looked down at the piece of paper in front of him. 'According to what you told the Desk Sergeant, you're staying at the Beaumarris Commercial Hotel. Is that right?'

'Yes, I always stay there when I'm in Whitebridge.'

'An' there are a number of pubs very close to it,' Woodend said. 'So what were you doing in a boozer more than half a mile from your hotel?'

'What's the point of all these questions?' Allcard asked. 'The woman hit me. I've reported it. That should be the end of the story.'

'My boss, the Chief Constable, likes us to get all the details down,' Woodend said. 'It might seem a little pernickety to you – old-fashioned even – but that's the way he is, and we're stuck with him.'

'I see,' Allcard said.

'So what *were* you doin' in the Drum and Monkey?'

'I fancied a short walk before I turned in.'

'And this woman . . . Monika, is it?

'That's right. Or at least, that's what she *said* her name was.'

'This woman, Monika, came right up to you in the pub and introduced herself?'

'No, it wasn't quite like that.'

'Then how was it?'

'I introduced myself to her, as a matter of fact. She looked lonely. I thought a little chat might cheer her up.'

'Very considerate of you,' Woodend said. 'And later you thought you might go for a little walk together, down to the canal?'

'That's right.'

'And what happened next?'

'The bitch hit me.'

'What caused her to attack you?'

'I've absolutely no bloody idea.'

'You didn't do anything to provoke the attack?'

'Not a thing.'

'It can't have been a robbery,' Woodend said pensively, 'or she'd have taken your wallet and made a run for it. And she plainly *didn't* do that, or we wouldn't have her in custody now.' He paused, as if a new thought had suddenly struck him. 'How is it that we *do* have her in custody?'

'Don't you know?' Allcard asked, his outrage growing again. 'Hasn't anybody told you?'

'As I think I've already explained, I've only just got here,' Woodend said smoothly. 'And since you, as the victim, were my prime concern, you're the first person I've talked to. No doubt there is a report on the woman's – this Monika's – arrest, but it would save time if you could give me the details now.'

Allcard sighed theatrically. 'After she attacked me, she offered to drive me to the hospital. But I was having none of that. I told her to take me to the nearest police station, which is what she did.'

'So she drove you here, knowing she was bound to be arrested,' Woodend mused. 'That was thoughtful of her.'

'Thoughtful!' Allcard said angrily. 'Is that what you call it? She broke my bloody nose.'

'Of course she did,' Woodend agreed. 'And she'll be punished very severely for it. We like to think of Whitebridge

127

as a law-abidin' town. We certainly can't tolerate prostitutes attacking respectable businessmen in this way.'

'She's a *prostitute*!' Allcard exclaimed.

'So I've been led to believe. The Duty Sergeant apparently knows her quite well. He's even on first-name terms with her.'

'A prostitute,' Allcard repeated thoughtfully. 'But if she's a prostitute, why did she argue with me? Why didn't she just ask me for some mon—?'

'What was that?' Woodend asked, pouncing.

'Nothing,' Allcard said quickly.

'You told me earlier she hit you for no reason. This is the first I've heard anythin' about an argument.'

'There wasn't one.'

Woodend nodded. 'Good, because if there had been, God alone knows what her defence brief might have made out of it when he had you up there on the witness stand.'

'What?!'

'I must say, I admire your public spirit,' Woodend said. 'Most men would think twice before filin' charges against a prostitute. They'd be too worried about what their friends and family might think, especially if they're married. Are you married, Mr Allcard?'

'Yes, I am.'

'Anyway, as I was sayin', they might worry their wives would think they'd actually been *consorting* with the woman. But not you! You know your duty! You won't be deterred by all the finger-pointin' and the sniggers. You'll stand up in open court and say exactly what happened.'

'I ... er ... I'm no longer sure I want to go ahead with this,' Allcard said uneasily.

'But you must,' Woodend said sternly. 'A crime has been committed, a prosecution must follow. Otherwise this has all been a waste of police time, which is a very serious matter indeed.'

'I ... er ... think that I might possibly have got a bit confused when I fell over.'

'Fell over?' Woodend repeated, mystified. 'I thought you said this prostitute *hit* you.'

'No ... er ... that's where the confusion comes in, you see. I *thought* she hit me, but now I see that I only fell over.'

'So it was an accident after all? And this whole thing has been nothing but a misunderstanding?'

'That's right.'

'And I can let the young lady go, can I, confident that I'll hear no more about it?'

'Yes.'

'Then perhaps you'd like to come with me to the cells.'

'What for?'

'To *apologize* to the young lady for all the inconvenience your confusion had caused her.'

'Do I have to?' Allcard whined.

'Strictly speaking, there's no obligation to,' Woodend admitted. 'An' thinkin' about it, I suppose you might be better off goin' straight back to your hotel and getting' a good night's sleep. After all, you've had a very difficult evening.'

'Yes, I have,' Allcard moaned. 'A *very* difficult evening.'

Nineteen

Woodend was in no mood to be messed about, and, if Jack the landlord had taken too long answering his knock on the side door of the Drum and Monkey, it was more than likely he'd have kicked the door in first and worried about the consequences later. Fortunately, no such drastic action proved necessary. Jack must have been listening for their arrival, and as soon as Woodend knocked there was the sound of the bolts being drawn back.

Sally Spencer

Woodend and Paniatowski stepped through the door, and the landlord quickly closed it behind them.

'By Christ, but you look like you really *could* use a drink, Mr Woodend,' Jack said. He turned his attention to Monika. 'An' you an' all, Sergeant Paniatowski – if you don't mind me sayin' so.'

'You can say what you like, as long as there really *is* a drink at the end of it,' Monika told him.

Jack led his two late-night visitors into the public bar. 'What'll it be? The usual? Or is it a whisky night, Mr Woodend?'

'I'll have a pint, but I'll pull it myself,' Woodend said. 'You get off upstairs to your missus, Jack. When we've finished here, we'll leave our money on the till an' let *ourselves* out.'

'You're sure that'll be all right?' the landlord asked.

'I'm sure,' Woodend replied.

Jack nodded and left. Woodend slipped behind the bar, pulled himself a pint and – while it was settling – drew a triple vodka from the optic.

Though the bar was empty, and Paniatowski could have sat wherever she wanted to, her legs took her automatically to their usual table in the corner.

'What happens now?' she asked, when Woodend had finished preparing the drinks and joined her.

'About the assault charges?'

'Yes, about the assault charges!' Paniatowski snapped. 'After all that's happened tonight, I'm not likely to be talking about the bloody *weather*, am I?' She took a deep slug of her vodka. 'I'm sorry, sir. I should never have said that,' she continued, contritely.

'After we discussed the matter at some length, Mr Allcard decided he didn't really want to press charges after all,' Woodend said. 'An' I've taken the extra precaution of ensurin' that there's no record of you an' him ever havin' been at the station.'

'Thank you, sir,' Paniatowski said sincerely.

130

'There's nothin' to thank me *for*. It's what you always do for one of your own,' Woodend said. 'But I would like to know *why* I had to do it.'

'Are you asking me why I hit him?' Paniatowski asked.

'Well, I'm certainly not talkin' about the bloody *weather*,' Woodend replied, giving her a taste of her own medicine.

'I hit him because he attacked me. I warned him not to do it, but when he refused to take that warning, I was forced to defend myself.'

'Well, that's an answer of sorts,' Woodend admitted, 'but it's certainly not the answer to the question I asked – an' you bloody know it isn't.'

Paniatowski nodded. 'You're right,' she admitted. 'I went down to the canal with him because I *hoped* he'd attack me – because I wanted to strike out at something, and he was a convenient target.'

'So why take him back to the station? Wouldn't it have been more sensible to drive him to the hospital?'

'It was the station he wanted to go to.'

'You could have insisted on the hospital. I imagine he'd have been too weak to argue. You could have dropped him off outside the casualty department, an' then just driven off into the night.'

Paniatowski sighed. 'What would have been the point of that? I'd have been caught eventually, whatever I did. The creep knew where he'd picked me up, and that's a strong enough trail for even our beloved Chief Constable to follow. Besides, I did it, and I wasn't about to pretend that I hadn't.'

She opened her handbag and took out her cigarettes. As she lit one, Woodend saw that her hands were trembling.

'Do you know what I think?' Woodend said.

'I don't really *care* what you think, sir!' Paniatowski said, with a sudden burst of anger. 'I thought we were here to discuss the case. Do you want to do that? Or should we just call it a night?'

'Which case do you mean?' Woodend asked.

'There *is* only one case that concerns us,' Paniatowski told him. 'The bloody Pamela Rainsford case!'

'All right, let's talk about that for the moment,' Woodend conceded. 'I'm findin' it difficult to form any clear impression of her. The way her boss talks about her, you'd think she'd never so much as say boo to a goose. Then there's her so-called best friend, who's so caught up between need an' jealousy that she doesn't know what she thinks. An' finally there's the feller I talked to earlier tonight. Mr Bascombe, his name is. Admittedly, I wouldn't automatically classify him as one of the world's most reliable witnesses, but he certainly seems to think that Pamela was little less than a nymphomaniac.'

'Bascombe's probably not too far from the truth,' Paniatowski said, and told Woodend about the discussion she'd had with Peter Tewson, the dead woman's ex-boyfriend from the town hall.

'What do you think to the idea that the killer in this case could have been a woman?' Woodend asked tentatively.

Paniatowski considered it for a second. 'It's possible,' she said. 'An ex-lover, driven mad by jealously, would certainly be capable of doing the kinds of things which were done to Pamela.'

Woodend almost choked on his beer. 'You think Pamela Rainsford was a *lesbian*?' he asked.

'I don't know, but it's certainly not something we should rule out,' Paniatowski replied. 'We already know that she was experimental in her sex life. Maybe her experimentation led her to trying women as well as men.'

'There are times when I think I'm getting' far too old for this job,' Woodend said.

'Why?'

'Because I'd never have come up with the idea that you just have. Because I was brought up in a world that was a lot less complicated than the one we're livin' in now. Take Bob an' Maria as an example.'

'I don't want to talk about Bob!' Paniatowski said fiercely.

'All right, let's talk about couples in general terms then,' Woodend said soothingly. 'It used to be the case that if a woman found out her husband was havin' an affair, she'd give him absolute hell for it. But she wouldn't think of leavin' him, because you just didn't do that kind of thing. You stayed together for the sake of the kids, an' because *economically*, you didn't have any other choice. But it's not like that now.'

'Where are you going with this?' Paniatowski asked suspiciously.

'I'm just tryin' to illustrate a point,' Woodend said. 'Take another example. I'm sure there were as many homosexuals an' lesbians around when I was growin' up as there are now, but we never heard about them. An' that's not just because they were cleverer at hidin' what they were doin', it was because most of them didn't *do* anythin'. You suppressed your urges, because society didn't approve – an' because you didn't really approve yourself, either. I'm not sayin' it was a better world we lived in back then – but, by God, it was certainly a *different* one.'

'I'm sure that's all very interesting – in its way – sir,' Paniatowski said. 'But your home-spun philosophy's not going to help us find out who killed Pamela Rainsford, now is it?'

'Christ, but you're ready to lash out at just about anybody who's standin' in your path, aren't you?' Woodend said, starting to feel an anger of his own coming to the boil.

The intensity of his tone pulled Paniatowski up short. 'No, I just—' she began.

'Shall I tell you why *I* think you took Allcard back to the station?' Woodend asked. 'You did it because you wanted to land yourself in the shit!'

'That's ridiculous. I—'

'You had no idea that good old Charlie Woodend would come ridin' in like a knight in shinin' armour to rescue you. You didn't *expect* to be rescued. You didn't *want* to be rescued. What you *did* want was to be suspended. Because if you were under suspension you'd be able to tell yourself that it wasn't that you *wouldn't* help Bob, it was that you *couldn't*.'

'Are you saying that I deliberately planned—?'

'Of course I'm not! I'm sure that on the conscious level you had no idea what you were doin'. But that *is* why you did it.'

'Not true!' Paniatowski said stubbornly.

'You've got a closed mind when it comes to Maria's murder,' Woodend said, 'an' that's just not like you. You've got to learn to rise above your own personal pain, an' seek out the truth.'

'We already know the truth.'

'If you really think like that, there's no real point to havin' bobbies at all, is there?' Woodend demanded furiously. 'If crime detection involves doin' no more than arrestin' some-body who *could* be the murderer, then school dinner ladies could do our job.'

'Please, Charlie, won't you just look at the facts of the case?' Monika pleaded.

'That's just what I intend to do,' Woodend told her. 'But first I've got to make sure I have all the facts available to me. An' I don't. Not yet! But I'm gettin' there.'

'Are you?' Paniatowski asked, almost pityingly.

'Yes, I bloody am. An' I don't think I'll even have to look very hard to find them. I think they're probably so thick on the ground that I'll practically trip over the buggers. So why hasn't DCI Evans found them? Because he isn't even both-erin' to look for them.'

'Or because he's right and you're wrong,' Paniatowski said. 'Because you *wish* that certain facts were there, and he *knows* they aren't.'

'You're such a smartarse, aren't you, Monika,' Woodend said. 'So sure you know everythin' there is to know. Well, let me tell you somethin' that I've *already* found out.'

'Don't do this to yourself,' Monika pleaded.

'This Bascombe feller, who I was talkin' to tonight, happens to live on Ash Croft,' Woodend said, ignoring her. 'An' do you know where Ash Croft *is*, Sergeant Paniatowski?'

'Yes, I know where it is.'

'It's very close to Bob and Maria's house. In fact, the only thing that *separates* it from Bob's house is a strip of buildin' land.'

'I know.'

'Good! I'm delighted to hear that you do at least know *somethin'*. Anyway, the point about Ash Croft is that there are very few houses on it which are occupied yet. Which means – an' I shouldn't need to tell you this – that very few cars will normally be parked on that road. So I asked this Bascombe feller if he'd noticed any strange vehicles parked there the night Maria was murdered. An' he bloody had, Monika! He bloody had! He'd spotted a dark-green Ford Cortina GT. One of the new models. An' before you ask how he can be sure of that, he's sure because he's a motor enthusiast, an' he went right up to it to get a closer look. Do you see where I'm goin' with all this, Monika?'

'Yes, I see where you're going,' Paniatowski replied.

There was a dull, almost lifeless tone to her voice, but Woodend was now so fired up that he didn't even notice it.

'It could have been the *killer's* car,' he said. 'The killer could have parked there, slipped across the buildin' site under the cover of darkness, an' murdered Maria. But does Chief Inspector Evans know anythin' about this green Cortina? Does he buggery!'

'You can't be sure of that,' Paniatowski said, her voice as flat and cold as an ice rink.

'Can't I? Then tell me this. If he knows about it, why hasn't he done a follow-up investigation?'

'Perhaps he has.'

'Bollocks! If he'd followed it up, he'd have had the driver in for questionin' by now. Findin' him would have been an absolute doddle, wouldn't it? Because, when all's said and done, there can't be *that* many new, dark-green Cortina GTs in the Whitebridge area.'

135

'No, there can't,' Paniatowski agreed heavily. 'But I know of one, at least.'

'Well, there you are then!'

'What kind of car do you think Bob drives?' Paniatowski asked.

'I *know* what kind of car he drives. A Vauxhall Victor. But what's that got to do with anythin'?'

'He *did* drive a Victor. But he's been planning to trade it in for something else for a quite a while, and he took delivery of his new car just a couple of days before Maria was killed.'

'An' what . . . what make of car is it?' Woodend asked, wishing he was dead.

'It's a Ford Cortina GT,' Paniatowski said. 'The latest model. And it's dark green.'

Twenty

The weather forecasters had been predicting a relatively mild autumn, but the weather itself was refusing to play along with them, and on the morning after Teddy Allcard had his nose broken, the air in Whitebridge was chilly and the sky heavy with thick grey clouds.

Monika Paniatowski, crossing town in her beloved MGA, found herself thinking about the nature of murder investigations.

It was a common belief in police circles that a squad assembled to deal with a homicide should strive to become a well-oiled machine. It was a belief she herself had shared, until she'd started working for Charlie Woodend.

'I don't like usin' the term at all,' Woodend had told her, back in their early days together. 'A well-oiled machine! It's too cold. Too mechanical. It makes what we do seem like a science.'

'And isn't it?' Paniatowski had asked.

'Oh, I'll not deny there's room for science an' logic in an investigation, but there's an *art* to it as well.'

'So if we shouldn't try to be a machine, what exactly *should* we try to become?'

'An organism,' Woodend had said. 'A livin' breathin' organism.'

'Like a cat or a dog?'

'No, more like an octopus. The way I see it, each member of the team is a tentacle, feelin' about in the murk, an' sendin' its impressions back to the brain. An' the brain's job is to put all these impressions together, an' build up a complete picture.'

He was right, of course. Cloggin'-it Charlie usually *was* right. And thinking back over the cases they'd investigated together, Monika Paniatowski could appreciate just how well the theory worked out in practice – just how well the tentacles and the brain had gelled with one another.

But that only worked as long as the brain was up to the job. And Woodend's wasn't – not on this particular case. Because the brain was ignoring the tentacles. It had no real interest in receiving the messages they were sending it on the Pamela Rainsford case. Its only concern was to try to prove that someone other than Bob Rutter had murdered Maria Rutter two nights earlier.

Paniatowski pulled up at a red light, and reached into the glove compartment for her cigarettes. She shouldn't have to be making this visit to Pamela Rainsford's flat, she thought, because that ground had already been covered by someone else. But now the brain had abdicated its responsibility, the tentacles were going to have to do more of the thinking.

Like the few of its original inhabitants who were still in residence there, Hebden Brow had seen itself go down in the world.

Once it had stood on the very edge of Whitebridge. There had been an uninterrupted view of the moors from bedroom windows, and the row of single-residence houses had been owned mainly by mill managers, doctors and rising businessmen. Now there was only an uninterrupted view of the new council estate, and most of the houses had been converted into flats.

This was not new territory to Monika Paniatowski – most of the Margaret Dodds case had been centred on Hebden Brow – and as she turned on to the street, she remembered the details of that investigation and felt an involuntary shudder run through her whole body.

Pamela Rainsford had lived on the top floor of number 33, Hebden Brow. Many of the occupants of upper-storey flats on the Brow were obliged to enter their houses through a communal front door, but Pamela had been lucky in this respect, since there was a cast-iron staircase running up the outside of the building which gave her a private entrance.

'Nice for her,' Paniatowski thought as she climbed the stairs. 'Nice for *her* – and unlucky for *us*.'

She had not known quite what to expect from the flat. Would it reveal Pamela's penchant for risky sex in public places? Would her flirtatious nature – so sourly noted by Mr Bascombe – be obvious from the décor? Or would the picture presented be one of the neat, thoroughly respectable, young woman who Derek Higson imagined had worked as his secretary?

She opened the door, and felt a wave of disappointment wash over her as she saw that, at first glance at least, it was the thoroughly respectable side of Pamela which was on show.

The furniture was light, modern and nondescript – more Whitebridge High Street than New Horizons Enterprises. There were scatter cushions in royal blue on the sofa and armchair, and a poster showing James Dean in *Rebel Without a Cause* on the wall. The curtains matched the cloth which covered the sofa, the carpet had been chosen to blend in with the curtains.

The kitchen revealed a tidy mind. The plates were neatly stacked in the appropriate place, the pans thoroughly scoured, the knives and forks laid in the drawer with almost military precision.

It was only when she reached the bedroom wardrobe that Paniatowski felt a quickening of interest. The wardrobe was clearly divided into two halves. On the left side were the clothes that Pamela must have worn to work – respectable dresses and almost severe suits. To the right were clothes of an entirely different nature – dresses which failed to cover the knees, blouses which plunged to reveal a dangerous amount of cleavage.

Yet what had the search really told her? Paniatowski wondered, as she paused to light yet another cigarette.

That Pamela liked to attract men? She already knew that.

That she kept her life as a secretary and her life as a vamp apart? That had been evident for some time.

What would Charlie Woodend – the *old* Charlie Woodend – had made of all this? Paniatowski wondered. She closed her eyes and tried to imagine that he was in the room with her.

'*Pamela Rainsford liked to show off, an' she liked to run the risk of bein' caught,*' Woodend's deep voice said in her head.

'I know that, sir,' Monika said softly, to the empty flat

'*You might know it, but you've not really* thought *about it – you haven't really put yourself in her situation,*' the voice rumbled on.

'Haven't I?'

'*No, you bloody haven't. Think about your own situation. What's the best thing, as far as you're concerned, about investigatin' a case?*'

'Bringing the criminal to justice?'

'*Save that sort of guff for your promotions board. What's in it for* you? *How often do you enjoy the case while it's in progress?*'

'Not very often. It's usually a bit like coming down with a bad case of the 'flu.'

'*So what* do *you enjoy?*'

'Reliving it.'

'*Reliving it* how?'

'If I'm honest, I suppose I'd have to say I like wallowing in the triumph of it all.'

'*Aye, a bit like a pig rollin' in shit,*' the imaginary Woodend said dryly. '*An' do you do this wallowin' alone?*'

'You know I don't. I do it in the Drum, with you and . . .' her voice choked slightly, '. . . and Bob.'

'*This is no time for emotionalism,*' the imaginary Woodend said sternly. '*Could Pamela relive her triumphs with anybody else?*'

'I don't think so.'

'*Why not?*'

'Because the only people she could have relived them with would have been the boyfriends. If the others are anything like the one I talked to, they wouldn't have been around any longer.'

'*So?*'

'So she'll have kept a diary!'

'*Aye, that's more than likely, isn't it?*'

The diary was hidden under a loose floorboard beneath the bedroom carpet. It wasn't the best hiding place in the world, Paniatowski thought, but perhaps that was precisely why Pamela had chosen it. Knowing how vulnerable it was – how easily a determined person could find it – would only add to the danger and enhance the thrill.

When the two constables heard the sound of footsteps at the other end of the police garage, they already had the boot of the dark-green Ford Cortina GT open and were examining the contents. As the footsteps drew closer, the constables straightened up and saw a large man in a hairy tweed jacket walking towards them.

'I never know what I'll find you doin' next, Beresford,' Woodend said jovially. 'Beat policeman, driver, forensics examiner – you're a jack-of-all-trades, an' no question about it.'

'I went on a Home Office course for this kind of work, sir,' Beresford said, in a flat voice. 'It's as well to have a number of strings to your bow.'

'Aye, it is,' Woodend agreed.

The constables did not resume their examination, but neither did they make any effort to continue the conversation.

'Nice set of wheels,' Woodend said, after what seemed like an unbearable amount of time had elapsed. 'Wouldn't mind ownin' one of these buggers myself. I expect you wouldn't mind one, either.'

'No, sir, I wouldn't,' Beresford replied, his voice still toneless.

Another silence followed.

'I hope you're not goin' to damage it,' Woodend said, trying his best not to sound too desperate. 'It'd be almost a crime in itself to pull a nice shiny new car like this to pieces.'

'We're not going to pull it to pieces, sir,' Beresford said.

'So what are you goin' to do with it? Polish the bodywork an' check the tyre pressures?'

Woodend laughed, to show he had been making a joke, but the constables didn't join in.

'No, we're not going to do that, either, sir,' Beresford said, unsmilingly.

'So what are you goin' to do?'

'We're going to *examine* it, sir.'

'Examine it,' Woodend repeated thoughtfully. 'That's an awfully general term, isn't it? What will you be lookin' for specifically?'

'Couldn't say *specifically*, sir.'

Woodend frowned. '*Couldn't* say? Or *won't* say?'

'With respect, sir, we're doing some *specific* work for Chief Inspector Evans.'

'There's very little difference between the two roads, you know,' Woodend said.

'I'm afraid I'm not following you, sir.'

'Elm Croft an' Ash Croft. They're on the same estate. Not a hundred yards apart, in fact. So any mud you find in the tyre treads could have come from either of them.'

'Sir, I don't think—'

'All I'm sayin' is, you shouldn't jump to any conclusions,' Woodend said hastily. 'Don't assume that the first thought that comes into your heads is necessarily the right one. Consider all the other possibilities. That's the essence of good detective work.'

'I don't think we're supposed to be discussing our work with you, sir,' Beresford said.

'Who's even askin' you to discuss anythin'?' Woodend said, aiming for hearty but merely sounding weak. 'All I'm doin' – as a senior an' more experienced police officer – is takin' the time to point out to you that there are certain pitfalls you should try to avoid.'

Beresford took a deep breath. 'With the greatest possible respect, sir, that's not what you're doing at all.'

'Then what *am* I doin'?'

'You're asking us to treat this examination differently to any other we might carry out.'

'Now why would I do that?'

'Because we both know this particular car belongs to a member of your team.'

Woodend bowed his head, ashamed. 'You're right, of course,' he admitted. 'I was askin' you to treat it differently, an' I apologize unreservedly for ever puttin' you two lads in such an awkward situation. You'll accept my apology, won't you, Beresford?'

'Of course we will, sir,' Beresford said. 'A boss should look after his team, and in your position, I'd probably have acted in exactly the same way.' He hesitated. 'But . . . er . . .'

'But you're still goin' to have to report this conversation to DCI Evans – an' possibly to Mr Marlowe as well?'

'Yes, sir. I'm sorry but—'

'Now there's nothin' for *you* to be sorry about,' Woodend told him. 'I'm the one who's overstepped the bounds. You'd be in dereliction of your duty if you *didn't* report it.'

'Under the circumstances, that's very understanding of you, sir,' Beresford said gratefully.

Woodend managed to produce a grin which was *almost* genuine. 'Understanding?' he repeated. 'Bollocks, lad, it's just common sense.'

Bob Rutter gazed at the chocolate-and-cream-coloured wall of the police station holding cell.

Several previous occupants – perhaps through boredom, perhaps through desperation – had left a record of their time in there by scratching words into the cement.

'I am inosent,' one of them had written.

'The police is bastards!' a second had gouged in large, angry letters.

'Forgive me, Alice,' a third had written.

And a fourth – someone with a sense of humour of sorts – had inscribed the word 'Exit', with an arrow below it pointing to the floor.

Rutter had read all the words many times, as if they were a favourite book he kept returning to. Blindfold him, and he could still have pointed to exactly where they were. But he was not reading them at that moment. Instead, he was thinking of the future.

The *future*? his mind mocked. *What* future?

In a little more than twenty-fours, DCI Evans would either have to charge him or release him. And from the conversations he had had with the bullet-headed Chief Inspector, he was in no doubt as to which of these two available options Evans would choose.

He thought about his interview with Evans. What had he been doing between the time he had left home and the time he had returned to the burnt-out shell? the DCI from Preston had asked him. He'd just been driving around, he'd replied. Driving around where? Evans had demanded. And he'd said that he couldn't remember. That had been true at the time. Shocked as he had been by Maria's death, he had no idea where he'd been the previous night. But slowly his memory had come back to him, and now he had filled in quite a number of the gaps. Perhaps he should ask to see Evans again, because surely what he had remembered would give him an alibi of sorts. But the DCI would never listen. Why should he, when he was already convinced he had his man?

Once the charges had been laid, Rutter thought, returning to visions of his gloomy future, he would exchange this cell in the police station – which was home ground – for another cell in a remand centre completely unknown to him. He would, in other words, be entering enemy territory without any means to defend himself.

The authorities in the remand centre might just keep quiet about the fact he was a policeman, since they knew full well what happened to bobbies who'd been locked up.

Of course, they could always choose to go the other way – could it make it perfectly plain who he was, because they'd decided that a policeman who had gone bad deserved all that was coming to him.

And a great deal *would* be coming to him, if that happened.

Scalding tea would be thrown on his crotch and into his face. He would be beaten up on a daily basis. He might even be gang-raped if the other prisoners sensed – quite rightly – that he would consider this to be the ultimate humiliation.

It was even possible that he would be killed before he ever went to trial. And that, in a way, would be a relief.

An escape!

He pictured himself standing in the dock and listening to the sentence being passed. He could almost hear the judge's words.

'*In all my years on the bench I have never come across a more shocking case than this one. The defendant was a senior police officer, in whom we had placed our trust. And he betrayed that trust by committing the most heinous of all crimes. He murdered a woman! A defenceless woman. A* blind *woman.'*

There would be no mercy shown to him. He would receive the stiffest sentence the law made it possible to impose.

How old would the baby be when he came out of prison – if he ever *did* come out? In her twenties, at least. A grown woman – a woman who would be a complete stranger to him, yet would hate him as much as one human being could ever hate another.

He looked around the cell. The custody officer had taken his belt and shoelaces from him, as was standard procedure, but if he wished to hang himself then the bed-sheets would prove a more-than-adequate substitute.

Perhaps that was what they all wanted, he suddenly realized.

Perhaps they were willing him to hang himself.

And perhaps he would oblige them.

Twenty-One

As Woodend drove towards New Horizons Enterprises, he had an uneasy feeling in his gut which was so alien to his normal self that for quite some time he had no idea what it was.

It's guilt! he thought with a sudden flash of insight, as he pulled into the car park. It's bloody guilt!

And it had every right to be there, he quickly decided. He owed it to Pamela – just as he owed it to every murder victim whose case he'd investigated – to see that the killer was caught. And *nothing* – not even Bob's desperate state – could absolve him of that responsibility.

Yet had he been doing his job as well as he might have done? Had he buggery!

He got out of his car and slammed the door brutally behind him. He would get to the bottom of this case whatever it cost him, he promised himself. Even if he couldn't save Bob, he would at least prove that justice could be done *sometimes*.

Woodend was struck by a feeling of *déjà vu* the moment he entered the upholstery workshop. Looking around him at the legion of small men – and they did all *seem* to be small – who were busily engaged in stretching fabric, hammering in studs and screwing pieces of wood together, he tried to work out *why* it should seem so familiar to him. And then he had it. The place reminded him of the picture books of his childhood. It was as if he'd walked into Father Christmas's workshop, and found all his elves hard at work.

'Can't you get a job here if you're tall?' he asked the foreman, Tom Doyle, who was no giant himself.

Doyle grinned good-naturedly. 'Big men aren't suited to it,' he said. 'Big men have big hands, you see, and for this kind of work you need to have the delicate touch. You'd be a rubbish ottoman-maker yourself.'

'I expect I would,' Woodend agreed. 'Seems to be a thriving business you've got here.'

'It is,' Doyle agreed. 'We go from strength to strength. Mind you, it was a different story a few years back. There was a period when I was almost convinced we'd go under.'

'So what turned things around?'

'Hard to say exactly,' Doyle admitted. 'One thing, of course, is that people started gettin' more money in their pockets, an' once they could afford it, they decided to buy quality. But there's more to it than that. When Mr Higson's first wife died, he seemed to lose most of his interest in the business. Things weren't bein' run as they should have been.'

'An' when did he start to get his interest back? When he got married the second time?'

146

'Yes,' Doyle said, slightly warily.

'You don't seem sure,' Woodend said.

'Look, I don't want to knock Mr Higson,' Doyle said. 'He's always treated his workers well. Besides, he's a brilliant sales-man, to judge by the amount of orders we keep gettin' in. And that matters, does gettin' orders, because even if you make the best furniture in the world – an' ours come pretty close to that, in my opinion – it's a wasted effort unless you can persuade somebody to buy it.'

'But . . . ?' Woodend said.

'But what?'

'But what is it you're holdin' back?'

Doyle sighed. 'He's got a lot goin' for him, as I said, but he's far too impulsive to handle the day-to-day runnin' of the company properly. An' that's where *Mrs* Higson comes in.'

'You think she's the one who actually keeps the factory tickin' over?'

'Think? I know it for a fact. But for God's sake, don't quote me.'

'Why wouldn't I?'

'Because she wouldn't like it to be generally known.'

'Any reason for that?' Woodend wondered.

'From what I've seen in this life, there's three kinds of women in the world,' Doyle said. 'There's the doormats, who let their husbands walk all over 'em. Then there's the dragons, who like everybody else to know their husbands don't fart without askin' their permission first. But there's a third kind – a rare breed indeed – an' Mrs Higson is one of them.'

Woodend grinned. Since the moment Maria Rutter's kitchen had exploded, he seemed to have inhabited a poisoned planet all of his own, and the chirpy foreman was a welcome breath of fresh air.

'So what do you call the third kind of women?' he asked.

'Angels,' Doyle said. 'I call them angels, an' Mrs Higson's the one right at the very top of the Christmas tree. She's one of them women who does everythin' she can for her husband, yet leaves him with the impression that his balls are still his own.'

'And what kind of woman was Pamela Rainsford?' Woodend asked.

'Depends on where she was, an' who she was with,' Doyle said, a little cautiously.

'Would you care to explain that?'

'I'm not sure I can.'

Woodend laughed. 'Come on, Mr Doyle! The way you've got with words, you could explain anythin' you put your mind to.'

Doyle thought about it for a moment. 'Mr Higson comes down the workshop now an' again,' he said finally, 'an' when he does he usually brings – he usually *brought* – Pamela with him to take notes. Well, you've never seen such a little mouse as Pamela when she was trailin' in the boss's wake. Doormat? She was more like a mud-scraper.'

'But there were other occasions . . .' Woodend prompted.

'She went out with one of my lads – young Malcolm Shirtcliffe – for a while an'—'

'Mrs Higson told me Pamela had nothin' to do with the shop-floor workers,' Woodend interrupted.

'An' no doubt she believes it,' Doyle countered. 'But how many bosses really know what's goin' on in the private lives of the people they've got workin' for them?'

'True,' Woodend agreed.

'Anyway, as I was sayin', she went with Malcolm, an' she was a real fire-breather to him. The poor lad never looked happy all the time they were seein' each other. Mind you, it was even worse when she broke it off. He was destroyed. In the end, he went an' took one of them assisted passages to Australia. I can only hope he found an angel waitin' for him there. Goodness knows, he deserves it, after what Pamela put him through.'

'You didn't like her much, did you?' Woodend asked.

'Oh, it probably wasn't her fault,' Doyle said hastily.

'I've never understood people who say that you shouldn't speak ill of the dead,' Woodend told him. 'Dyin' doesn't

Dying in the Dark

suddenly turn an arsehole into a saint. The fact that somebody's gone doesn't suddenly mean they didn't do harm while
they were here.'

'You misunderstand me,' Doyle protested. 'I said it probably wasn't her fault, an' I meant it.'

'Then who's fault was it?'

'Nobody's I suppose. Unless you're keen on blamin' God
or nature – an' neither of them's ever done any harm to me.
You see, there are some lads you meet who are so soft an'
gentle that you can just tell they'd have been happier if they'd
been born girls. An' there are some women – even nice-lookin'
ones like Pamela – who'd have been much better adjusted in
life if they'd come out of their mothers' bellies with somethin' hangin' between their legs.'

'You're a philosopher, Mr Doyle,' Woodend said.

'I'm an upholsterer, Mr Woodend,' the little man replied.

Woodend looked around at Doyle's elves again. 'What's
that he's usin'?' he asked, pointing to one of the workers who
was bent over a chesterfield.

'It's special adhesive tape,' Doyle said. 'We use it to hold
pieces of wood together while we're workin' on them. The
advantage of it is, you see, that when we strip it off again, it
doesn't leave any marks.'

'Could you spare me a roll?' Woodend asked.

Doyle grinned again. 'You should never try fixin' things
yourself, you know,' he said. 'Leave it to the craftsmen. That's
what we're here for.'

'I really would appreciate it,' Woodend said.

'All right, if that's what you want,' Doyle agreed cheer-
fully. 'But don't blame me if your sofa collapses when you're
havin' a bit of downstairs how's-your-father with your
missus.'

As Woodend walked towards the door, the tape in his hand,
he realized he was now more focused on the case than he
had been at any point since Bob Rutter was taken in for
questioning.

'Special adhesive tape', Doyle had called it. It was strong

149

enough to hold two heavy pieces of wood firmly together, yet could be stripped off without doing any visible damage. Ideal for furniture making – and ideal for immobilizing and gagging your victim while you tortured her.

He paused near the doorway, to examine a row of tools hanging on a rack. Some – like the tack hammers and chisels – he recognized, but others were so specialized that he had no idea what they were used for. But at least half of them *could* have been used for the terrible things that were done to Pamela Rainsford.

Monika Paniatowski put the diary into the glove compartment of her MGA. Under normal circumstances, she thought, she would have taken it straight back to Woodend. But these were not normal circumstances, were they? Since the diary didn't relate to the Maria Rutter murder, it would be of very little interest to the man who had taught her almost all she knew about detection – and now seemed to have forgotten most of those rules himself.

So what should she do? She would drive out on to the moors, she decided, park in a wild, elemental spot, and study the dark secrets of Pamela's diary in seclusion.

She was on the point of turning the key in the ignition when she noticed the curtain twitch in the flat below Pamela's. A nosy neighbour! Every investigating officer's dream. Paniatowski got out of her car, and marched up to the downstairs' neighbour's front door.

The woman who answered her knock was in her mid-sixties. She was wearing a padded housecoat and huge, fluffy slippers. Her hair was set in a tight, blue-rinsed perm, and the edges of her mouth were turned down in a permanently dissatisfied expression.

'Are you the police?' she asked.

'Not all of it,' Paniatowski replied, with a smile. 'There are a couple of fellers who help me out now and again.'

The woman did not return the smile. 'I don't like people using the term "fellers",' she said. 'You should have called them "gentlemen". That's the proper thing to say. Do you have a warrant card?'

Paniatowski produced it. 'Could you tell me your name, please?' she asked, as she held it out.

'I'm Mrs Walton,' the woman said. She examined the warrant card carefully, but did not look impressed.

'Is something wrong?' Paniatowski asked.

'A sergeant!' Mrs Walters said disdainfully. 'I would have thought they'd have sent a much more senior officer to talk to me.'

'I'm just here to do the preliminary work. My boss'll be along later,' Paniatowski lied.

'You should not refer to him as your "boss",' Mrs Walters rebuked her. 'That's common. The correct term is "superior".'

'My *superior* will be round later,' Paniatowski said. 'In the meantime, I was wondering if you could spare me a few minutes of your valuable time.'

Mrs Walters hovered between the desire to give the impression of having a full social calendar and the urge to have someone to talk to. The latter won. 'If you would like to accompany me into my withdrawing room, I believe I can accommodate you,' she said.

The front parlour was as close to looking like a room from the pages of *Country Life* as could be managed on a limited budget and in a limited space. The sofa was large, and far too bucolic for a ground-floor flat in a declining neighbourhood. The hunting prints on the wall would have looked more at home in a pub lounge. Paniatowski searched in vain for a mounted stag's head on the wall, and – since Mrs Walters would not have appreciated it if she'd suddenly burst out laughing – was quite relieved that she didn't find one.

Mrs Walters gestured her to a seat. 'No doubt you are wondering why I choose to live here,' she said.

'No, I—' Paniatowski began.

But it was only the sound of her *own* voice that Mrs Walters was interested in hearing.

'I did have a little place in the country,' she said. 'Nothing too grand, you understand, though the neighbours were kind enough to say that it was charming. But, alas, things have gone completely downhill since the war. The government seems determined to make the better class of person pay through the nose, in order that the dregs of society can live in luxury, and I was forced to abandon my lovely home and move here.'

'It must have been a bit of a trial for you,' Paniatowski said, with mock sympathy.

'It was a *great* trial,' Mrs Walters corrected her. 'But I make the best of it, as I was brought up to do. I keep myself to myself, and avoid the riff-raff who live around me as much as possible.'

'Would you describe Pamela Rainsford as one of the riff-raff?' Paniatowski asked.

'I would use quite another word for her,' Mrs Walters said severely. 'One that I would never even dream of voicing out loud.'

'Could you give me a little clue as to what that word might be?' Paniatowski wondered.

'I met the late Mr Walters at church,' the other woman said. 'For the first six months of our acquaintanceship, we were never alone. And when we did finally decide to walk out together, Mr Walters – always a gentleman – came to our house to ask my father's permission first.'

'That wouldn't have worked in this case. Pamela Rainsford didn't live with her family,' Paniatowski pointed out.

'I used to know any number of young men who went out to work in the colonies,' Mrs Walters said. 'They told me that even when they were in the depths of the jungle, with no one but a servant to attend on them, they would still dress formally for dinner.'

'What's your point, exactly?'

'That there is never any excuse for letting your standards slip, whatever circumstances you find yourself in. Not that I suppose Miss Rainsford had any standards in the first place. When I lived in the country, I saw bitches on heat show more restraint.'

'She had a lot of boyfriends, did she?' Paniatowski asked.

'A positive stream of them. They were always calling for her. Not that they went to her front door to call, of course. That would have been a far too gentlemanly thing to do. No, they sat in their cars on the street and hooted their horns – not caring who they disturbed.'

'Did she ever take them upstairs?' Paniatowski wondered.

'She most certainly did not take them upstairs! Even she was not quite as shameless as that!'

Or to put it another way, she much preferred to lose all restraint in places where there was a risk of getting caught, Paniatowski thought.

'Could you tell me anything about her last boyfriend?' she asked aloud. 'The one she was seeing just before she died?'

A look of grave distaste came to Mrs Walters face. 'It wasn't a man at all,' she said. 'It was a woman!'

Who's to say the killer was a man? Woodend had asked. Why couldn't it have been a woman?

'Could you describe this woman to me?' Paniatowski asked.

'No, I could not. She stayed in the car, just as all the men had. Made Miss Rainsford come to her. No respect! Not that I necessarily believe the baggage from upstairs *deserved* any respect.'

'You knew she was a woman,' Paniatowski prodded, 'so you must have seen something of her.'

'I may have caught just a quick glimpse of her,' Mrs Walters reluctantly agreed.

'So what did you see?'

'She had long blonde hair. No natural blonde, of course. That would have been too much to expect.'

'Then what colour was it, exactly?'

'It was what I believe is called "platinum" blonde – like those cheap American film actresses used to have.'

'There's just one thing about what you've said that I don't quite understand,' Paniatowski confessed.

'And what might that be?'

'From the way that you talk you seem to assume she was Pamela's *girlfriend*.'

'And that's a polite way of putting it,' Mrs Walters said.

'But why couldn't she just have been Pamela's girl *friend*?'

'Girl *friends* don't kiss,' Mrs Walters said.

'Actually, they do,' Paniatowski said.

'Not in the way that they did,' Mrs Walters insisted. 'It wasn't just a peck on the cheek with them. They went at it hammer and tongues. It seemed to last forever. I was so disgusted I can hardly bear to look.'

Twenty-Two

Woodend was just draining his first pint when the phone rang behind the bar of the Drum and Monkey. It could have been absolutely anyone, calling about absolutely anything, but his instincts told him it was for him, and by the time Jack the landlord glanced across the counter to see if he was at his usual table, he'd already got out of his seat.

'Woodend!' he said, into the phone.

'Go to Melton's Garage,' a vaguely familiar voice on the other end of the line said.

'Now why should I want to do that?' Woodend wondered.

'Ask them about the spot of trouble they've been having with their new Cortina GTs.'

'Who is this?' Woodend demanded.

'Say you want to look at the service records for any recent work they've done.'

'An' what good will that do me?'

'If you're even half as good as they say you are, you should be able to work that out for yourself, sir.'

Sir? Woodend repeated in his mind. *Sir?*

'Who are you?' he asked. 'Are you a bobby?'

But the line had already gone dead.

Melton's Garage was located just off the Whitebridge bypass. It was very much one of the 'new' businesses – a combination of car salesroom and workshop – which had sprung up in the previous ten years, as motor cars had made the transition from luxury to necessity. A large sign on the forecourt proudly proclaimed that it was an *official* Ford dealer.

When Woodend arrived, the salesroom had closed for the day and the workshop was very definitely shuttered, but there was still a light burning in the office. When he knocked on the office door, a voice from the other side of the door called out, 'Bugger off! We're closed.'

Woodend turned the handle. The door was not locked. He pushed it open and entered the office.

The man seated at the desk was in his late forties. He was wearing a loud check suit, and had a thin moustache of the kind that spivs sported at the end of the War.

He glared at the new arrival. 'What's your problem?' he demanded. 'Are you deaf – or just thick?'

'I rather like to flatter myself that I'm neither,' Woodend said, producing his warrant card.

The man examined the card carefully. 'Oh, I say, a chief inspector!' he said, his voice losing some of his irritation. 'We are honoured!'

'Would you mind tellin' me who I'm talkin' to?' Woodend asked.

'I wouldn't mind at all. I'm Paul Melton, of Melton's Motors, provider of quality, reliable vehicles to the cream of Whitebridge society. Or to put it another way, if the buggers who come in here can just about scrape together the deposit, I'll sell them the motor.'

Woodend grinned. 'You don't seem to be exactly encouraging new customers.'

'I've no need to. To tell you the truth, I've got more work than I can handle. There's a waiting list for the new Cortina GT, and some of the impatient sods on it are ringing me up every single bloody day, demanding to know if their wheels are here yet.'

'Good car, is it?' Woodend asked.

'Good car? It's a bloody great car!' Melton said enthusiastically.

'That's funny,' Woodend said.

'What is?'

'Well, somebody I've just been talkin' to led me to believe you've had to do a lot of remedial work on these new models recently.'

'Oh, that!' Melton said dismissively.

'That,' Woodend agreed.

'I wouldn't call it "a lot" of work. The new model had a bit of teething trouble, that's all.'

'What kind of teething trouble?'

'A slight technical hitch in the gubbins.'

Woodend grinned again. 'Well, that's certainly made it clear enough,' he said.

'Look, there's no point in askin' me about technical matters,' Melton said. 'I drive the cars and I sell the cars, but I leave my grease monkeys to work out what's going on under the bonnet. Anyway, as I said, it turned out there *was* this itsy-bitsy problem.'

'They were worried the wheels might fall off or somethin'?' Woodend suggested.

Melton looked horrified. 'Nothing like that!' he protested. 'Nothing to do with safety at all. There was just a slight adjustment which needed to be made in order to ensure driver convenience. A piffling little job, really. Didn't take my lads more than a couple of hours to put it right on each vehicle, and when the customers drove them away again, they were as pleased as punch.'

'Was Bob Rutter one of those customers?'

Melton pursed his brow. 'Rutter?' he repeated. 'Rutter? That name sounds familiar. Wait a minute! Are we talking about *Inspector* Rutter? The man who was arrested for murdering his wife?'

'We're talking about the Inspector Rutter who's helping the police with their *inquiries* into the murder of his wife.'

Melton grinned. 'Oh I get it,' he said, winking. 'Official terminology. We use a lot of that in the motor trade. Helps to confuse the punters.'

'*Is* he one of those customers?' Woodend repeated.

'Yes, I think I do remember him now. Late twenties, early thirties? Dark hair? Snappy dresser?'

'That's him,' Woodend agreed.

'He didn't say he was a policeman – well, you don't do you, it makes people feel uncomfortable – so I didn't connect him to the feller who'd topped his wife.' Melton paused, then grinned again. 'Sorry, I didn't connect him with the feller who's *helping the police with their inquiries.*'

'Was his car in for one of these revisions of yours?'

'Definitely. Unless my memory fails me, he'd only had the vehicle for a matter of days.' Melton swivelled on his chair, opened a drawer in the filing cabinet, and extracted a file. 'That's it. Said he couldn't be without a car, because he needed it for work, so out of the goodness of my heart I lent him one of my old bangers while his was being fixed.'

'When exactly was this?'

'Day before yesterday. Brought his Cortina in first thing in the morning, picked it up the same evening.'

'*What time?*' Woodend demanded.

Melton consulted the file again. 'Signed for it at half eight.'

Woodend glanced at his watch. 'It's just after half eight now, and you're closed,' he said.

'True,' Melton agreed. 'But I was around then like I'm around now – we work hard in the motor trade – and I didn't see any harm in letting him have his vehicle back.'

'And you're *sure* about the time?'

157

'Absolutely. I left straight after that, and was in the Roebuck, ordering my gin-fizz, by a quarter to nine. Besides, look at the record. It's all down here in black and white.'

So Bob was picking up his car just ten minutes before the explosion at his house, Woodend thought. Which meant that there was no way that the car Bascombe had seen parked just up the road from his house could have been Bob's.

No way at all!

Bob Rutter had often wondered how habitual criminals could almost seem to *welcome* a fresh term of imprisonment, but his own incarceration had given him a small insight into their minds.

It was the routine they liked, he decided – the fact that they knew when they would eat and when they would be allowed to exercise, what privileges they would be granted automatically over time and which they would have to do something extra to earn. Prison, he now saw, took away the need to make decisions for themselves, and for those of them who found life outside difficult to handle – and sometimes even incomprehensible – such order must come as something of a relief.

Even the amount of light they were granted was both regular and dependable. At that moment, the overhead lamp was providing him with sufficient illumination to write by. But that wouldn't continue for long. Soon, at the preordained time, it would be dimmed. Not extinguished, just dimmed. There would be enough light for him to find his way from his bed to the toilet – and enough light left for anyone looking in the through the spy-hole to see him doing it – but not so much that sleep would be impossible.

So if he were going to finish his letter – the letter they would find later, when it was all over – then he had better do it while the bright light lasted.

He looked down at what he had written so far. The letter was addressed to Charlie Woodend. It started with an apology for the inconvenience he was causing, and went on the thank Woodend for all the help and encouragement he had given over the years.

'We were a good team,' he wrote, then instantly crossed it out.

It didn't *matter* that they'd been a good team, he told himself. It didn't matter that they'd shared jokes, and drinks, and problems. What had happened to Maria was now the only important milestone in his life, and everything which had gone before it was as nothing.

Besides, none of that was the main point of the letter – none of that had anything to do with leaving his affairs in order.

He didn't have much of an estate to pass on to his daughter, he wrote – a house with twenty-three years of mortgage payments still outstanding, a new car which it would probably be easy enough to sell, a few savings in the bank – but he would like Woodend to be the trustee of what little there was until the child was old enough to handle it herself.

He wondered if he should close by proclaiming his innocence, as the half-literate previous occupant of the cell had done on the wall.

But there wouldn't be much point in that, would there? Because Woodend either already believed that, or he didn't – and mere words would not sway him one way or the other.

He thought of writing a letter to his daughter – but what would he say?

I didn't kill your mother!

By the time she was old enough to read the letter herself, her mother would be someone else entirely – someone she hadn't even met yet. If she knew about her natural mother – the beautiful Spanish woman who had struggled and strained to give birth to her – it would only be because she had been told about her by someone else. And as for her natural father – the man accused of taking her mother's life – it would be better if she never learned of him *at all*.

The light over his head dimmed right on schedule, and he heard the sound of footsteps in the corridor outside.

Constable Fletcher – *Fatty* Fletcher, as he was known to everyone at the station – making his rounds. If he followed his regular routine that night, he would walk to the end of the corridor, then turn around and walk back, stopping to check each spy-hole on the way.

Rutter climbed into his bed and pulled the sheet and blanket over him. He shut his eyes and remained perfectly still when he heard the shutter on the spy-hole being slid open. Once the shutter had slid closed again, he counted slowly up to twenty. Finally, sure it was now safe to do so, he threw off his bedding and swung his legs on to the floor.

Fletcher would have reached his office by now, he calculated. The next step would be to brew himself a cup of tea, and once he firmly ensconced his fat arse on his padded chair, he would be very reluctant to get off it again for at least a couple of hours.

But what if a new prisoner was admitted to the holding cells? Rutter thought with a sudden wave of panic. Wouldn't Fatty Fletcher, once he had locked the man safely way, decide that – since he was on his feet – he might as well check the other cells again?

Rutter trembled at the thought of being discovered – hanging, but not yet dead. Of all the humiliations he might expect to suffer, that would be the worst.

He forced himself to calm down – to consider the matter rationally. Prisoners weren't brought in and then locked up straight away, he reminded himself. There was a whole admissions procedure to be gone through. They had to be photographed. They had to be fingerprinted. Forms had to be filled in. Even in the hands of the speediest officer – and Fletcher was far from that – it would be half an hour before the prisoner could be locked up. And half an hour was more than enough time for a man to take his own life.

Rutter separated his sheet from his blanket, and then began to twist the sheet into something resembling a rope. It was a rough sheet, he thought as he worked, but it was strong enough. It would certainly hold *his* weight.

Twenty-Three

It had been a mistake to drive out on to the moors, Paniatowski told herself.

She'd thought, when she'd made the decision, that the isolation would provide the right atmosphere in which to study Pamela Rainsford's diary. But it hadn't worked out like that. Not at all. The sight of the stark, savagely beautiful, landscape had not cleared her head – it had filled it with memories of Bob Rutter.

They had walked there – she and Bob – hand in hand. And as they walked they had both tried to forget that in little more than an hour – or two at the very most – they would have to part again, she to drive back to her lonely flat, he to return to his wife and child.

They had made love in isolated spots, not – as Pamela Rainsford had – because they were thrilled by the prospect of discovery, but because they had nowhere else to go.

It had been a desperate affair from the start. They had both known that. Had known, too, that it would have to end eventually.

Yet they had never imagined it would end in the way that it had – would never have dreamed that their passionate couplings would lead to the death of Bob's wife and the destruction of his own life.

And my life too! Paniatowski thought. Mine is destroyed because I'll carry with me to the grave the knowledge that if I'd left Bob alone, Maria would still be here.

She sat in the driving seat of the MGA, wracked by her sobs, hugging herself tightly. The watery autumn sun made its descent over the horizon, and darkness began to fall. She did not notice it. Wrapped up as she was in her misery, she did not even register how cold it was getting. Why should she register it, when her whole world was cold – and would remain cold for now and evermore?

Finally, at around eight o'clock, she saw a solution to her problems. There was a piece of rubber tubing in the boot of her car, she remembered. She had used it once or twice to siphon petrol. Now she would put it to quite some other use.

She ran through the steps in her mind. Switch on the engine. Take the rubber tubing from the boot. Place one end of the tubing over the exhaust, and feed the other end through the window. Close all the windows, then sit back and relax.

She switched on the engine. The air which blew though the heater was cold at first, but as the engine warmed up, so did the car, and she felt some life begin to return to her numb arms and legs.

She lit a cigarette. The thought came to her mind that it would be foolish to kill herself quickly, when she could do it more pleasurably – though infinitely more expensively – through excessive drinking and smoking.

She laughed. She had not intended to, but she took it as a good sign. It appeared that, contrary to all the evidence, there was still some fight – some spirit – left in her.

She reached for the torch she kept in the glove compartment, switched it on, and picked up Pamela Rainsford's diary.

It was not so much a diary as a thick, leather-bound notebook which Pamela had *used* as a diary. Nor was there an entry every day. Sometimes a fortnight would pass without her feeling the need to put pen to paper, then there would be a number of passages on consecutive days.

It soon became clear that Pamela had never felt any desire to comment on the weather, where she had been or what she bought. The book served simply as a record of her sexual exploits. No more and no less.

Paniatowski resisted the urge to start reading from the end of the journal, and began with one of the earlier entries. Pamela had written in her small, tight handwriting:

7th June, 1961. First time with PT. Did it on the back seat of his Morris. He was terrified someone would see us. That only made it better for me! The more frightened he grew, the more excited I was. We only just finished before the breakdown truck arrived. The AA mechanic was big and rough. I could see his muscles bulging under his shirt. Did he know what we'd been doing before he arrived? I think so. I could see it in his eyes. And he wished it had been him instead of PT!

And so did you, Pamela, Monika thought. I've met Peter Tewson, with his concerns about his modest career and his honeymoon in Bournemouth already booked. He didn't seem to me to be the kind of man who could keep a woman like you happy for long!

13th August, 1961. We did it in the woods. This time we were both naked. I insisted on that. And some lads saw us! I don't know how long they were watching, but I think they must have seen the whole thing. We ran away – because that's what PT wanted to do! When we'd got our breath back I was still so excited that I wanted to do it again. But he wouldn't. To be honest, I don't think he could have, even if he'd wanted to. I'm getting rather bored with him.

Other entries followed. More men, more love-making in places where the lovers were likely to be discovered.

Some readers of the diary might have found it stimulating, Paniatowski thought, but to her it seemed both dreary and really rather sad. It was only when she got to a series of entries which began a year earlier that she started to feel a real prick of interest.

Went out with Lulu tonight. God, what a bitch! And God, how right we are for each other! And all the time we've been together at New Horizons, I never suspected! Never even imagined! I thought I was daring, but I'm nothing compared to her. She runs risks I'd never have thought of taking. And I love it!

Paniatowski flicked through to the end of the journal – to the last few entries Pamela made before she died.

7th October, 1964. Lulu's the one! I'm sure of it. I want her with me always. I'll never grow tired of her.
9th October, 1964. I told Lulu how I felt. I expected her to be deliriously happy, but she wasn't. When I talked about the two of us going away together, a blank look came into her eyes. She said there were other people involved, not just us and we had to think about them. I told her she'd better *think about them. She asked me what I meant by that, and I said that I wondered how these* other people *would feel if they found out what she was really like. That set her thinking!*
19th October, 1964. Lulu's given in! She says she'll do whatever I want! She's asked me to meet her by the canal, after work, tomorrow. I said, 'Why the canal?' and she said she had something special planned. I can hardly wait.

Paniatowski closed the journal.

You went too far in the end, Pamela Rainsford, she thought. You should never have tried to blackmail Lulu in the way that you did, because that's what cost you your life.

Constable Fletcher was sitting in his chair, pleasantly dozing, when he felt the finger prodding into his arm. At first he tried to ignore it, but when it persisted he opened his eyes and saw the big man in the hairy tweed sports coat standing over him.

'Oh, hello there, Mr Woodend, sir,' he said. 'Is there somethin' I can do for you?'

'Yes, there is, Fletch,' Woodend told him. 'I need to have a talk with Bob Rutter.'

'At this time of night?'

'We can't all sleep on the job, you know,' Woodend said. 'Some of us have *real* work to do.'

'Are you sayin' I was asleep, sir?'

'Weren't you?'

'No, I most certainly was not,' Fletcher said, looking as dignified as his podgy frame allowed. 'I was just thinkin'. An' I find I always think better when I've got my eyes closed.'

'Then no doubt it wasn't really snorin' that I heard comin' from that mouth of yours,' Woodend said. 'Can I see Mr Rutter now?'

'Inspector Rutter's Mr Evans's prisoner,' Fletcher said. 'Have you got his authorization to make the visit?'

'Do I need it?'

'I'm not sure.'

'Then let's assume that I don't.'

'Strictly speakin' I'm not certain I can do that, sir.'

'An' strictly speakin', I suppose I should report you for *thinkin'* on the job,' Woodend countered.

Fletcher winced. 'Old hands like us don't always stick to the book, do we?' he asked, struggling to his feet and reaching for his keys. 'You won't want long with Mr Rutter, will you?'

No, Woodend thought. Just long enough to have Bob confirm that he didn't pick up his new car until eight thirty, thus making it impossible for it to be the *same* car that Bascombe had seen. And once that had been established – once he was *really* sure of his ground – he would go after that bastard Evans.

'I'll only need about five minutes,' he told Constable Fletcher. 'Will that be all right?'

'Five minutes isn't long,' the fat constable agreed. 'It's hardly worth botherin' notin' *five minutes* down in the record book.'

'No, it isn't, is it?' Woodend agreed.

Constable Fletcher headed for the holding cells, with Woodend close on his heel.

The fact that Bob's car hadn't been the one on Bascombe's street did not prove that Rutter couldn't have killed his wife, Woodend cautioned himself. But it did raise serious questions about the way DCI Evans had been conducting his case. And it was certainly enough of a mistake on Evans's part to give him grounds for demanding that all the other evidence the chief inspector from Preston had collected should be gone over again with a fine-toothed comb.

'Here we are, sir,' Fletcher said, stopping in front of one the metal doors. 'Holdin' Cell Number Three. The best room in the house.'

'Do you think it's funny that one of your colleagues may be facin' a murder charge?' Woodend growled.

'Well, no, not exactly,' Fletcher said, surprised by Woodend's change of mood. 'But you can't always treat life as if it was deadly serious, can you?' he asked hopefully.

'Probably not,' Woodend agreed. 'And I hope you won't mind if *I* don't treat it seriously the next time *you're* up shit creek.'

'There's no need for you to take offence, sir,' Fletcher said huffily, as he slid back the eye hole. 'I was only tryin' to . . . Oh, my God!'

Woodend pushed the fat constable roughly to one side, and peered through the spy-hole himself. What he should have seen was a bed and a small table. But he didn't. He couldn't – because his view was blocked by a pair of hanging legs.

Twenty-Four

From his vantage point inside the Chief Constable's office, Woodend had a perfect view of the early morning sky. He watched as the heavy grey clouds massed as a prelude to launching their first angry attack of the day on the ground below. It was going to be one hell of a storm when it got started.

A single drop of rain – an advance guard – hit the Chief Constable's window with all the force and determination it could muster, but to no avail. The glass remained totally unmoved by the encounter. The raindrop itself spattered on impact, then slowly and brokenly trickled downwards.

It never had a chance, Woodend thought, watching its progress with morbid fascination. *It never had a bloody chance.*

The Chief Constable – who had spent the previous five minutes on the phone, firming up the arrangements to meet a friend of his at some conference or other – finally said goodbye and placed the receiver back on its rest.

'Well, you were the one who requested this meeting, Mr Woodend,' he said. 'And as I'm only here to adjudicate, I suppose that you're the one should get us started.'

Only there to adjudicate! Woodend thought with disgust. The Chief Constable was only there to *adjudicate* – only to see that there was fair play between him and DCI Evans. So why were Marlowe and Evans both sitting on the same side of the Chief Constable's bloody desk?

Woodend cleared his throat. 'I'm unhappy with the way that DCI Evans is conductin' the Maria Rutter murder investigation,' he said.

167

'From what I can recall of your previous escapades, the only officer who you're *ever* happy to see conducting a case is *yourself*,' Marlowe said, showing right from the start just how even-handed he actually intended to be. 'But we'll leave that aside for the moment. What, specifically, is the nature of your complaint against Mr Evans?'

'He's not gone into the investigation with an open mind. He's lettin' his pre-existin' prejudices determine the way the case develops.'

'Interesting,' Marlowe said. 'And I trust you have some examples to back this up.'

'Yes, I do. He set his forensic team to work on Bob Rutter's Cortina GT without even botherin' to establish whether or not it was that car which was seen on Ash Croft on the night of the murder. He probably *still* doesn't know whether they were examinin' the right car or not, do you, Evans?'

'As a matter of fact, I do know,' DCI Evans said. 'The Cortina on Ash Croft couldn't have been Rutter's, because Rutter's car was at Melton's Garage at the time, undergoing some minor adjustments.'

'An' how long have you known that?' Woodend asked, feeling as if the ground he'd been so sure of was slipping away beneath him.

'I've known since yesterday afternoon.'

'I don't believe you.'

'You may believe – or disbelieve – whatever you choose, Mr Woodend,' Evans said calmly.

'If he – or any of his team – had actually been to Melton's Garage, Paul Melton would have mentioned it to me when I was there myself,' Woodend told Marlowe.

'Well, Mr Evans?' Marlowe asked.

'We didn't need to waste valuable police time going to the garage,' Evans said. 'We found the documentation for the adjustment work in the glove compartment of the Cortina.'

Overhead, there was a crash of thunder, followed rapidly

by a searing bolt of lightning. And then it began to rain in earnest.

'Any comment you'd care to make at this juncture, Mr Woodend?' the Chief Constable asked.

'It's sloppy police work,' Woodend said.

'What is?'

'If Bob Rutter had put the documentation anywhere other than in the car, DCI Evans's team wouldn't have found it.'

'Yes, I should have thought that was obvious.'

'An' they'd have gone on treatin' Rutter's car as if it was the one which was spotted on Ash Croft. Which would have meant they wouldn't be lookin' for the Cortina that really *was* there.'

'Nobody can actually say that this other Cortina *did* have anything to do with the murder,' the Chief Constable pointed out.

'An' nobody can say for certain that it *didn't*,' Woodend countered. 'Nor *will* they be able to, until they've conducted the kind of investigation which should have been conducted in the first bloody place.'

'Mr Woodend does have a point, you know,' Marlowe said to Evans. 'It could be claimed, if one were feeling uncharitable, that you had in fact made a mistake there.'

'Yes, sir,' Evans agreed. 'It's noted, and I'll see it doesn't happen again. And I've already sent a man up to the garage to get a list of all the other Cortina GTs which were *not* there are the time.'

'Good. Well, that seems to settle the matter, then.'

'Is that it?' Woodend demanded incredulously. 'Is that all you're goin' to say to him? "*Good. Well, that seems to settle the matter, then*"?'

'It's all I'm going to say to *Mr Evans*, certainly,' Marlowe told him. 'But I still have a few words I'd like to direct at you.'

'You've got *what*?' Woodend asked.

'It is no doubt useful to DCI Evans's investigation that you've raised the question of the car on Ash Croft,' the Chief

Constable said. 'But the fact of the matter is, you should never have put yourself in a position to ask the question in the first place.'

'I don't believe this!' Woodend said.

'You're supposed to be investigating the Pamela Rainsford murder, not the Maria Rutter murder,' the Chief Constable reminded him. 'And then there's the question of what happened last night.'

'Last night!'

'You had no business to be visiting DCI Evans's suspect without clear permission from DCI Evans himself.'

'You do realize that if I *hadn't* gone – or even if I'd gone and arrived a couple of minutes later – Bob Rutter would be dead now?' Woodend exploded. 'You do *understand* that, don't you?'

'It was certainly very fortunate that you arrived at Rutter's cell when you did,' Marlowe said. 'I'm delighted that you were able to save his life.'

'Delighted!' Woodend said, disgustedly.

'Nevertheless, that is an entirely separate issue from the one we're discussing. You had no business being there, and I am contemplating beginning a disciplinary procedure.'

'Would you like my bloody resignation?' Woodend shouted.

'Are you *offering* it?' Marlowe asked.

Was he? Woodend wondered. No, he bloody wasn't! How could he, at this crucial stage of the game?

'No, I'm not offerin' to resign,' Woodend said. 'I'll take my chances with the discipline board – *if* an' *when* you convene it.'

'Oh, it will be convened. You can be assured of that,' Marlowe said.

'So what happens now?' Woodend asked.

'What I'm tempted to do is suspend you,' the Chief Constable admitted. 'Unfortunately, I happen to have two murders on my hands at the same time as I'm battling against serious staff shortages. So what I'd like you to do, Mr Woodend

– what I'm forced to *allow* you to do – is to continue with the Pamela Rainsford investigation. But if you go beyond your remit again, I *will* suspend you, even if it means taking over the investigation myself.'

'Now that I *would* like to see,' Woodend said.

Marlowe scowled. 'You're being insolent, Chief Inspector,' he said.

'I'm not followin' you, sir,' Woodend said innocently. 'How can it be insolence to say I'd like to sit back myself an' watch a real professional tacklin' the job?'

'Get out!' Marlowe said.

'On my way, sir,' Woodend replied.

I shouldn't have done that, he told himself as he was reaching for the door handle. I shouldn't have done it – but, by God, it felt good.

The Duty Sergeant told Woodend that Constable Beresford was on his tea break and would very likely be in the canteen. And so he proved to be, playing cards with a couple of his mates.

Woodend slid into a free chair at their table. 'If you wouldn't mind, lads, I'd like a few words with Beresford in private,' he said.

The other constables looked at each other, then at Beresford, then stood up and left.

Woodend waited until they were well clear of the table before he said, 'I've just been to see the Chief Constable about the Cortina.'

Most constables would have directed their gaze at the table, but Beresford looked him straight in the eyes.

'I told you I'd have to report our conversation, and that's just what I did, sir,' he said. 'I wasn't doin' anything behind your back.'

'Not behind *my* back, no,' Woodend agreed.

'I beg your pardon, sir.'

'You don't trust DCI Evans, do you?'

Now Beresford did turn away. 'Mr Evans is my superior,

sir,' he said. 'We are told to trust our superiors. We're told that if we don't, the whole system will collapse.'

'Is that a "no" or a "yes"?' Woodend wondered.

'I suppose you'll take it to mean whatever you want it to mean,' Beresford said.

'Aye, I probably will,' Woodend said. 'So you didn't trust DCI Evans. An' that's why findin' the service sheet in Mr Rutter's car presented you with a problem. You see, bein' the smart lad that you are, you'd already worked out that it would be helpful to DCI Evans's case if the Cortina on Ash Croft turned out to be Mr Rutter's. An' you were worried that he might accidentally-on-purpose lose any evidence which proved that it wasn't. Now I happen to think you were worryin' unnecessarily – Evans may not be your kind of bobby, an' he's *certainly* not mine, but I don't think he's bent. Still, your concern does you credit.'

'No comment,' Beresford said.

'I'm not surprised,' Woodend told him. 'So where were you to go from there? Well, you decided that the best way to make sure the evidence didn't go missin' was to make another senior officer aware of its existence. That's why you rang me at the Drum, an' told me about Melton's Garage. I couldn't quite pin the voice down at first, but now I'm sure it was you.'

'But I dis—' Beresford began.

'You did *what*?'

'Nothin', sir.'

'You disguised your voice. But you didn't disguise it very well. An' you called me "sir", which was a mistake.'

'We all make mistakes,' Beresford said.

'Aye, we do,' Woodend agreed. 'But you shouldn't suffer too badly from this one, young Beresford, because if you ever need a friend in the Central Lancs Police, you've only to whistle an' I'll come runnin'.'

Provided, of course, I'm still *in* the Central Lancs Police when this case is over, he thought, as he made his way to the door.

Twenty-Five

The storm which had broken when he'd been in the Chief Constable's office was continuing to vent its spleen on the inhabitants of Whitebridge more than an hour later. Rivers of angry water rushed headlong through the gutters, cascades of it gurgled furiously down the drains. Woodend, his collar turned up ineffectively against the deluge, strode rapidly towards the Yew Tree Café.

He would have preferred a different venue for what would probably turn out to be a difficult meeting with Monika Paniatowski, he thought as he hurried along. The Drum and Monkey came immediately to mind, but since that blessed haven wouldn't be opening its doors for another hour, the café would just have to do.

Monika was already there when he arrived, sitting at a table by the window and gazing out at the storm without really seeing it. He would have said she looked rough, but that would have been rather like saying that Derek Higson's Rolls-Royce was a moderately expensive car.

He sat down opposite her.

'Have you seen him?' she asked without preamble.

There was no need to ask who 'he' was, so Woodend merely nodded and then said, 'Yes, I have.'

'And how is he?'

'Considerin' he was probably no more than a minute or two from death when I found him, he's not in bad shape.'

'Have there been any . . . any . . .'

'Permanent effects? They don't think so. He'll be speakin' with a bit of a croaky voice for a while, but as far as they can tell at the hospital, there's been no brain damage.'

'He didn't do it!' Paniatowski said, letting the words gush from her mouth as if they'd been bursting to break free for quite some time.

'Didn't do what? Didn't try to kill himself? Well, there was nobody else in the cell when I got there, an' as much as I feel nothin' but contempt for bobbies like Fatty Fletcher, I can't actually see him just sittin' back while somebody tried to commit murder on his watch.'

'That's not what I meant.'

'Then what *did* you mean?'

'Bob didn't kill Maria!'

It was the last thing that Woodend had been expecting his sergeant to say to him.

'What's brought you round to this sudden change of mind?' he asked, amazed.

'The fact that he tried to hang himself last night,' Paniatowski said, as if that explained everything.

'There are those who'd say that was a confession of guilt, rather than a protestation of innocence,' Woodend pointed out.

'But I'm not one of them,' Paniatowski countered. 'Look, sir, you don't know Bob like I do. I'm sorry, you may not like to hear that, being as close to him as your are, but it's true.'

'I'm not arguin',' Woodend said. 'Let's hear the rest of what's on your mind.'

'If Bob had killed Maria, he'd have taken his punishment like a man,' Paniatowski said fiercely. 'But he never *would have* killed Maria – I see that now I've started looking at the case through the eyes of a woman who loves him, rather than the eyes of a policewoman.'

'If it wasn't guilt that made him try to top himself, then what was it?' Woodend asked.

'Despair!'

'Because he couldn't face the thought of all them years in gaol for a crime he didn't commit?'

'Maybe.'

'Have you got another theory?'

'It might just have been that he couldn't bear the thought of everybody looking at him and *thinking* he was guilty.'

It didn't ring true, Woodend thought. It just didn't ring true.

'Now tell me what it is that's really eatin' away at you, Monika,' he said gently.

'Perhaps he tried to kill himself because he simply didn't want to go on living now that Maria's dead,' Paniatowski said bitterly. 'And what lesson can you draw from that, sir?'

'I'm not sure that I can draw any—'

'Then I'll spell it out for you! He could tolerate life without me, but not life without her. He said he loved me, and perhaps he meant it. But she was the one who had his heart. She was the one who had his soul.'

Monika was on the verge of tears.

'Listen, lass—' Woodend began.

'I don't want your sympathy!' she said, a burst of anger driving away the tears. 'You asked why I thought he tried to kill himself, and I've told you. That's the end of the matter. Can we now turn our minds to the problem of proving that he didn't kill his wife?'

'If you feel up to it.'

'Of course I feel up to it! We've got a job to do, so let's cut out all the emotional crap and get down to hard cases, shall we?'

'Whatever you say,' Woodend agreed. 'Let's talk about the Cortina GT, shall we? We know it wasn't Bob's, and it didn't belong to any of Bascombe's neighbours – so who *did* it belong to, and what the bloody hell was it doin' there?'

'The driver could have been a friend of one of Bascombe's neighbours, just paying a social call,' Paniatowski suggested.

'In that case, he'd have parked in front of the house he was visitin', instead of in front of one of the buildin' shells. Nobody would have walked further down that muddy lane than he had to. Besides, if it belonged to a visitor, Evans would have found out about it from one of his team.'

'How do you know he hasn't?'

'Because he assured Marlowe that he'd sent for the list of owners from Melton's Garage. An' he'd have no need to do that if he already knew whose car it was.'

'Even so, the Cortina could have been parked there for a completely innocent purpose,' Paniatowski said.

'Even so, it's the only bloody lead we've got!' Woodend reminded her.

Paniatowski nodded. 'You're right.'

'Since Paul Melton's garage is the only official Ford dealer in this area – and since there's a long waitin' list for the new GT – we have to assume that's where the car came from,' Woodend continued.

'So we need to know who he's sold them to, and which of the cars he's sold weren't in the garage, being checked over, at the time of Maria's murder.'

'Exactly.'

'And the only person we can get that information from is Paul Melton himself.'

'Yes.'

'But will he give it to us?'

'I don't see why he shouldn't.'

Paniatowski lit up a cigarette, and took a deep, thoughtful drag. 'But there's also no reason why he shouldn't tell DCI Evans that we've asked to see the list,' she said.

'True,' Woodend agreed.

'And Mr Marlowe's already warned us off sticking our noses into the investigation.'

'True again.'

'So if Melton does tell Evans, we're finished.'

'No, we're not,' Woodend corrected her. 'If he tells Evans, *I'm* finished – because I'll be the one who does the askin'.'

'You're taking a big risk,' Paniatowski cautioned.

'I'm takin' a bloody *huge* risk,' Woodend said.

'And it still might not lead anywhere, because the Cortina could be just a red herring.'

Woodend grinned weakly. 'Are you tryin' to talk me out of it, Monika?' he asked.

Paniatowski shook her head. 'No, I'm not. Getting our hands on that information may just give us a chance. It might be a bit like drawing the three-legged horse in a sweepstake, but when it's the only horse you've got, you just have to believe it will come through.'

Paul Melton was sitting behind his desk, munching his way through a plateful of thick-sliced toast, heavily ladled with strawberry jam.

'One of the perks of being the boss is that you indulge yourself whenever you feel like it,' he said with relish. 'Would you fancy a piece of toast yourself, Chief Inspector?'

'No thanks,' Woodend said. 'But there is something I would like.'

'The list of people who've bought the new Cortina GT?'

'That's right.'

Melton nodded, and crammed another piece of toast into his mouth. When he'd chewed it up enough to speak again, he said, 'The other bobby who was here told me you might come around and ask for it. He said that if you did, I wasn't to give it to you.'

'Did he, now?' Woodend asked neutrally.

'Which puts me in a sticky situation,' Melton continued. 'The thing is, I've always gone out of my way to avoid offending the police, but as matters stand, I can only avoid offending one bobby by offending another. So the question I have to ask myself is, which of the two bobbies is the more important? Would you like to help me out there?'

It would be pointless to lie, Woodend decided. 'The lad who came round to see you probably isn't as important as me, but he has the backin' of the Chief Constable, an' I don't,' he said.

'Well, there you are then,' Melton said, sucking some jam off his fingers. 'There's nothing I can do for you, is there?'

'The other night, somebody killed a defenceless blind woman in Elm Croft,' Woodend said. 'That same somebody robbed a little baby of her mother. The Chief Constable an'' his cronies think Bob Rutter did it, but those of us who know him well are sure that he didn't. Would you like to see the real killer brought to justice, Mr Melton?'

'Well, of course I would. Anybody would. But given the pressure that's been put on me, I don't see how I can help you.'

'Suppose this isn't a one-off,' Woodend said. 'Suppose the killer strikes again, an' it's a child he kills this time. Will you be able to sleep at night, knowin' you could have prevented it, but decided not to?'

'You play a dirty game,' Melton said.

'I'm in a dirty business,' Woodend told him.

Melton wiped his hand on a paper towel, then stood up and extracted a single sheet of paper from his filing cabinet. He read through it quickly, then laid it down on his desk.

'I'm going out on to the forecourt for a while,' he said. 'When I get back, I expect you and this piece of paper will be long gone.'

'Thank you,' Woodend said.

'I'm not sure I'm due much thanks,' Melton told him, 'because I need to cover my own back – and the best way to do that is to report to your boss that the list's gone missing and you're the only person who could have taken it.'

'When will you make this report?' Woodend asked.

Melton thought about it. 'I suppose I could leave it for twenty-four hours, at a push. Will that be long enough?'

Probably not, Woodend thought, but it was the best deal he was likely to get out of Melton.

'Twenty-four hours will be fine,' he said.

Melton looked out on to the forecourt. 'It's a nice car, that Wolseley of yours, but you'll need to trade it in eventually for something a bit more modern,' he said reflectively. 'And when you do, I hope you'll consider bringing your business to Melton's Motors.'

'I wouldn't think of takin' it anywhere else,' Woodend promised.

'Well, that just about wraps it up,' Paul Melton said, opening the door and stepping outside.

Woodend waited until Melton had closed the door again before picking up the list. There were a dozen names on it. He had not been expecting to recognize any of them, and when he *did* recognize one – when one stood out as if it were in lights – he felt as if he'd been smacked in the face with a shovel.

Back in the café, Woodend told Paniatowski about Paul Melton's list of Cortina GT owners, and Paniatowski told Woodend about Pamela Rainsford's diary. For perhaps half a minute, they fell into a profound silence, then Woodend said, 'Of course, it could all be a coincidence.'

'Yes, I suppose it could,' Paniatowski agreed.

'But I distrust coincidences at the best of times,' Woodend told her, 'an' this one really does stretch the bounds of credulity to breakin' point.'

'So if we accept that it *isn't* a coincidence, what conclusions do we have to draw?' Paniatowski asked.

'That we thought the two murders – Pamela's and Maria's – were unconnected, but they're not,' Woodend said heavily. 'That we thought there were two killers, but there's only one. An' how do we know this? Because the maskin' tape an' the implement which were used to kill Pamela almost definitely came from New Horizons, an' because the car which was parked on Ash Croft almost certainly belonged to Lucy Higson.'

'Lucy – Lulu – was Pamela Rainsford's lover,' Paniatowski said, spelling it out. 'They'd been seeing each other for about a year, and things were going fine. Then Pamela decided that she wanted Lucy all to herself.'

'But Lucy wasn't prepared to give up the luxurious life that she had as the wife of one of the richest men in Whitebridge.'

'And she was probably afraid that if she turned Pamela down, Pamela would tell Derek about their affair, and he would kick her out.'

179

'If he divorced her for adultery – especially adultery with another *woman* – Lucy would walk away from the marriage with nothing. So she decided to kill Pamela.'

'But why did Lucy mutilate Pamela in such a ghastly way?' Paniatowski asked.

Woodend shrugged. 'Maybe she thought that it would cloud the issue – that it would make us think that the murderer, instead of being her lover, was a ravin' nut-case. Or maybe she really *did* hate Pamela by that point, an' that hatred came though in the mutilation.'

'Then, one night later, she parks her new car – the Cortina GT – on Ash Croft, walks across the rough land, and murders Maria,' Paniatowski said. 'Why do you think she did that?'

'It had nothin' to do with Maria *as* Maria,' Woodend told her, 'but it had *everythin'* to do with Maria as the wife of one of the investigatin' officers. As I see it, Lucy calculated that if she presented us with a new murder – one we were more personally involved in – it would distract us from investigatin' Pamela's death. An' it worked, didn't it?'

'Why Maria?'

'Because she was the ideal candidate. Lucy could have chosen you, but she probably figured out that as a trained police officer, you might put up a good fight. She could have chosen my Joan, but that would have involved travellin' out to the sticks, where it's much more difficult to commit a murder without bein' noticed. Besides, she may have found out that Joan's away. So that left her with Maria, who lived on an anonymous estate, an' wouldn't even be able to see her killer comin'.'

'Lucy couldn't have known Bob would be arrested for the murder,' Paniatowski pointed out.

'She could have made a pretty good guess at it,' Woodend countered. 'When a woman's murdered in her own home – for no apparent reason – it's usually the husband who falls under suspicion, isn't it? An' you don't have to be a bobby to know that – all you have to do is read the papers!'

'The woman's a monster!' Paniatowski said.

'There's not much doubt about that,' Woodend agreed.

'But how do we prove it?'

Woodend sighed heavily. 'Buggered if I know,' he admitted. He paused for a moment. 'Maybe we should go back to basics. Where did Lucy live before she married Derek?'

Paniatowski flicked through her notebook. 'Pemberton,' she said.

'That's in enemy territory, isn't it?'

Paniatowski smiled at Woodend's instinctive reaction to the people of the neighbouring county. 'Yes, it *is* just inside Yorkshire,' she said.

'Well, at least it shouldn't be too long a drive.'

'You think we should go to Pemberton?'

'Yes.'

'Why?'

'Because maybe we can find out what it was that made Lucy the monster she is now. Maybe we'll find somethin' in her dark past that we can use to put leverage on her in the present.'

'Like what?'

'It could be anythin'. Possibly this isn't the first time she used violence on an unwanted lover. Possibly she's even *killed* before. We won't know until we get there an' start askin' questions.'

'It's a bit of a long-shot, isn't it, sir?' Monika Paniatowski asked sceptically.

'It's one *hell* of a long-shot,' Woodend agreed. 'But have you got a better idea?'

'No, I haven't.'

'That's what I thought,' Woodend said grimly.

Twenty-Six

Pemberton was one of those picture-postcard towns that Yorkshire had more than its fair share of. It owed its development to wool, rather than cotton, and whereas places just the other side of the county border had dark satanic mills as their legacy of the past, Pemberton was blessed with pretty stone cottages and all the animation which comes from being a small market town.

Woodend and Paniatowski arrived in the centre of Pemberton just before noon. It had been raining when they left Whitebridge, but Pemberton was basking in the kindly glow of an autumn sun, and the small corner of Woodend which was fervently Lancastrian took it as almost a personal insult.

'If the local bobbies find out we're operatin' on their patch without their explicit permission, there'll be hell to pay,' the Chief Inspector said as he manoeuvred the Wolseley into a parking place in the town centre. 'So we'll have to be sneaky, won't we? An' just how do you think we should go about that, Sergeant Paniatowski?'

'I've got a few ideas,' Monika replied. 'But when it comes to being sneaky you're a master, so what have you come up with?'

Woodend, fired by an optimism born from the belief that they were finally getting somewhere with the case, grinned.

'The best way to get people to talk to you is to pretend that you're a newspaper reporter,' he said. 'But that'll only work as long as you look enough like one to be able to carry it off. An' let's be honest, that's somethin' I'd never be able to do in a month of Sundays.'

'But I would?'

'I think so.'

Paniatowski, herself caught up in the new-found enthusiasm, sighed theatrically.

'You're right, of course,' she admitted. 'A pretty young thing like me could be anything she claimed to be, whereas nobody would ever take you for anything but an old-fashioned flat-foot.' She lit up a cigarette. 'So while I'm out playing news-hound, what will you be doing?'

'I'll be in there,' Woodend said, pointing to a large stone building with a sign on the side of it announcing it was the library. 'I'll be searchin' through the back copies of the local rag for any references to our Lucy.'

'It's a big job,' Paniatowski said doubtfully.

'A very big job,' Woodend agreed. 'I could use a whole team on it. But I haven't got one, have I? So I'm just goin' to have to skim-read – an' hope I get lucky!'

'And what, precisely, will you be searching for?' Paniatowski wondered.

'A good question.'

'And what's the answer?'

'I really have no bloody idea.'

Derek Higson looked across his desk at the bullet-headed man who was sitting opposite him and said, 'So how exactly can I help you, Chief Inspector?'

'It's actually your wife I came to see,' DCI Evans said.

'Unfortunately, she's not here at the moment. Might I ask what this is all about?'

'A car matching the description of your wife's was seen to be parked on Ash Croft the night Maria Rutter was murdered.'

'Yes?' Derek Higson asked quizzically, as if he didn't quite know where all this was going.

Evans cleared his throat. 'We'd like to establish for certain whether or not it *was* your wife's car, sir.'

'Are you seriously suggesting that Lucy could be involved in the murder in some way?' Higson asked, his voice showing just the beginnings of anger. 'Can you actually sit there and tell me that you suspect my wife of killing a woman she didn't even know?'

'Of course not,' Evans said. 'All we're seeking to do is to eliminate her from our inquiries.'

'Well, that should certainly be easy enough to do. It couldn't have been my wife's car on Ash Croft, because she was at home all night, and her car was parked in the garage.'

'How would you know that, sir?' Evans asked.

'Possibly because I'm married to her? Possibly because we live in the same house and share the same bed?'

'But, as I understand it, sir, you yourself were abroad at the time.'

Higson's eyelids gave the briefest of flickers. 'Quite right, I was,' he admitted.

'So you can't actually know for a fact that your wife was at home, can you, sir?'

For a moment, Derek Higson was silent. Then he said, 'I can confirm she was at home, as a matter of fact. Because when I rang her up, she was there to answer the call.'

'At what time did you make this call?'

'The call began at around eight o'clock, and it must have been about ten to nine when I finally hung up.'

'That's a long time to be on the phone, especially when you're ringing from abroad,' Evans said suspiciously.

Higson sighed. 'We run a business here, Chief Inspector. And when I say "we", I mean my wife as well as myself. We discuss that business every day, whether I'm here or in Europe. And by their very nature, those discussions can be quite extensive.'

'So you're saying it was a business call?'

'We may have discussed a few domestic matters – I really can't remember – but the bulk of the call was about business, yes.'

'And you're sure about the time?'

'Absolutely. The call was sandwiched between dinner with one client and drinks with another.'

'Eight o'clock is a bit early to have finished dinner, isn't it?' Evans asked. 'I thought they ate later on the Continent.'

'The Dutch don't eat as late as most Europeans,' Higson said. 'Besides, there's a time difference, so although it was only eight o'clock here when I rang, it was nine o'clock in Holland.'

'I hadn't thought of that,' Evans admitted. 'I assume your wife will confirm that this conversation took place.'

'Why wouldn't she, when that's what happened?'

Evans stood up. 'In that case, I'll leave you to get on with running your business,' Evans said.

'Will you be back to see my wife?' Higson asked.

'No, I don't think that will be necessary,' Evans told him. 'But if you wouldn't mind asking her to give me a ring at headquarters . . . ?'

'Of course,' Derek Higson agreed. 'I'd be delighted to.'

The girls' grammar school was on its lunch break when Monika Paniatowski arrived, but the headmistress, Miss Pringle – a grey-haired woman who must have been close to retirement – was more than willing to see her in her study.

'I wanted to be a journalist myself, when I was younger,' Miss Pringle told her, 'but Father was against it. "It's not the sort of profession a young lady should ever contemplate entering," he said, and in those days, of course, a father's word was law. And I suppose I can't complain about the path I did take. I've had a very fulfilling career in many ways, and helped thousands of young minds to develop.' She sighed. 'Still, there are still occasions when I wish I'd showed a little more spirit and stood up for myself.'

The sound of a young girl, screaming excitedly that she wanted the ball, drifted in through the window. The words seemed to remind Miss Pringle of where she was.

'We have a very good netball team,' she said. 'Fearsome, almost. Now, would you like to tell me what I can do for you, my dear?'

'I believe Lucy Higson – Lucy Watkins, as she used to be – was once a pupil at this school,' Monika Paniatowski said. 'You don't happen to remember her, do you?'

185

'But of course I remember her. Lucy was one of the outstanding pupils of her year. I was very sorry indeed when her mother took her away and put her into private education.' The headmistress's eyes narrowed slightly. 'Can I ask what *your* interest in her is?'

I want to find a way to prove that she's a cold-blooded killer, Paniatowski thought.

But aloud, she said, 'You know that she's married to a very successful businessman in Whitebridge, don't you?'

'Yes. I remember reading an account of her wedding. From the photographs, her husband looked somewhat older than her. Is he?'

'Yes. Nearly twenty years older.'

Miss Pringle nodded. 'Yes, I suppose it was always going to be that way,' she said.

'What do you mean?' Paniatowski wondered.

'Just that . . .' Miss Pringle brought herself up sharply. 'Nothing really. I've never been married myself, so I don't really think it's my place to comment on the matches that my girls choose to make. But you still haven't told me why you're so interested in Lucy.'

'We're running a series of articles called "The Woman Behind the Man Behind the Business".' Paniatowski giggled girlishly. 'The title's not mine, I promise you. I'd have preferred something snappier, but my editor liked it, and he's the boss. Still – ' she grew more serious again – 'I do think it's basically a good idea, and I'd appreciate any help you could give me in producing an accurate portrait.'

Miss Pringle thought about it for a moment. 'I'm not sure I'm the right person to talk to.'

'But surely, if you were her teacher—'

'Teachers like to think they know their pupils, but I'm increasingly coming around to the view that, for most of the time at least, we only know what our pupils *want* us to know,' Miss Pringle said. 'So while I could tell that Lucy was very good at history – she won the prize two years running, as a matter of fact – I'm not sure I could give you an accurate picture of what she was like as a *person*. In fact, I think you'd find out much more by talking to one of her contemporaries.'

'No doubt I would – in an ideal world,' Paniatowski agreed. 'But I write to a deadline and—'

'The girl I have in mind was not only Lucy's closest friend, but also teaches at this school,' Miss Pringle said firmly. 'I'm sure she wouldn't mind giving you a few minutes of her time.'

The first mention Woodend could find in the *Pemberton Guardian* of Lucy Higson, née Watkins, was a photograph taken in 1930, the year that she was born. Above a short piece announcing her birth was a grainy photograph of the proud parents holding up the baby for the world's inspection.

Lucy herself was little more than a white blob of a head wrapped in swaddling clothes, but the parents were much clearer. Lucy's mother, with a happy grin covering her face, looked very much like an old-fashioned version of the woman that Lucy had grown up to be. Her father was wearing a wide-lapelled pre-war suit, and looking much more serious. He reminded Woodend vaguely – and slightly troublingly – of someone else, though the Chief Inspector couldn't quite put his finger on who that someone else was.

There were various other peripheral references to Lucy over the next few years – she'd been Mary in the school nativity play and had won the egg-and-spoon race on sports' day – but it was not until 1952 that she featured again prominently. This time, she was photographed standing next to a soldier who looked a good few years older than she was. His name was Captain Clive Thornton, the newspaper said, and he and Lucy had decided to announce their engagement sooner than planned because the Captain was due to be posted overseas. Again, Woodend was struck by the fact that there was something familiar about the face.

The engagement did not last long. Clive was posted to

Malaya, and was killed in the jungle, by communist insurgents. There was a long article in the *Pemberton Guardian* about the funeral of the dead local hero.

There was just one more photograph of Lucy to be found in the newspaper. This time she was standing next to Derek Higson, on the eve of her engagement to *him*.

And suddenly, Woodend saw the pattern! He checked back on the previous photographs, but even before he'd started the comparison, he was convinced he was right.

The three men, Lucy's father, her first fiancé and her eventual husband, could never have been mistaken for one another – could never even have been taken for brothers – but they were very much the same *type*.

Right from the beginning of the investigation, Woodend had been wondering what there had been about Derek Higson which led Lucy to want to marry him. Now he had his answer – and it was not an answer he welcomed.

'We were about as close as close friends could be,' Mandy Miller told Paniatowski. 'But we were very different.'

'Different how?'

'I could have told you, even back then, that I'd probably end up teaching art back at the old school, but Lucy always had a bit more about her. She'd got an inner strength most of us don't have. You'd only have had to see the way she handled her father's death to know that.'

'When did her father die?'

'When she was ten. It wasn't a long lingering illness or anything. One day he was there, and the next he was gone. The autopsy revealed he had a weak heart, but nobody had even suspected that before he actually died. It would have been a terrible thing for most girls to have gone through, but it was especially hard for Lucy, because she really did worship him. In fact, I don't think she ever got over losing him like that.'

'What was she like as a person?'

'Outgoing. Strong. Kind. Generous. The sort of girl I like to have in my classes, but so very rarely do.'

'Boyfriends?'

'Nothing serious. There were plenty of boys who would have given their right arms to go out with her, but she wasn't really interested. She said they all seemed so immature. But she had a terrific crush on my dad at one time. And on a couple of our friends' dads, now I come to think of it. Not that you can read much into that. Remember what you were like when you were thirteen or fourteen?'

'Yes,' Paniatowski said, as the horrors of her childhood flashed briefly through her mind.

'I'm afraid I can't tell you much about her *late* teens,' Mandy Miller said. 'First she was sent off to boarding school, then she and her mother moved away from Pemberton. We swore we'd keep in touch, but you never do, do you?'

'I was wondering what made her mother decide to send her off to boarding school,' Paniatowski said.

'Oh, I think she'd *always* wanted to send her,' Mandy Miller said. 'She just couldn't afford to until she got the legacy.'

'What legacy?'

'Lucy had a great-uncle living in Australia. When he died, he left all his money to Lucy and her mother. By all accounts, it was an absolute fortune. People around here used to joke about how they'd never realized they'd been rubbing shoulders with a future millionaire.'

'So Lucy's mother was suddenly rich?'

'Not her mother, so much. She was left comfortably off, but most of the estate went into trust for Lucy, until she was twenty-one.'

'So Lucy's a rich woman in her own right?'

'Loaded!' Mandy Miller said, sounding surprised. 'Didn't you know that?'

The pub in the centre of Pemberton was called the Barley Mow. It had thick stone walls, and a log fire was burning merrily in the grate. Under normal circumstances, Woodend would have relished being there, but at that moment he was hardly aware of his surroundings at all.

189

'We started out with two basic assumptions,' he said gloomily to Paniatowski. 'The first was that Lucy Higson married Derek because of his money. Now we know that's not true. If anythin', it was the other way round. That upholsterer I talked to said what saved New Horizons from goin' belly-up was Lucy's managerial skills. An' that may have been part of it. But I'd be willin' to bet that a fair amount of her cash went into the business, too.'

'I wouldn't be at all surprised,' Paniatowski agreed.

'An' our second theory's been proved to be just as wrong,' Woodend continued. 'We assumed that Lucy was a lesbian by nature, an' that marryin' Derek was a cover for that. Well, we couldn't have been more off-target, could we? There's no evidence at all that Lucy showed any inclination to fancy girls when she was growin' up. On the other hand, there's every indication to suggest that what she was lookin' for in a mate was a father-figure. An' Derek Higson fits that description to a T. Which tells us what?'

'That she probably *does* love her husband just as much as she appears to,' Monika Paniatowski said. 'That she probably wasn't having an affair with Pamela Rainsford at all. That it was another woman who Pamela was seeing. A woman she *nicknamed* Lulu for some reason of her own – though now she's dead we'll never know what that reason was.'

Woodend nodded. 'It's like a house of cards, isn't it?' he said. 'You take away one of the bottom ones, and the whole bloody structure collapses.'

'In other words, if Lucy didn't kill Pamela, she had no reason to kill Maria, either?'

'Exactly,' Woodend agreed. 'The Cortina GT parked on Ash Croft probably didn't belong to Lucy at all. There's absolutely no reason why it should have. It might not even have been supplied by Melton's-bloody-Motors. The fact is, we've been relyin' on it bein' a local car, but it could have come from anywhere.'

'So what do we do now?' Paniatowski asked.

'What *can* we do now?' Woodend replied. 'We go back to Whitebridge with out tails between our legs.'

'Never mind,' Paniatowski said, trying to sound optimistic. 'Tomorrow is another day.'

'Aye, it is,' Woodend agreed. 'It's the day that Paul Melton informs the Chief Constable that I nicked his list of GT owners. It's the day I find myself under suspension, pendin' the settin' up of a board of inquiry.'

Twenty-Seven

They didn't say much on the journey back to Whitebridge, because there wasn't a lot to say.

They had no leads.

No new ideas to bounce off each other.

Nothing.

And the closer they got to home, the more an air of despondency descended on them, until it was almost suffocating.

They would never crack this case, Woodend told himself, as they drove back into the depressingly persistent rain.

They would never find out who killed sweet, helpless Maria. Bob Rutter would spend the best years of his life rotting away in some stinking gaol for a crime he never committed. And after so many close scrapes with the Chief Constable, he would finally go down in flames himself.

It was already dark by the time they reached Whitebridge centre, and the rain showed no signs of easing off.

'Do you fancy a quick one at the Drum an' Monkey?' Woodend asked his passenger.

'Not really,' Paniatowski replied.

'Neither do I, as a matter of fact,' Woodend admitted.

'But I think I might as well go an' have one anyway, because I don't particularly feel like doin' much of anythin' else, either.'

He dropped Paniatowski off at headquarters, and drove on alone to the pub. He had no plans for what to do when he'd finished drinking, so maybe he'd just keep on drinking until some sort of plan came to him.

He was at the bar, ordering his first pint of best bitter, when he felt a tap on the shoulder.

'Hello, hello, hello. I'm afraid I must ask you to accompany me to the police station,' said a voice behind him, in the mock-pompous way that uniformed policemen always speak in cheap films, but rarely do in real life.

Woodend turned round. The man who'd addressed him had a roundish red face, and thinning red hair. They were of an age, Woodend guessed, and the other man seemed vaguely familiar.

'Don't you want to ask me *why* you have to accompany me to the station?' the man said.

'Why do I have to accompany you to the police station?' Woodend asked, playing along with the obvious gag because he really couldn't be bothered to do anything else.

'Why do I have to accompany you to the police station, *officer*?' the other man said.

'Why do I have to accompany you to the police station, officer?' Woodend repeated dutifully.

'Because I can't find my way on my own.' The red-faced man laughed. 'The old jokes are always the best, aren't they, Charlie?'

'I'm sorry, but—' Woodend began.

'You surely haven't forgotten who I am, have you?' the red-faced man asked, in a tone of voice which fell neatly between amazement and umbrage.

'Yes, I think I must have done – but I'm almost certain that we've met before.'

'Met! Met? I should say we have! We *met*, as you put it, every school day for nine years. I'm Terry Dawes!'

Of course he was, Woodend thought.

Foxy Dawes! The school bully! The nasty little bastard whose teeth he'd once knocked out.

'How are you doin', Foxy?' he asked.

Dawes frowned. 'Nobody's called that for years,' he said. 'As a matter of fact, I'd rather you didn't call it me now.'

'Well, I'll do my best not to,' Woodend promised, 'but old habits die hard, don't they, *Foxy*?'

Terry Dawes looked like a man considering whether or not he should take offence.

'The thing is,' he said, plainly having decided not to, 'I was reading in the paper about how the grammar school is having a reunion, and I asked myself why the toffs should have all the fun.' He waited for Woodend to make some comment, and when it was plain that none was forthcoming, decided to plough on. 'It's been nearly forty years since we said goodbye to the dear old school, you know, Charlie—'

'The *old* school, anyway,' Woodend interrupted.

'. . . and I saw no reason at all why we shouldn't copy the snobs from the top of the hill and have a reunion of our own.'

'Didn't you?' Woodend asked, noncommittally.

'I did not,' Dawes said over-emphatically. 'I had a bit of trouble tracking down some of the lads, but a famous man like you was easy enough to find. Just popped into the police station, and announced I was an old friend of yours. They said right away that I'd probably find you here. Apparently you've become a world champion at quaffing the wheat and the hop, and this is well known to be your favourite watering-hole.'

'You weren't strictly tellin' them the truth at the station, were you now, Foxy?'

'Wasn't I?'

'No, you weren't. There's a lot of words I could think of to describe our relationship, but "friends" isn't one of them.'

Dawes looked a little downcast. 'I wouldn't have put it quite like that,' he said.

'I would,' Woodend told him. 'So you're organizin' a reunion, are you? What do you hope to get out of it personally?'

Dawes tried to seem shocked by the question, and didn't quite make it. 'Nothing,' he said. 'Nothing at all.'

'Pull the other one,' Woodend said. 'You always had an angle, even when you were a nipper. So if you're goin' to all this trouble, you're doin' it for a reason. My guess is that you're either sellin' or beggin'. Which one is it?'

'I wouldn't call it *begging*,' Dawes said haughtily. 'Far from it, in fact. I thought I might take up a few minutes of the meeting to make my old friends aware of a unique business opportunity in wholesale carpeting, but that would be to their advantage, rather than mine. After all, a lot of you must have quite a bit of spare cash lying about doing nothing, and most people would welcome the chance to double or triple it in less than a year.'

'The banks all turned you down, did they?' Woodend asked.

'These *provincial* banks can be very short-sighted sometimes,' Dawes said. 'I could, of course, easily raise the money in London, but I'd much prefer to use local capital.'

'Have you contacted Derek Higson about this "unique business opportunity" of yours?' Woodend wondered.

'As a matter of fact, I haven't.'

'An' why is that?'

'I read in the papers about one of his workers getting murdered. I thought he probably had enough on his plate for the moment.'

'Very considerate of you,' Woodend said. 'But I can't help wondering if that was the real reason.'

'Of course it was. As I said—'

'I can't help wonderin', you see, if you'd worked out that after makin' his life a misery like you did, he probably wouldn't piss in your mouth if your throat was on fire.'

'I think you're overstating the case there, Charlie,' Dawes said. 'I might have had a bit of fun at his expense, but I wouldn't go so far as to say that I made his life a misery.'

'Wouldn't you? Well, I bloody would,' Woodend said relentlessly. 'None of our families were particularly well off, but Derek's mother had to struggle to get by more than most. An' it showed in the way she turned him out for school, didn't it? His clothes were always beautifully clean, but they were always very nearly threadbare as well. Which, of course, was one of the main reasons that you an' your nasty little mates decided to pick on him.'

'I think you're making a bit of a mountain out of a molehill,' Dawes said feebly.

'No, I'm bloody not,' Woodend told him, in full flow now. 'I remember one incident in particular. His mam must have run out of underpants for him to wear, an' she sent him to school in a pair of his sister's navy-blue knickers. Of course, it didn't show on the outside, but you an' your mates must have found out about it, some way or another – because when I went into the bog for a slash, three of you had grabbed him. An' do you remember what you'd done to him, Foxy?'

'Yes, I remember.'

'You'd pulled his shorts down, so that everybody else could see what it was wearin'.'

'Yes, but—'

'I knocked your teeth out on the spot, an' I've never once regretted it. You deserved far more than that for humiliatin' him the way you did.'

'He was asking for it,' Dawes said sullenly.

'Askin' for it!' Woodend repeated. 'How the bloody hell could he have been askin' for it?'

'His mam didn't *make* him wear the knickers. He *wanted* to. He stole them from his sister's drawer. That's how we found out about it. She was the one who told us.'

'I don't believe you,' Woodend said.

'And it wasn't a one-off, either. He started doing it regularly, after that time in the bogs. Well, he could afford to, couldn't he?'

'How do you mean?'

195

'He knew we wouldn't dare touch him again, because we were all afraid of you.'

'If Derek had been wearin' girls' clothes on any kind of a regular basis, I'd have known about it,' Woodend said – but he was starting to sound unconvincing, even to himself.

'Who'd have told you?' Dawes asked, sensing his uncertainty and going on to the attack. 'Would Derek have told you himself, do you think?'

'No, but surely somebody else—'

'You didn't hit people very often, Charlie. But when you did, you hit them hard. Nobody was going to risk that. Nobody was even going to *mention* what Derek was doing in your hearing.'

'If you're makin' this up . . .' Woodend said menacingly.

'I'm not,' Dawes protested. 'It's all true. We used to call him Gloria when you weren't around. No, that's not right. It wasn't Gloria at all. What was it now? It was Lulu.'

Woodend put his hand to his forehead.

'Oh sweet Jesus!' he groaned.

Twenty-Eight

The Higsons' house was located on the northern edge of Whitebridge. It was architect-designed, and had been cunningly constructed so that most of the major windows looked out on to the moors, rather than down into the grimy industrial town where Derek Higson had made his money. The house was large – even by the ostentatious standards of the local extravagantly rich. It had two swimming pools – one outdoors for when the Lancashire weather was kind, one indoors in acknowledgement of the fact that it usually wasn't

– and was surrounded by gardens which were almost extensive enough to have been called 'grounds'. Pleasant paths snaked through these gardens, passing a small orchard and a medium-sized waterfall. There were lights to illuminate these walks, but they were not turned on at that moment, so anyone looking out of the house would not have seen that there were uniformed policemen all around the edge of the property.

Woodend and Paniatowski walked up the Higsons' drive on foot. At the front door, the Chief Inspector rang the bell. He'd been hoping it would be either Derek Higson or the housekeeper who came to the door, but it was poor, bloody Lucy Higson who actually did.

Not that she *looked* like poor, bloody Lucy, Woodend thought.

Dressed in a shot-silk blouse which emphasized her bosom, and a black skirt which showed off the shape of her sculptured legs, she was as stunning as ever.

Not that she even *saw* herself as poor, bloody Lucy, he added mentally.

She had all the poise of a woman with the strength to ride out her difficulties and the determination to finally get what she wanted. But all she *really* had was delusion. She hadn't realized that yet – but she soon would.

'Is your husband at home, Mrs Higson?' Woodend asked.

Lucy smiled – still poised, still confident. 'No, he's out as it happens, Chief Inspector,' she said. 'But I *am* expecting him back at any time. Would you and your sergeant like to come inside and wait?'

Woodend sighed, and held out a piece of paper in front of him. 'I'm sorry, Mr Higson, but we've got a warrant to search your house,' he said.

'A warrant?' Lucy Higson repeated, a puzzled expression coming to her face. 'To search my house?'

'I'm afraid so.'

'But what could you possibly be looking for?'

'I'd rather not say, at the moment.'

Puzzlement was slowly being replaced by mild outrage. 'The mayor is a personal friend of mine, you know,' Lucy said.

'I'm sure he is,' Woodend agreed. 'You're probably quite pally with the Chief Constable, an' all. But that's neither here nor there.'

'Is there nothing I can do to stop you searching?'

'Nothing at all.'

'Then I suppose you'd better come in,' Lucy Higson said resignedly. 'But if you think that I'm going to allow you wander around my house completely unsupervised, then you've got another think coming. I shall insist on accompanying you wherever you go.'

'I'd be grateful if you would.'

Lucy Higson shook her head slowly from side to side, as if she still didn't *quite* believe all this was happening.

'I don't know whose orders you're acting on, but to search the house of one of the most prominent, respectable and law-abiding men in Whitebridge is just plain ridiculous,' Lucy said. 'Wouldn't *you* call it ridiculous, Chief Inspector?'

'No, I wouldn't.'

'Then what *would* you call it?'

'I'd call it bloody tragic,' Woodend said

They went straight upstairs to the master bedroom.

'Why, of all places, are you starting here, Chief Inspector?' Lucy Higson asked.

'Please don't ask me questions you know I'm not goin' to answer,' Woodend replied.

It was a large room – and it needed to be in order to accommodate the two huge wardrobes it held.

Woodend and Paniatowski checked the one on the left. Men's suits, shirts, jackets, ties and trousers, all of them expensive.

'That's my husband's wardrobe,' Lucy Higson said, with just a tinge of sarcasm to her tone.

'I think we could have worked that out for ourselves,' Woodend answered, deadpan.

The wardrobe on the right contained dresses, skirts and blouses.

'Could you please identify all these clothes as yours, Mrs Higson,' Woodend asked.

'Who else's are they likely to be?'

'Just do as I ask, if you wouldn't mind.'

Lucy Higson sighed and gave her wardrobe no more than a cursory inspection. 'Yes, they're all mine. Are you satisfied now?'

'I'm afraid I'm not. Do you have any other clothes than the ones which are here?'

'There are my dirty clothes, of course. I imagine the maid will have taken them to the laundry room.'

'Any others?'

'There may be a few items I'll never wear again, but which I haven't got round to giving away to charity yet.'

'*May* be a few items?' Woodend said.

'There *are* a few items.'

'An' where will I find them?'

'Where does anyone put things they don't want any more? They'll be in trunks in the attic.'

'Then that's where we'll go next,' Woodend said.

All the clothes in the attic trunks were Lucy Higson's size, and she identified them as belonging to her.

They moved on to the laundry room, and Paniatowski and Woodend carefully went through the dirty clothes hampers.

'What a glamorous life you police officers really do lead,' Lucy Higson said, and the sarcasm was much more in evidence this time.

She was starting to become uneasy, Woodend told himself. She was starting to suspect that there might actually be something wrong.

'Do you send any of your clothes to an outside laundry?' he asked.

'No, the maid does everything.'

'An' there are no clothes anywhere else in the house?'

'What *is* this obsession of yours with clothes?'

'Just answer the question, please.'

Lucy Higson sighed again. 'No, there are no clothes anywhere else in the house.'

'Is there any part of the house where your husband doesn't like you to go? Anywhere he considers his private space?'

'I don't know what kind of marriage you and your wife have, Chief Inspector, but my husband and I keep no secrets from each other,' Lucy Higson said witheringly.

That's all *you* know, Woodend thought.

'Does Derek have an office in the house?' he asked.

'He has a *study*, if that's what you mean.'

'An' how often do you go in there?'

'Not very often.'

'Because he doesn't like you to?'

'Because I see no *need* to.'

'We'll look at that next,' Woodend said.

Derek Higson's 'study' was all that might have been expected of it. A large mahogany desk dominated the centre of the room, and there was space enough in one corner of it for a half-sized snooker table. There were framed photographs of various stages of the factory expansion on the wall, as well as a map of Europe with several coloured pins stuck in it.

'The map shows the places we conduct our criminal activities from,' Lucy Higson said. 'The red pins indicate where we have brothels, the blue ones where we fence all our stolen property.'

'I'd thought it might just be places you shipped your furniture to,' Woodend said.

'Well, aren't you a clever little policeman. You should go straight to the top of the class.'

'Please, Mrs Higson,' Woodend said.

'Please what?'

'Please don't make this any harder than it has to be.'

There was a full-length cupboard built into the wall. Paniatowski opened it to find several fishing rods and a set of golf clubs.

'Derek's a keen sportsman, Chief Inspector,' Lucy Higson

said. 'You should try developing a few outside interests your-self. It's very healthy for the mind. And a man who's totally obsessed with his work does come up with some very strange ideas, you know.'

Paniatowski tapped the back of the cupboard with her knuck-les. 'It's hollow,' she said.

She removed the fishing rods and the golf clubs, and exam-ined the panel at the back of the closet.

'It's got a false back,' she told Woodend.

'Can you remove it?'

'No problem at all. It's only held in place by a couple of clips.'

'Your warrant gives you permission to search the house, not to dismantle it,' Lucy Higson said, with an edge of panic to her words now.

She doesn't *know* about her husband for a fact, Woodend thought, but she certainly *suspects* that something isn't quite right.

'Did you hear me?' Lucy Higson demanded. 'I will *not* have you pulling my house apart.'

'We're only goin' to remove one panel, an' if we cause any damage, we'll pay for it,' Woodend said.

Lucy Higson walked towards the door. 'Well, I'm certainly not going stand around and watch while my home is destroyed,' she said.

'Stay where you are,' Woodend said.

'You can't—'

'Stay!' Woodend repeated.

Paniatowski removed the panel from the cupboard, delved into it again, and emerged holding two dresses and a wig. The dresses were cheap and garish. One of them was covered with shiny blue sequins, the other with shiny red ones. Both of them were so large that they would have swamped Lucy Higson. The wig was made up of long, platinum-blonde, hair.

'Are these your clothes, Mrs Higson?' Woodend asked.

'You know they're not,' Lucy Higson replied.

And then she burst into tears.

Twenty-Nine

The rain had eased off slightly. Now it was no more than a slow persistent drizzle, the kind of rain it was almost possible to ignore, but which still managed to soak those exposed to it right through to the bone.

In Interview Room Three, which had no window to the outside, they didn't even know it was raining. But then, as Woodend often reminded himself, that was the point of the place.

An interview room was a world of its own; a world in which all the complexities of life were stripped down to a single issue; a world in which one man rained his questions down on another man until he was sodden with them – until he lost the will to resist.

When Woodend entered the interview room, Derek Higson was already sitting at the table. He looked perfectly calm, and perfectly in control of himself, but then many men before him had felt exactly the same at the *beginning* of the process.

Woodend sat down opposite Higson. He didn't speak. He didn't reach into his pocket for his cigarettes, though he desperately wanted to. The silence filled a full minute, then stretched to two. Higson was doing better than Woodend had thought he ever would, but then the man was a salesman – and all salesmen know the value of silence.

It was somewhere in the middle of the third minute that Derek Higson finally spoke.

'Well, Charlie, here we are, two old mates from Sudbury Street Elementary, back together again,' he said.

'Is that how you see it?' Woodend asked.

'Isn't it how *you* see it?'

'No. I see it as a chief inspector sittin' across a table from a man he'll soon charge with murder.'

Derek Higson laughed. 'Come on, Charlie, we both know that's not really going to happen. I wasn't even in the bloody country when poor Pamela was murdered.'

'You don't really think I'll buy that story, do you?' Woodend asked, almost sadly.

'Why shouldn't you, when it happens to be the truth?'

'When you drive to Europe, you do it in your bloody *Rolls-Royce*, for God's sake!'

'I know I do, and there's a very good reason for that. It impresses the clients over there, you see. That's the trick to successful selling, Charlie. You must never let the customer know how eager you are to make the sale. So when the Germans or the Dutch see me arriving in the Roller, they say to themselves, "Here's a man who doesn't *need* to do business with us. Here's a man who'd almost *doing us a favour* by doing business with us." Do you understand what I'm saying?'

'Grow up, Derek,' Woodend said wearily.

But perhaps that was the problem, he thought. Perhaps Derek Higson had *never* grown up. Perhaps he'd learned early on – or, at least, *thought* he'd learned – that if you had a protector there was no need to take responsibility for your own actions.

And who had been one of the first people to teach him that lesson?

Little Charlie Woodend!

'You still don't see the point about the Rolls-Royce, do you?' Woodend asked. 'So maybe I'll explain it to you. Even if your foreign clients were prepared to lie for you, and say you were in Europe at a time when you weren't – and they won't, Derek, trust me, they won't – it doesn't really matter. Even if HM Customs and Excise at Dover have lost all the records of your disembarkation at the

203

port – which they won't have – it makes no difference. And why is that?'

'You tell me.'

'Because people notice Rolls-Royces. People *remember* Rolls-Royces. Without even breakin' into a sweat, the Dover police should be able to collect a dozen statements on exactly when you landed.'

Derek Higson thought about it for a moment. 'So perhaps I did come back to England earlier than I've previously claimed I did,' he said. 'In fact, if it'll make your job any easier, I'm perfectly willing to *admit* that I did. But that's not to say that I killed anybody, is it?'

'So what *did* you do when you got back to England?'

'I wanted a little time to myself, away from all the responsibilities of the factory. I went touring in Cornwall.'

'Touring? In *October*?'

'The Cornish coastline can be very beautiful, you know, even in bad weather.'

'So where did you stay? Do you have any receipts for the hotels you spent the night at?'

'I slept in the car.' Higson chuckled. 'You could almost *live* in a Roller, you know.'

'You didn't dare drive all the way back to Whitebridge in the Rolls, because someone would have spotted it,' Woodend said, as if the other man had never spoken. 'So my guess is that you left it somewhere like Manchester, an' made the rest of the journey by bus or train. That's why, when you got here, you had to use your wife's Cortina to get around.'

'I was in Cornwall,' Higson said stubbornly.

'But you can't leave a Rolls on the street, like you might an ordinary car,' Woodend continued. 'You'll have to have parked it in a secure garage. It shouldn't take us too long to find where that is.'

'Why are people always trying to fit me up for things I didn't do?' Higson asked, as if the question genuinely puzzled him.

'Is *that* what they do?'

'You know it's what they do. They were even doing it back in elementary school. Don't you remember what happened in the bogs?'

'Remind me.'

'Foxy Dawes and his mates grabbed me and pulled my pants down. Then they slipped a pair of girls' knickers on to me, and tried to say I'd been wearing them all along.'

'You know, you said all that so convincingly that I could almost believe you,' Woodend told him. 'But you see, Derek, when we searched your house, we found the dresses.'

'What dresses?'

'The red one an' the blue one. *Lulu's* dresses.'

'My wife's name is Lucy. She's never called herself Lulu. She wouldn't dream of it.'

'*You're* Lulu,' Woodend said. 'It's the name Foxy Dawes an' his mates gave you back at Sudbury Street. I've been wonderin' why you started to apply it to yourself, an' I think I've finally worked it out. Would you like me to tell you what I've come up with?'

'No!'

'Well, I will anyway. There's two things you like about havin' a protector. One is obvious – he or she protects you. But by the same token, you have to put yourself in your protector's power to a certain extent – an' I think you rather enjoy that, too.'

Higson smiled. 'Let me see if I've got this straight,' he said. 'I always seek out protectors. Is that right?'

'Yes.'

'You protected me from Foxy Dawes's gang. And my wife Lucy protected me from . . . ?'

'From your business goin' under. New Horizons was on the verge of bankruptcy when you married Lucy. She ploughed money into the firm, an' now she runs the parts of it you can't be bothered with.'

'And what about Pamela?'

'What about her?'

'Well, if I had the kind of relationship with her you seem

to think I have with most people I come into contact with, she must have been protecting me from something herself, mustn't she?'

'Yes.'

'And what was that, exactly?'

'She was protectin' you from ruinin' your marriage.'

'What rubbish you do come up with sometimes.'

'You daren't tell Lucy you were a transvestite, because she'd never have accepted it. But you *could* tell Pamela. An' as long as one of the women in your life knew your little secret, that was enough for you. But then things came to a crunch, didn't they? Pamela began insistin' that you had to leave Lucy. If you'd said you wouldn't, she'd have told your wife about your little quirks, an' Lucy would have left *you.*'

A tear slowly began to run down Derek Higson's right cheek. 'I love my wife, Charlie,' he said. 'It's not just her money I'm interested in. I truly do love her for herself.'

'I believe you,' Woodend said.

'If she could just have accepted that I liked to dress up now and again – that there was no harm in it – I wouldn't have needed Pamela at all. But I knew she never would.'

'How could she accept that, when both the dad she worshipped, an' her first fiancé, who was a hero, would never have considered doin' such a thing?' Woodend mused, almost to himself.

'What's that supposed to mean?' Derek Higson demanded.

'Nothin',' Woodend said. 'Or, at least, nothin' that should concern you. Let's get back to the way you killed Pamela Rainsford.'

'I didn't kill her,' Higson insisted. 'All right, I may have lied about not being in Whitebridge when she died, but I certainly didn't kill her. I was with my wife the whole evening. Lucy will confirm it.'

'I can see how you might believe that,' Woodend said. 'Why shouldn't she continue to lie for you, when she's told so many lies already?'

'She hasn't told any—'

'I don't know what cock-and-bull story you told her to explain your unexpected return to Whitebridge – and why she had to keep that return a secret – but she believed it. Because she *wanted* to believe. Because she *needed* to believe. But any power you once had over her has gone for ever.'

'Has it really?' Derek Higson asked, making no attempt to hide his scepticism.

'Yes, it has,' Woodend said firmly. 'It's gone because she's seen Lulu's dresses for herself.' He paused for a second. 'You know, I think we both might have been wrong about her never acceptin' your need to dress up,' he continued. 'It would have been hard for her, but it's possible she might have come to terms with it. But what she'll *never* accept is that you shared a secret part of your life – a part that was vital to you – with another woman. She won't protect you any longer, Derek. She hates an' despises you. An' if we still had public executions for people like you, she'd queue up all night just to get a good view of you droppin' through the trap-door.'

It was as if the bones in Derek Higson's face had suddenly begun to crumble. His jaw fell, his skin slackened, and his eyes seemed to want to retreat into the back of his head.

'Help me, Charlie,' he said.

'I'll do what I can for you,' Woodend promised, 'but you're goin' to have to be honest with me.'

Higson nodded. 'All right.'

'When Pamela issued her ultimatum, you knew you were goin' to have to get rid of her. She couldn't be bought off, because – in her own twisted way – she loved you just as much as Lucy did. So you decided you had no choice but to kill her. Am I right so far?'

'Yes.'

'You arranged to meet her down by the canal. You not only strangled her but you raped her with one of the upholstery instruments you'd brought with you from the factory. An' then you messed up her face so much that it didn't even look human any more. Now why did you do all that?'

207

'You already know.'

'Tell me anyway.'

'I thought it would confuse matters. I thought it might make you think that her killer was deranged.'

He bloody well *is* deranged! Woodend thought.

'An' then, as an extra refinement, you even suggested to me that the murderer might be a woman,' he said aloud.

'Yes, I was quite proud of that particular touch,' Higson said, managing a weak smile. 'I'm a salesman, Charlie, and as every salesman knows, you're not selling a product, your selling an *idea* – a feeling. You have to paint a picture in the customer's mind of what it would be like to possess what it is you want him to buy from you. I sold you the idea that the killer might be a woman, but you soon made it your own, didn't you?'

Oh yes, Woodend thought, with self-disgust. Oh yes, I most certainly bloody did!

'Now you've heard my confession, I expect you'll want me to put all this down in writing, won't you?' Derek Higson said.

'Not yet,' Woodend told him.

'Why ever not?'

'Because first I'd like to hear the rest of it.'

'What rest of it?'

'I want to know why you killed Maria Rutter.'

Thirty

It's a grey October afternoon. They're walking in the park together. He has told Pamela this is a dangerous thing to do – that even being seen together is a risk for him. He has said it because it is what she likes to hear – because she thrives on danger – but he's not unduly worried himself. She is his secretary, he is her boss. They have a perfect right to be walking together, and anyone who sees them will probably deduce – from their serious expressions – that they must be talking about business. Why should they think anything else?

'Have you decided when it's to be yet, Lulu?' she asks.

There are times when he regrets telling her his secret name, because he sometimes doesn't like it when she talks to him as if he really were a woman. But, then again, he sometimes does like it – sometimes positively revels in it. He wishes life were not so complicated — wishes he were not so complicated.

'I'm waiting for an answer, you bitch,' she says.

'It's not that easy,' he protests.

'Of course it's that easy,' she says scornfully. 'You just tell her you're leaving her. And if you won't tell her, then I will!'

They have drawn level with a bench. No one is sitting on it. In fact, there are very few people in the park at all. In this weather, most folk prefer to be indoors, warming their hands in the heat of a glowing coal fire.

'I want to do it,' she says. 'I want to do it now!'

'Here?'

'Yes, here!'

They have made love in dangerous places before. But never so close to home. Never where there was any chance of their being discovered by people who would recognize them.

He bites back the comment that it's too risky. That would only excite her more.

'It's too cold,' he says.

'We won't be at it long. And it's not as if I'm asking you to take all your clothes off. We only need to expose the important bits.'

'I'm not wearing my dress.'

'*You don't wear your dress every time.*'

'*I know, but—*'

'*Are you turning me down?*' *she asks.*

'*Not exactly turning you—*'

'*Because if you won't make love to me, I'll have to find something else to do to amuse myself. There's a phone box on the edge of the park. Maybe I'll go and ring your wife.*'

He looks around desperately. There is a small plantation of holly bushes some distance from the path. Once they are in the middle of them, they will be invisible.

'*Let's do it in those bushes,*' *he suggests.*

'*Doesn't holly prick?*' *she asks.*

'*Not if you're careful,*' *he replies.*

A small smile comes to her face. It's the first one he's seen there for quite a while.

'*I think we* will *get pricked,*' *she says gleefully.* '*I think you want us to get pricked.*'

'*No, I—*'

'*It might be rather interesting,*' *she says.*

She steps off the path and begins to walk towards the holly bushes. He watches her for a second, as if making up his mind whether or not he wants anything to do with this, then meekly follows. It is half-way between the path and the bushes that he decides he has no alternative but to kill her.

They make love quickly and – from his point of view at least – unsatisfactorily. But he can't let that show, because if he does, she will want to do it all over again.

'*That was lovely, wasn't it?*' *he says.*

She doesn't reply.

'*Just like it used to be,*' *he says, trying not to sound desperate.*

'*You said I was the only one who mattered to you.*'

Doesn't the risk he's just taken mean anything *to her? He would have thought it would have bought him at least a* little *time.*

'*You* are *the only one who matters to me!*' *he says.*

'*You said we'd be together for ever.*'

'*We will be.*'

'Then what about her?'

Back to the old theme again. Will Pamela never give him even a minute's peace?

'She's a complication,' he says. 'No more.'

'She seems like more than that to me.'

He has zipped his fly and smoothed down the rest of his clothes. Cautiously, he raises himself above the level of the holly bushes.

And is horrified by what he sees!

There had been no one on the bench when they went into the bushes, but there is now. A young, dark-haired woman is sitting there.

He bobs down again. 'We have to go to the other path, on the far side of those trees,' he tells Pamela, who is in the process of readjusting her bra.

'The path we came off's much closer,' she says.

'A bit of an extra walk won't kill us.'

'I know it won't. But I don't see the point.'

He daren't tell Pamela about the dark-haired young woman, because if he does, the reckless bitch will probably instantly incorporate her into the game. She might even go up to the woman and ask her if the noise of their love-making had disturbed her.

'If we keep our heads down and run to the far path, there's always a chance someone will see us,' he says.

'So?'

'So they'll wonder what we've been doing. They'll imagine all sorts of things. Won't that be exciting for them? Won't it be exciting for us?'

'Yes, it might well be,' Pamela admits. 'All right, we'll do it.'

No one does see them, and when they reach the far path Higson says, 'I have to go.'

'Go where?'

'It's none of your bloody business!'

She is about to protest, then decides against it.

Oh, I can read your mind, you bloody cow! he thinks. You're

211

telling yourself that if you allow me to treat you badly now, you can make all kinds of unreasonable demands on me later. Well, think what you like, you whore. You won't be able to demand anything, because you'll be bloody dead!

After Pamela has flounced off, he retraces his steps, and gets back to the holly bushes just in time to see the young man and the baby in the pushchair approaching the bench. He recognizes the man instantly, through having seen his picture so often in the local paper.

'Oh God, let him have nothing to do with the woman on the bench,' he prays. 'Let them be strangers to one another.'

And then the man stops directly in front of the bench, and he knows that they are husband and wife.

'I told myself it didn't matter,' Higson said to Woodend. 'That even when Pamela turned up dead, nobody would be able to put two and two together. But however much I tried to convince myself, it simply wouldn't work. Mrs Rutter was a detective inspector's wife, you see. And the more I thought about it, the more I could see that she was the only weak link in my plans.'

'Go on,' Woodend said heavily.

'It was easy enough to find out where they lived. They're in the telephone book. And once the investigation had begun, I rang up my old friend, the Chief Constable, to find out which officers were involved. When he told me Inspector Rutter was part of the team, I knew I no longer had any choice but to act. There was always a danger Rutter would talk to his wife about the investigation, you see, and that she'd provide him with the missing piece of the puzzle. Besides, it seemed as if I was *destined* to kill her.'

'What gave you that idea?' Woodend asked bleakly.

'Isn't it obvious? If Rutter was working on the case, he wouldn't be at home. It was almost as if Fate was inviting me to take my opportunity.'

'An' you did.'

'Yes, I did. I drove Lucy's car down to Ash Croft. I almost

lost my nerve when I saw that people had actually moved into some of the houses, but I told myself that if I parked far enough away from them, I wouldn't be noticed.'

Nor would you have been, if Mr Bascombe hadn't been a fan of the new Cortina GT, Woodend thought.

'You reached Bob Rutter's house by cuttin' across the buildin' site?'

'That's right, I did. I'd been worried I might leave foot-prints, but the ground was so hard that I realized there was no chance of that. Fate again, you see.'

It was as much as Woodend could do not to throttle the man where he sat.

'How did you get into the house?' the Chief Inspector asked.

'Through the French windows. There was a catch on them, but when you've been in the furniture trade for as long as I have, that kind of thing presents no problem at all.'

'What happened next?'

'I could hear noises from the kitchen. The radio was play-ing quite loudly, but there was also the sound of pots and pans banging. I crept across the living room into the hallway. That's when I got my first glimpse of Mrs Rutter. The kettle was on. There were two cups on a tray, and she was reaching up into the cupboard. It looked as if she were getting ready to enter-tain someone.'

Me! Woodend thought. She was gettin' ready to entertain *me*.

'It struck me at the time that she was moving rather slowly and carefully,' Derek Higson continued, 'but some women are like that. She had her back to me. I had a hammer in my hand. I brought it down hard on the back of her head. It was very merciful, in a way. Onc second she was alive, and the next she was dead. She probably didn't feel a thing.'

'An' when you'd killed her, you tried to make it look like an accident?'

'Yes, I did. I fixed up the cooker so there'd be an explosion shortly after I'd left. I thought the fire might obliterate the traces of what I'd done. I didn't make a very good job of it, did I? Though in my own defence, I have to say that I was rather hurried, because I knew she was expecting a visitor.'

'What about the baby?' Woodend asked.

'What about her?'

'Didn't it bother you that she might be somewhere in the house you were just about to set fire to?'

'To tell you the truth, I didn't think about that.'

'To tell me the truth, you didn't *care* about that,' Woodend said, his head pounding and his hands itching to fasten themselves around Higson's throat.

'I think you're being a little unfair to me, Charlie,' Higson said, sounding hurt.

Woodend took a deep breath. It would soon be over, he told himself. He would soon walk out of the room, and this loathsome creature would be somebody else's problem.

'I still don't see why you thought you had to kill her,' he said.

'She was a witness!' Higson replied exasperatedly. 'She'd been there in the park, and heard me arguing with Pamela. She could have tied us together. She could have linked me to the murder.'

'You thought that hearing you argue from a distance would have been enough for her to be able to make a positive identification of you?'

'No, of course not. I thought she'd *seen* us. Or at least seen *me*!'

'She was a blind woman, for God's sake!'

'I know that. But I *didn't* know it until I read the account of her murder in the paper.'

214

Epilogue

It was still raining, but instead of rushing to the protection of his Wolseley, Woodend stood in the centre of the car park, and let the weather do its worst. He was not sure how long he was there – though his body remained rooted to the one spot, his mind was ranging far and wide – but by the time he did make a move towards his vehicle, the shoulders of his hairy tweed jacket were sodden, and his boots squelched as he walked.

He would probably have a heavy cold in the morning, he thought as he turned the key in the ignition, but he didn't really care. Standing out in the rain had been a good thing – standing out in the rain had done a little to wash away the layer of disgust, despair and desperation which had been clinging to him since he left the interview room.

As he drove into central Whitebridge, he found himself thinking about his career. He had saved himself yet again. However much the Chief Constable might yearn to discipline him for interfering in the Maria Rutter murder instead of devoting all his energies to investigating Pamela Rainsford's death, he could no longer do it – because the two cases were inextricably linked. There should be some comfort to be drawn from that, but he hadn't found it yet.

He had reached a roundabout. The first exit off it led to the Drum and Monkey. He longed to take it, but instead drove past and took the second exit instead. The case was not quite over, he reminded himself. There was still some unfinished business to deal with.

*   *   *

He'd fully expected Elizabeth Driver to be propping up the bar at the Clarence Hotel, and she didn't disappoint him. The journalist was drunk, but it was not, he thought, the drunkenness of desperation she'd been displaying the last time he saw her. No, this was quite different. This drunkenness had a celebratory – relieved – air about it.

She greeted him like an old friend.

'I've just been talking to my contact at police headquarters,' she said, slightly slurring her words. 'And do you know what he told me? He told that Cloggin'-it Charlie's come through again – that the brilliant Chief Inspector Woodend has arrested the big bad man who killed poor, blind Maria Rutter.'

'You never did get around to telling me what you were doing in Whitebridge,' Woodend said.

'No, I never did, did I?' Elizabeth Driver agreed.

'So let me take a guess. There were no stories to chase, so you went about creating one of your own.'

'Maybe.'

'Last year, when I was investigatin' the bonfire murders, we made a deal,' Woodend reminded her. 'I gave you an exclusive on the killer, and you agreed in return to forget that you'd ever known that Bob Rutter and Monika Paniatowski had had an affair. Isn't that right?'

'Yes, it is.'

'Only you never stick to your deals longer than you have to, do you? The Monika and Bob story wasn't that big a news item, but it was certainly made more poignant by the fact that Bob's wife was blind, and you decided it was worth resurrecting it. But how would you go about it? How would you bring the story to the surface again? The answer's obvious when you think about it, isn't it?'

'Is it?'

'Somebody told Maria about Bob and Monika's affair, and I think that somebody was you.'

Elizabeth Driver blinked. 'You can't prove it,' she said.

'I think I just did,' Woodend told her. 'All you were expecting from your mischief was for Maria to institute divorce proceeding against Bob,' he continued. 'Then Maria was murdered, and Bob was the chief suspect. You thought it was all your fault, and for once in your life, you learned what it was like to feel guilty. That's why you were so upset, wasn't it? Because you thought Maria's death was partly your fault.'

Elizabeth Driver lurched slightly. 'But it *wasn't* my fault, was it? Whether I told Maria or didn't tell Maria has nothing to do with anything. She'd have been dead whatever I'd said. So no harm done, and it's a case of all's well that ends well.'

No harm done! Woodend repeated bleakly to himself.

A baby had been left without a mother, a husband without a wife. Monika and Bob would be carrying around their guilt for the rest of their lives, not because they were wholly – or even partly – responsible for a lot of what had happened, but because that was what decent people like them did.

He couldn't lay any of that at Elizabeth Driver's door, but there was one thing he *could* blame her for.

'*I hit her on the back of the head, as hard as I could,*' Derek Higson had said. '*She probably didn't feel a thing.*'

But that was where he was wrong. For the last week of her life, Maria had been carrying around with her a burden of unhappiness, brought on by knowledge of her husband's affair. And *that* had been unnecessary.

'Say it!' Elizabeth Driver demanded.

'Say what?'

'Whatever it is that's going on in that head of yours.'

'All right, I will,' Woodend agreed. 'If somebody *had* to be in the park to overhear Pamela Rainsford and Derek Higson, then I wish that somebody had been *you*.'